On the Edge of Truth

Ileana M. Leon

When life does not make sense Trust in God Psalm 121

D1292452

BOOK REVIEW

On the Edge of Truth will take you on a journey through the ups and downs in their life. Ileana's detail of her characters allows you to walk in their shoes.
This author's descriptive style of writing places you in each environment she presented. There is a genuine sense of love and loyalty throughout. The realization of faith and how we cannot live life without it, is spread across the pages from start to finish. This novel was realistic and emotional. To be completely honest, it offers hope and opens the door to trusting God with everything.

Kim Doran
Author of LEAD and Pack your Suitcase

"Such a captivating read. I loved all the subtle tributes to important topics."

Always,
Paula Jean & Jess
Author of Hard Learned Lessons Learned

DEDICATION AND ACKNOWLEDGEMENTS

This book is dedicated to all the people who lost their lives inthe 9/11 Terrorist attacks, their families, and all First Responders.

I want to thank my Lord and Savior, Jesus, because, without Him, I could not have written this book. He inspires me and leads me daily to the places and the people he wants me to bless.

I want to thank my husband, Frank, and my children, Joel, and Kat, for believing in my desire to touch lives through my words.

A special thank you to these three ladies:

My Spiritual sister who has gone to be with the Lord way too soon, Doreen Franklin. She edited and encouraged me to keep fleshing out my characters and cover up the plot holes.

Paula Jean Ferri, helped with editing as well as answered a lot of random questions I threw her way.

Kim Doran, was my sounding board and gave me the push I needed to finally publish this labor of love.

1

He is not who he claims to be. The words battered her mind. She looked over the copy of the anonymous email tucked away in the pages of her reading book. Normally, she would blame it on SPAM, but this one came too close to her wedding day. Jumbled thoughts stuck to her like sticky cobwebs. Julienne raised her eyes. They found the window.

The concrete jungle below was wrapped in a patchwork of color. Swanky marketing murals, to advertising logs, stamped on city busses added to the illusion of endless progression. Street vendors and swindlers peddled everything from used phones to Rolex watches. The never-ending race of commercialism coursed through New York's metropolitan veins. Clouds swept by extinguishing the sun.
A brush-stroke of gray painted the prosperous city. Inclement weather was approaching.

"Have you finished the Fashion Week entry?" Angelo's voice interrupted her thoughts.

She turned her chair, dropping the paperback on her desk.

"Don't tell me you are still wasting time with that silly book?"

"It's not a crime to read spy novels."

"It is filling your head with garbage."

Julienne stared at her fiancé. Angelo D'Marco sat on the loveseat reading the New York Times. She swiveled taking in his chiseled features. If truth be told, he was the most handsome man she had ever seen. Instead of crunching numbers for a living, he could have been glossing the pages of magazines. But in the five years they had been dating, not once did he show up to the photoshoots, she had lined up for him.

"Juls, are you going to be ready to show those sketches to Veronique?"

"Uh-hum," she replied as his six-foot, toned body occupied the space in front of her. He lifted her off the chair; his hands hung loosely on her waist.

"So, what did you read that has you all flustered? I know, in the last scene, before he drops dead, he chokes out those three little words..." He took a few steps backward pulling her with him.

"I love... you," he uttered, with a voice deeper than his own. He clutched his chest with his free hand pretending to have been shot. He fell against the back wall taking her with him. His cell phone beeped extinguishing their laughter. The twinkle in his eyes vanished; he brought it to his ear. He would continue the conversation in the other room.

Julienne sat back down at her credenza. The guest list peeked out from under a stack of papers. She lifted it out from the pile and looked it over. Before she could tackle rearranging the names on the tables, she had to put the finishing touches on her sketches. Julienne rubbed her temples. So much still to do between wedding dress fittings and picking out flowers. Then there was that email. It had brought up all kinds of questions filling up her already busy mind.

Angelo came back carrying his favorite tie. "Got to fly to Madrid to reel in the big fish. He wants to go over a few details before signing the contract."

Julienne threw the list back on the table. *Here he goes again putting work before everything else.* It was wonderful that he was so responsible, but why should she get stuck planning their wedding on her own?

"What's up?" he asked, bending down so she could slip the tie under the collar of his shirt. She evened out the sides and continued maneuvering it until she tied the perfect knot. She held it tightly against his Adam's apple.

"Wow, so much hostility," he taunted, giving a playful tug to one of her curls. "You know if you choke me, I am not going to be able to get that promotion so we can honeymoon like the rich and famous," he said removing her hands.

Julienne bit her bottom lip and looked down toward the paperback concealing the troublesome message. She wanted to show it to him. But she couldn't. He would laugh and tell her it was a joke, and to forget about it. He would blame her worry on the stress of the wedding. He would suggest something practical like more fiber in her diet and less reading. The last thing she needed was a lecture from Mr. Perfect.

"You're gonna love Europe," he said, taking his umbrella. "It's going to rain all this week, but for our honeymoon, it is supposed to be nice and sunny."

3

"Who cares? My sketches are a flop. Our wedding is in less than a week and now you're leaving again!"

Angelo took her in his arms. Julienne nestled her head on his chest. "Juls, you will get it all done. I have faith in you. Your work will be as phenomenal as always. If all else fails, you can throw in burlap and sackcloth dresses to the mix," he chuckled, tapping her nose.

"Thanks a lot."

"Now don't you go getting all stressed out. These deals take time. Don't worry, I'll be back before the wedding. We'll meet up at One Serving or Two and finalize the seating arrangements." He checked his tie in front of the entrance mirror and gave her a goodbye kiss.

"And Juls? Stop fantasizing; your life is more exciting than you think."

***

Julienne sat at her kitchen table staring at the smudge on her countertop. She had spent hours making sure the color palette was radiant on her sketches. But was that good enough? She checked her watch. Frustrated, she rubbed the smudge with her finger. It only made it more noticeable. She wanted to pick up the marble cleaner and give the counter a thorough cleaning, but she was already running late. She tried rubbing it with a paper towel in a circular motion. It just made the smudge bigger. She took the sponge from the kitchen sink, dropped a few drops of dishwashing detergent on it, and scrubbed the counter. She checked her watch again. Julienne threw the wet sponge in the sink, gathered her designs, stuffed them in her briefcase, and headed out the door.

The restaurant was only a few blocks away on foot. Being a New Yorker meant she was used to long walks and taking taxis. It was much too expensive to own a car in Manhattan. Not to mention, the nightmare of finding a decent parking space. She walked fast, dodging the other pedestrians occupying the sidewalk. When she arrived, Alfie's typical weekend crowd was milling around outside. *Has anybody ever heard of making a reservation?*

"Miss. Veronique is waiting in Table 6. She doesn't look happy," the hostess warned before escorting her back to the private dining area.

A raven-haired woman in her late sixties sat behind the table powdering her nose. Veronique Sorié was known as the powerhouse behind Imperial Designs. She was a veteran designer who prided herself in grooming upcoming designers. At first, the young illustrator thought working under the prestigious fashion boss was an answer to prayer. Now she knew better.

"Finally! I was ready to go," Veronique complained in her thick French accent.

"Sorry I'm late," Julienne answered sliding into the chair the waiter had pulled out for her. She opened her briefcase and handed her the documents. Veronique perched her glasses on top of her aristocratic nose and began to edit the drawings. In the middle of the summer ensemble, she lifted her marking pen and flashed her subordinate a condescending look.

Renata. That was the private nickname Julienne had given her boss. She had named her after the cruel villain from the espionage trilogy she had been reading. But Veronique did not need the coldness of an interrogation room to make her subordinates quake.

5

"This is… "Veronique began, removing her spectacles and folding her hands before her. "Ridiculous… the design is chaotic, and the fabric is blah. What were you thinking?"

"I admit the color is a bit dark for the season, but I think it makes a bold statement, "she explained shifting uncomfortably in her chair.

"Julienne, do not insult my intelligence. This work is Infantile. You can do better. What does your boyfriend think? Would he like to see *le femmes* wearing this…" she twirled the pen searching for the English vernacular, "…trash?"

Julienne hid her indignation under a pasty smile. "He's my fiancé, not the designer."

"*Non*, but he would make an excellent model."

"I have tried, he just not interested. He likes his numbers." Julienne flipped open the menu, avoiding another confrontation.

"So where is *Monsieur* D'Marco today?

"Working."

"What a pity. I'd like to dress him in Armani and watch him walk the catwalk."

I bet you would …you've always had a thing for him.

The snapping of Veronique's fingers brought Julienne out of her mental rant.

"*Excusez moi,* are you going to order?"

"Sorry," she apologized handing the waiter the menu. "I'll have Alfie's Bowtie pasta with Marinara sauce."

"How quaint." The senior Designer scowled. "Antonio, I want the dolphin grilled and my salad, very green with rosemary and olive oil. *Si'l vous plait*, don't toss it until you are ready to serve it."

"If you want that kind of service La Travietta down the block offers a la carte." Julienne offered.

The sophisticated woman pursed her Botox injected lips " *Non et non!* What fun is that? Antonio can make more cash tonight than he makes all week if I like his service."

Julienne winked at the waiter, scurrying to reset the table with European champagne flutes and porcelain plates. In one fluid movement, the atmosphere was transformed from the everyday eatery to an elegant five-star restaurant. An Italian musician entered the room playing "Solo Mio" on his accordion. Veronique clapped her hands in rhythm to the music.

"How can they afford all this? Some nights they can't even break even," Julienne muttered.

"Not my problem. If they want my business, they will do as I wish. You need to worry about designing *magnifique* garments and leave Alfie to *moi.*"

By the time the musician was done with his act, the food had arrived; but Julienne had lost her appetite. The three years she had been working for Veronique had been hell. It all started during her internship. Madam Sorie noticed Julienne's attention to detail, as a result, she became her favorite intern. During her internship, Veronique used her to run personal errands and pick up her lunch. She also arranged meetings and answered all of Veronique's calls. It left her little time to work on actual designs. However, as an apprentice, she must have stood out, because right before her term ended, she was offered a position as a Junior Designer. Working for a prestigious fashion house had always been her goal. So, she accepted the offer. At first, Veronique took her under her wing, showing her all the tricks of the trade. But as time progressed her antagonistic nature became apparent. Nothing the novice designer created pleased her critical eye.

7

Julienne pushed around the sauce covered pasta, thinking of a rebuttal.

"I know you think I am ruthless," Veronique began. "It's my job to make sure every piece that goes to the Fashion Week show is perfect. So, I am inflexible, and you can hate me all you want." She put down her fork and wiped her mouth clean. "You think, I don't know what they say about *moi,* what they call me?" She picked up the sketches again and studied them. "You're a romantic *chérie*. This type of clothing needs fabrics with a strong backbone and colors that breathe *Je suis* beautiful, I am Imperial, *n'est-ce pas*? If you cannot believe in your heart, you can't create. If *vous* cannot produce, *belle* Fashion Week merchandise. I will not let you disgrace our Imperial line. You have talent, now show it."

Did I hear right? The Ice-Queen admitting I have talent?

"What changes do you suggest? Julienne asked encouraged by the woman's admission.

Veronique shook her finger, "Oh no my *petite,* this is your *présentation*. If you can't wow me, you don't deserve to be in the show. There is always next year, but then you will be *histoire*."

Julienne frowned, stuffing a piece of the cannoli that had just been served in her mouth to keep from screaming.

"You have to decide, now, *tout de suite*, the wedding or Fashion Week? Come in the studio. Give me your very best." Veronique insisted, tasting the Tiramisu. "Tonio, service four stars today. Chef Luca, three. A little less mascarpone cheese next time."

They ate the rest of the meal in silence. When they were finished, Veronique threw a wad of cash on the table and left. Julienne gathered her work and asked for a box. She would take home the leftover dessert. Angelo could have it. Eating with Veronique always upset her stomach.

2

Angelo opened his untraceable phone. He typed in a string of alpha characters and waited. The screen lit up. The map feature showed him where he was to meet his contact in Madrid. He opened the attachment and read the file.

The flight attendant appeared offering beverages which he declined. Angelo studied the voices coming from the side aisle. It was standard procedure to check out every passenger on board. The two university students were returning home from studying abroad. The conversation revolved around their budding relationship. The man had traces of nicotine under his fingernails and jittery hands. A sign he needed a fix. His girlfriend flashed her credit card and ordered two drinks before the plane had left the runway. He had seen her type before. She was a product of old Basque money, a pampered, wealthy debutant rebelling against her parents' strict-up-bringing. A pre-arranged marriage was somewhere in her future.

Angelo felt for her. She would end up hitched to one of her father's associates. Most young women in the Basque region were married off to older men with larger inheritances. Her youthful beauty would entertain the old goat, but eventually, he would become bored and restless. She would return to the bottle or drugs, he would cheat on her and when she would try to leave him, he would beat her back into submission.

Angelo wanted to call Julienne and let her know he missed her, but duty called. He placed the earbuds on his ears and listened to the audio surveillance report. He had to keep his mind on this job. After committing to memory, the location, he deleted the files and put away his phone.

Most passengers were asleep or watching the movie playing. It was a Spanish Melodrama, with English subtitles. He had seen it before. The poorly made movie was not keeping the attention of the love birds either. For the guy with holes in his jeans and sand underneath his flip flops, the girl reading the tourism magazine was his whole world. Angelo wondered just how long it would take before Mommy and Daddy froze her accounts, and Romeo had to find a job flipping burgers to keep them afloat while she gave birth to their illegitimate child. Could they survive on love and minimum wage? Could Julienne's love for him survive the next few weeks? Would it survive the truth? Angelo lowered his gaze towards the walkway between the isles giving the couple some privacy.

He recalled moments when only the thoughts of his wife had kept him breathing. He owed her so much. Once he finished the Madrid assignment, he would tell her everything. He pulled up a picture of her on his phone. It was the first picture he had copied from her dossier. It was the one taken

11

by the newspaper when she won the Cattleman's Fashion show in Vineland, New Jersey. Her face was naturally flushed from the cold. Her honeycomb eyes though partially hidden under her cowboy hat were large and soulful. The tempest of ruby curls surrounding her slender shoulders, made her appear of high school age but she was in her twenties. He had no idea back then that one day she would own his heart.

***

He had officially met her in the fall of 1997. She was a college freshman with big dreams of becoming a Fashion Designer. She worked part-time in a boutique in SoHo and also attended NYU. Due to her excellent writing skills, her professor had gifted her with a column in the NYU newspaper. As an extra credit assignment, she was asked to write an article about the plight of the homeless in New York City.

Angelo's pastor had just bought a warehouse and was converting it into a soup kitchen. Julienne doubted that one soup kitchen could turn a place as jaded as Downtown New York around. Her skepticism was met with a challenge. The pastor asked her to become a volunteer. If she stayed the whole six months serving the poor, he would allow her to report her findings. Not only would her article be featured in her column, but the pastor would give her permission to share the story with the New York Times!

It was during her time volunteering at the soup kitchen that Angelo got to know the cocky college student. At first, they spent a lot of time arguing politics and religion. She didn't hold a very high opinion of God, but like most people she was curious. Angelo decided instead of tackling her unbelief with his human effort; he would let God do the work. He invited her to a Bible study led by the founder of One Serving or Two soup kitchen. Questions poured out of her like an open faucet. Between Bible Studies and witnessing the transforming power of God in some of the homeless, her soul was stirred. The gentleness beneath her armor of enmity; drew Angelo like a magnet. His feelings for her grew. Feelings that were forbidden.

It was on the Ferris Wheel in the Italian Festival where for the first time he let his feelings dictate his actions. It could have been the way her honey-colored eyes looked at him, or the way her hair was tossed about by the wind. Perhaps the lure was the tenderness he had found in her heart. Whatever the case, he was hooked. Suspended above the glow of the city lights, he pointed out the Brooklyn Bridge and kissed her. Most women he had kissed had responded favorably. Not Julienne. The minute their car reached the ground, she bolted out of the cart and lost herself in the crowd. The next day, he found a note attached to his windshield. It was an apology with an explanation. In the note, she shared how her father had abandoned her family and how her prayer for his return had never been answered. She did not believe in love. She did not want him to waste his time on her.

He crumbled the letter. He identified with the pain of abandonment all too well, but he would not sacrifice their love on the altar of her past. He was a man of action and he would not be easily deterred. He wanted Julienne to become a bigger part of his life. Therefore, he put a plan in motion to fight any obstacles that stood in the way of winning her heart. The plan was built on a lie. A lie fabricated to protect her. One that had given him five glorious years with her. But lies always had a way of coming out.

The pilot announced they were circling Barajas Airport. Angelo's throat felt dry. He lifted his eyes to the heavens and prayed. *Here I go again, God. Protect me from danger. Keep me alive so I can finally be honest with her.*

3

Julienne returned home from her early dinner to an empty apartment. She removed her heels and placed the fridge. She chewed on two anti-acid tablets while sizing up the blurry smudge still sitting on her counter. She buffed the marble until all she could see was her face on the shiny slab.

While she tidied up her kitchen, she daydreamed about her upcoming nuptials. Angelo was standing at the altar. Two perfect emeralds beckoned her. The bride walked in, blushing among rainbow flowers and virginal lace. Fairy tale perfect. Then a thin vein of mist made its descent. It twirled like a tiny tornado, expanding with each turn until it reached the altar. The fog whirled around the groom. It began to rise higher and higher carrying him away until he was gone!

Settle down, it's just stress. She told herself turning on the dishwasher. She twisted her hair into a bun and changed into her comfortable sweatpants. She brought out her laptop and found a cozy spot on the balcony chaise.

Julienne opened her computer. Out of habit, she checked her inbox for any last-minute RSVPs or work-related mail. There were twenty. She would read them later. Just before she clicked off, a new email popped up. It was from *Indigo@source.net*. She recognized the sender right away.

He is not who he claims to be

The earlier message rattled around her brain. Fingers itched to open the new message. Angelo loved her, so nothing that the second email contained could change that. She dried her perspiring fingers on her pants and clicked it open.

Lies come easy to those who are skilled.

"Lies? What lies? Angelo is an open book. Sure, may he travel a lot, but that's because he's a financial consultant who specialized in foreign markets!" She told herself," silencing the intrusive thoughts. *What about all those bizarre accidents that happen when he travels? Coincidences? What if they are not?*

Julienne tapped the screen. *Lord, do I need to pay attention to this?* A list began to form in her head. She opened a Microsoft Word document and began typing. She counted all the multiple times Angelo had to fly off to a last-minute meeting across the globe. It was during those meetings he usually came back with an accident-prone souvenir or two. The horse that had kicked him in Italy and the trolley that overturned in England. Snake bites in Paraguay, quarantine for Malaria in South Africa, and who could forget the slip and fall into a hot tub in Japan? Just how normal was it

for a person to always return from abroad bruised and battered?

She picked up her cell phone. If anybody could find out
who was behind the emails, it would be Dream Chaser. She
had met the computer genius at the library while working on
a project for her History of Fashion class two years ago. They
both had been perusing the fiction section. He was intrigued
as to why a designing major would be interested in espionage
books. After he had introduced himself and expressed his
obsession with that genre, it did not take long for them to
become friends. They met frequently at the nearby donut and
coffee shop to exchange conspiracy theories on the inner
workings of the CIA.

What Julienne liked about her geeky friend was that in
his spare time he hacked computers. Then he would share the
information he had learned with her.

"This should be a piece of cake. Just forward it to me. No
worries, it's probably some cyber joker." Dream Chaser told
her after she had explained about the mysterious emails.
Julienne thanked her friend and hung up. She was worrying
about nothing. Angelo was probably enjoying a celebratory
meal with his new client. Feeling a little more settled, she
picked up the sketch Veronique had decorated in red and
began correcting her work. It was 8:00 P.M. when the horn
of an irate driver woke her up from her unplanned nap. She
closed the computer and dragged herself inside. Tomorrow
would be a more productive day.

4

It was 2:00 a.m. by the time Angelo had finished going through customs and had rented the taxi. Madrid with its large fountains and old architecture had always been one of his favorite places to work in. He signaled the taxi to let him off at Alcala Street and walked on foot to the center of the square. In front of the City Hall building was Cibeles Fountain. The brightly lit fountain was built at the end of the 18th Century during the reign of King Carlos III. Angelo looked at the marble goddess being pulled by a lion-drawn chariot. The last time he was in front of Cibeles was last year when the Real Madrid soccer team won *La Copa Mundial*. The square had a merry atmosphere that night, as the players and enthusiasts alike celebrated their win against the Italians. Tonight, however, the Roman mythological deity rode alone.

Angelo met his contact under the slice of a crescent moon. He joined the Spanish Consular in one of the outside tables of *El Gallego Restaurant*. He was a portly man with graying sideburns. Madrid, like New York, was known for some great middle-of-the-night cuisine. Angelo ordered Seafood *Paella*. As they waited, he made a mental note. He would bring Julienne during their honeymoon. His beloved would be enthralled by the view of the lights dancing on the streams of water coming from *Cibeles*.

The consular drank down his Sangria in one greedy gulp. He dragged his Castilian Z's spitting food out of his mouth. He complained about his work schedule, his nagging wife, the lousy Soccer season, and how the crime rate had risen in the city since the new mayor had been elected. After he had consumed all the food on his plate, he handed Angelo his business card. On the back of the card, he had written the coordinates. On their way out, the consular shook Angelo's hand slipping him the keys. Angelo excused himself to use the men's restroom and exited through the back door of the restaurant.

The Audi was left parked in the employees' parking lot. He pulled out the case underneath the seat and made sure the vials of yellow liquid inside were tightly secure in the compartment. He programmed the GPS and followed directions.

Miraflor De La Sierra was thirty miles from the capital. The target's hideout was a small hacienda overlooking a small fishing village. He turned off the motor and cut the lights. He opened the glove compartment, pushed in the false wall, and removed the case hidden there. He fiddled with the comb nation until it popped open. With his pointer finger, he fished out the brown contacts and put them on. Next, he put on a pair of thick-rimmed glasses and a wig. Pouring gel in his hands, he slicked back the long ponytail hairpiece. He placed his Glock in the waistband of his pants and inserted the prosthetic mouthpiece extending his jaw forward. The lift inserts in his shoes would make him taller and produce Don Miguel's distinctive limp. It was uncanny the way he was able to impersonate or create new identities. It was an art he had learned to perfect and one that he hoped he would never have to use to protect his future wife.

Angelo stepped into the crisp Mediterranean air. He moved through the trees and shrubs skillfully. Silent footsteps brought him to the front door. He used the heel of his hand to knock. When the enemy opened the door, he was greeted with a kiss on his cheek and a hardy handshake. He estimated it would take about three hours from start to finish, but in the end, everyone would curse the moment they had crossed over to the enemy's side.

The cavalry arrived when he was finishing off the last thug. Angelo held his ribcage. Probably one or two ribs were cracked he assessed, stepping over the dead body of a teen-age boy. There were times he hated his job. Tonight, was one of those nights. The cleaning crew would arrive soon, and the trail of dead bodies left behind would disappear under the fizz of the acid bath. The agent knelt to close the eyes of the dead boy. He wondered, what kind of a monster he was for depriving the kid of a decent burial.

The agent wiped his bloody brow. He needed stitches which meant having to sell another tale of the clumsy fiancé to Julienne. The embassy would provide first aid and patch him up. Normally, he would rest in a comfortable suite and be ready to fly out in the morning, but he received an unantici-pated text, altering his plans.

***

Inside the American Embassy, Angelo was taken to the infirmary where he was checked over and sewn up. Shortly after, he was placed in an interrogation room with two-way glass. He was told to remove his shoes and was stripped searched. The men found nothing incriminating. He was told to shower and was given a new set of clothes. When he was finished dressing, a black hood was placed over his head. He was led through several winding hallways. They took him on an elevator ride down to the bowels of the Embassy. Once inside the clandestine quarters, his hood was removed.

Angelo blinked surveying the opulent room. Handcrafted wooden shelves filled with priceless first editions aligned the left wall. On the right, a mammoth jade statue of a warrior created an interesting focal point. Deer antlers and a cougar's taxidermized head completed the hunting wall.

Behind the Mahogany desk sat the most influential man Angelo had ever known. From the vintage phonograph, the sound of Beethoven's Ninth Symphony ebbed and flowed with precision. The man with the receding hairline and eyes closed, lifted his callous hands as if conducting the concerto. Angelo's shoes sank into the plush carpet. He made his way to the velvet armchair.

"I gather things went well in Madrid?" He asked, one hand still directing the instruments.

Angelo's eyes shifted sideways to the gold-plated book inside the glass display case.

"It went as planned... Congratulations, I see you acquired a copy of the Gutenberg Bible," he noted eyeing the rare masterpiece.

"Yes. And my bank account still has the scars to prove it," the older man chuckled.

"Do you plan to read it?" Angelo asked.

21

He walked around the desk, uncorked the Brandy bottle, poured it into a crystal sniffer, and offered it to his protégée.

"No thank you."

"That's very commendable of you. The others take to my Brandy like water. They end up telling me all sorts of things once the booze kicks in…but *you* have always been the exception."

He leaned on the glass casing and downed his Brandy. "I may take up Bible reading someday. But regardless of your optimism my young friend, I have committed so many sins that I am going straight to Hell. No stops at the pearly gates for me."

"Do you remember what I told you when you were laying on that gurney, full of holes?" Angelo asked.

He brought down his gaze, "I have the book turned to that page precisely."

"Good, then you know John 3:16 can be your saving grace, Javier… if you let it; but you didn't call me here to discuss your faith."

The enigmatic man moved away from the Holy Book. The hand with a missing finger tapped the intercom.

"Bring my friend a bottle of water."

A chilled bottle of Perrier was brought in on a silver tray. Angelo helped himself.

"What an absurd paradox I find myself in. I owe you my life," Javier said, refilling his thirst-quencher. "You broke the rules. If would have been anyone else, I would have had you eliminated on the spot. So, have you told her yet?"

Angelo leaned forward and stretched his aching back. The job in Madrid had been easy compared to other missions, but he had underestimated the extent of the injury from the kid's brass knuckles. It had left him welts that would take time to heal.

"I plan to tell her as soon as I get back," He answered between sips.

"I won't tolerate manipulation of any kind. If she negates your offer, you will graciously exit. I have made other arrangements."

"As you wish," he answered, forcing a smile. Though he showed no outward emotion, the light clank of the empty bottle on the tray gave away his irritation.

Javier smirked, swirling the ice cubes in his glass. "You have always exceeded my expectations. But if you fail her in any way, I will nail your head to the wall myself."

He drank the last drop and threw the expensive crystal into the fire.

"Tell me, do you think she will love you with the same intensity, once she knows?"

Angelo met his steely eyes. "It could never be the same. In some ways, it might be... I don't know. Regardless of the outcome, the truth *will* set us both free."

5

One day it will be my label on these dollies, she thought, revising the drawings scattered on top of her desk. She had managed to compile a nice collection using pastel colors with bright bold accents. The garments had rich textures that would surely win her entrance to the coveted Fashion Week. Julienne leaned in to sign her designs. When she had finished the round loop of her last E, she realized what she had done. Those designs didn't belong to her! She worked for Imperial. Her designs were owned by the fashion house.

Those who had been privileged enough to leave the house and set up their firms had the backing of very influential people who were willing to invest their money in them. But her fiancé detested socializing with the superficial industry breed. The only other way to earn enough cash to leave Imperial would be to throw her morals out the window as some of her classmates had done. They would frequent the after-hour parties in search of wealthy donors who would

24

fund their visions. The problem was every time a check was written, it would come with an invisible contract that read, "You will do whatever I ask when I ask, and how I want it done." Her friends went from aspiring designers to the prostitutes of the affluent and powerful. She flipped the pencil upside down and erased her handwriting. Very gently she blew on the paper until all the eraser dust had flown away.

The pensive designer stood by the large windows that opened to the veranda. From the twentieth floor of Imperial Designs, the world looked very small. The rain pelted the windows, as the temperature dropped down to the 30s. The soup kitchen would be filled with those wanting shelter from the weather and a warm meal. It was not her intention to make them wait, but sacrifices had to be made. Especially because impressing Veronique could secure her a spot on the runway of the biggest fashion show of the year. Satisfied with her finished product, Julienne bent down and retrieved a box from her drawer. Last month, Angelo had brought her a delightful gift from Dubai. Inside the box, nestled in velvet, was a silk scarf. The scarf had been hand sewn especially for her. Its peacock blue and gold strands, unknown to most, had been the inspiration for the collection she would be showcasing. When she tied the scarf around her neck, her eyes caught the light bouncing off the diamond on her finger. Her stomach tightened. She opened her purse and took out the paperback. Julienne turned to the page she had dog eared and removed the folded piece of paper.

"He is not who he claims to be. Lies come easily to those who are skilled."

It was useless. She had read them out loud in hopes that the words would release the hold they had on her. But hearing them from her lips cemented her fears. She should have listened to Dream Chaser and let it go, but the words owned her. Julienne refolded the paper and placed it back inside the novel. It was close to six; if she didn't leave now, she would not make it in time to help with dinner. She shut down her computer and put on her raincoat. She locked her office door and walked down the hallway.

The elevator doors opened. Her heels clicked loudly as she walked into the monstrous cavern. The elevator stopped on the next floor. A boyish-looking man carrying three large rolls of purple cloth entered, followed by a few lingering workers from different departments. Once on the ground floor, they flooded out, hurrying to catch the last bus or train home. Julienne also hurried her pace. Muggings in empty buildings were not uncommon in the Garment District.

Rain fell steadily upon the heavy evening traffic. The blasting wind whipped her coat. She ran, her leather boots splashing against the wet pavement. Pedestrians held on with two hands to their swaying umbrellas as they waited under the torrential downpour to cross the intersection. She took cover under the ledge of a nearby bakery. Taxis lined up to pick up drenched passengers. Julienne darted across toward a yellow one waiting at the curb. It was bumper to bumper for a few streets before the taxi began to pick up speed.

***

Only a light sprinkle of rain remained from the afternoon thunderstorm. One Serving or Two Kitchen Ministries was located inside a vast warehouse. It served the metropolitan area with food from donating grocery stores. Volunteer cooks and servers rotated every week to help feed the homeless.

Julienne removed her coat and wrung out her damp hair. She took one of the aprons hanging from a hook and put it on. Then she picked up a shower cap from the box beneath the aprons. With her fingers, she opened it and stuffed her hair underneath the cap. Julienne washed her hands and arms up to her elbows and dried them with a paper towel. Ever since the church had shown a documentary on illnesses contracted by unsanitary food preparation, she was extra careful.

Placing a pair of plastic gloves on, she scanned the room. She found Angelo in the serving line. Their eyes met. She silently thanked God he had returned safe and sound. He winked at her, mouthing the words "I Love You." Julienne lifted her pointer fingers bending them into a heart shape. She squeezed through the crowd and found her place between the vegetable salad and roasted potatoes server. A man with vacant eyes and missing teeth handed her his bowl.

"Don't forget them carrots," he said, watching her fill the bowl with chicken soup.

She handed it back to him. Sad eyes looked down at the steamy mixture. Carefully she scooped out a generous second helping of carrots and deposited them in his bowl.

"This girlie knows what I like." He beamed and blew her a kiss.

Angelo watched as Julienne conversed with those going through her line. He wiped his hands on a kitchen rag and went over to her.

"Hey, what's the hold up over here? He teased, wrapping his arms around her midriff. Apart from when they were alone, the soup kitchen was one of those rare places where Angelo felt relaxed.

27

She pushed him away playfully, "Hands off buddy, can't you see I'm working?"

"Yo, Angelo, when is the big day, man?" called out the teenager handing out hot chocolate at the end of the line. The buzzing from the noisy crowd grew more intense. The old man with the soup made uppercut boxing gestures, almost knocking his meal over. The rest of the hungry bunch hurried down the line to be served.

"September 15th. Right Juls?" Angelo answered loud enough for everyone in the place to hear.

"I'll think about it and let you know."

"She cut you deep, man!" The teenager snickered. The crowd began to whistle and hoot.

"Okay keep the line moving. If you come back on the 16th you can all have some wedding cake," Angelo instructed, serving the last person in line.

Pandemonium broke out in the crowded hall. People clapped and stomped their feet. A bold teen with dreadlocks stood on a chair and began to rap about the happy couple. A little one broke away from her parents and pushed her way to the front of the crowd. She handed the bride-to-be a package.

Julienne gently tore open the newspaper wrapping. Inside lain a cross made from popsicles sticks and painted white. Scribbled in second-grade penmanship was the verse Psalm 121v1.

I look up to the hills where does my help come from? My help comes from the Lord maker of heaven and earth.

"This is the most beautiful cross I've ever seen; do you know why?"

The little girl swung her matted braids back and forth.

"Because God's little princess made it with her own two hands."

Julienne hugged the small child. Her eyes moistened. The crowd before her had come into her life as foul-smelling, drug addicts, and mentally unstable individuals. But Angelo had taught her to look beyond the outward appearance. Through the years among the homeless, there had been success stories but also major losses that touched her deeply. They had become family, and she had grown to love them more than she had expected to.

While everyone was finishing their meal, Julienne helped pick up the used trays. Once the building had cleared, Angelo lifted the chairs on the table so the cleaning volunteers could mop the floor.

"Hey Juls, how about if we go to my place, we can catch a movie or finish that puzzle we started?" Angelo said taking out his keys.

"I would love to, but I have to get the mockups ready for tomorrow. Veronique is out for blood."

Throwing on his coat, he ushered her outside the ware-. house. "Don't worry 'bout it. I 'll get some of my boys on it,"

"You're gonna make her an offer she can't refuse?"

"Something like that."

Julienne giggled. "Okay, Godfather. But not tonight."

He held her close. "This can't continue. Between your work and mine, we hardly see each other."

She nuzzled his neck, enjoying the smell of his after- shave. "After Friday, you will have me every night and every day for the rest of your life."

"I am going to hold you to that, Miss Gutierrez."

"It's Julienne Juls, remember?"

"Right. J.& J. Designs... But let's keep it simple for now, at least until you take my last name."

"Been thinking about that. I want to hyphenate it. How does Julienne-Juls-D'Marco sound?"

"It has a nice ring to it." He agreed, opening the door of his Porsche.

"Wait a minute," She said, brushing the hair away from his forehead. The fluorescent light from the street lamp shined on Angelo's skin making visible the tiny line of stitches above his eyebrow.

"How did it happen, Angelo? And don't tell me some crazy story."

Angelo repositioned his hair. "There is no story. I walked into a pole."

"A pole?"

"Do you want to drive?" he interjected, throwing her the keys.

"Yeah, I do. At the rate you're going, you'll be in traction for the wedding."

Angelo blew off her comment. It was okay he had to play the injury-prone wimp for one more night. Soon enough his fiancée would see how coordinated her future husband was. Would she be frightened once she knew how those injuries truly happened? She was enjoying the feel of the leather steering wheel underneath her hands, way too much. He chuckled to himself. The woman found joy in the simplest things. Driving his car was one of them.

"Hey," he crossed his eyes and stuck out his tongue sideways. "Will you still love me if I end up like this?"

"I will love you even if you end up in a full-body cast," she answered, fixing the mirrors. "Now hurry up and get in; I want to hit the road."

30

***

The NY skyline glimmered like thousands of diamonds suspended in columns reaching as far as the eye could see. After the rainstorm, the Big Apple had transformed into the pulsating, fun-filled city it was known for. People from all nationalities traveled on foot from one hotspot to another in search of entertainment. Three-dimensional Billboards and holographic images bounced off each high rise, as a blend of musical pieces poured out of large, mounted speakers creating a festive atmosphere.

"You know Grease is playing at the Radio Music Hall tonight," Angelo commented, pointing toward the colorful marquee as they drove by.

A grin appeared on her face. Angelo pushed the button lowering the windows. The music filled the car. Julienne pretended not to hear it. But the music was so catchy it didn't take long before she was belting out Sandy's part of the duet. Angelo joined in, taking over the part of Danny Zuko. By the time they arrived at their destination, they had sung their off-key version of the whole play.

Her building was the tallest of the three that loomed above them. In the car, the devious Italian had waged a tickle war on her unsuspecting ribs. Julienne bolted out of the car. He caught up with her at the stairs. Laughter burst from her lips as he continued to tickle her.

'Stop!"

"Give me your ID card or your armpit gets it next." He jested.

She handed him the card that gave them access to the building after hours. He placed it in the slot and the magnetic double doors whizzed open. The sensor lights came on. As they were walking toward the elevator, Angelo scooped her up into his arms. Humming a lullaby, he rocked her back and forth. Coming out of the elevator he pretended to trip and almost drop her. The unskillful man regained his balance. As soon as they were inside her apartment, he threw her on the couch and turned on the lights.

"Are you sure you don't have a concussion?" Julienne asked standing up.

Angelo wrapped his voice in his Italian accent and thrust his hands outward, "Whatsa matter, Juls, you don't like the new improved Angelo, eh?"

What had gotten into her levelheaded fiancé? Julienne wondered, hanging up her coat on the coat rack. She took a moment to boot up the computer before returning to his side on the couch.

"Do you know how beautiful you are?"

The muscles in her body tensed up. He stroked her hair, playing with the ringlets. She tried looking away, but his fingers coaxed her face toward his, "Did you hear me, you *are* beautiful. Why can't you believe me?"

The young woman shrugged, picking at her cuticles.

He tickled her again. "Smile for me."

Julienne faked a smile then wiggled out of his arms taking residence on the other side of the sofa.

He took advantage of the space and stretched out his body on the cushions. He lifted his legs and propped his size eleven shoes on her lap.

"Angelo, why do you love me?" she asked, removing his shoes.

"Cause you're smoking baby."

"I'm serious. You could have had any woman you wanted," Julienne added rubbing his feet. "They all find you irresistible. So why me?" *And why am I getting emails saying you are not who you say you are?*

"You're the complete package. Beautiful, talented, and smart."

The intensity in her brown eyes begged for more than just a pat answer.

"Okay, let me try to explain this to you for the hundredth time. I love you cause underneath all that beautiful skin you have a selfless heart. I know you gripe about your boss, but I also know that you work as hard as you do because you don't want to let anyone down. You give 100 percent of yourself and rarely ask for anything in return; that's a real turn-on."

"Ang..."

"Shh, I'm not finished. You make me want to be a better man. You're a gift I don't deserve." He planted his feet back into his shoes.

So, he's a gorgeous Klutz, Lord, that is not a sin. I know he is a good man. Dream Chaser would have told me if he was iffy. "Promise me, no matter what, you will never leave me."

He brought his arm around her. He brushed her cheek, capturing a tear with his finger.

"Listen to me, Juls, I am never gonna leave you. We are going to grow old together and get on each other's nerves, I promise."

In one fluid motion, she was up. Julienne walked over to the paper pattern on her sketch board. She laid out the multi-colored metallic brocade and began cutting away the excess material.

"I have a lot to catch up on, and you probably have jet lag."

His expression stilled, and grew serious, "Why are you shutting me out?"

"I'm not. I love you, and we will have plenty of time for the mushy talk after the wedding. It's just... I have to get these done."

Angelo held his tongue; if he didn't leave soon, he would implode. With each day that passed, the secret grew bigger and more insurmountable. It was torture to keep lying to her. But it was not the right time for disclosure. She was too wrapped up in her self-doubt to think rationally. He could not give her another reason to blame herself, at least not tonight. Most likely she would work for a bit, then return to the pages of her novel. His fiancée would read long into the night allowing the mystique of the characters to bring out the adventurous woman in her. In the morning, when her subconscious would be flowing with thoughts of traveling through distant lands and facing dangerous situations, he would tell her.

"Make sure you get some sleep. The next few days are going to be extremely important" Angelo uttered, dropping a kiss on the top of her head, before letting himself out.

6

The shooting pain down her back woke her. She lifted her head, curls hanging like a curtain in front of her eyes. She flipped her hair back and thrust forward giving her body a good stretch. What she needed was a hot bath to get the kink out of her neck.

The sleepy woman turned on the shower, then peeled off the wrinkled shirt and skirt she had worn all night. The water felt good on her tense muscles. Lathering her hair, she washed away the traces of an all-night workathon.

***

The sunlight was filtering through the kitchen window, reflecting off the stainless-steel appliances. She turned on the coffee pot, allowing it to percolate. Tossing a bagel in the toaster oven, she glanced at the clock. It was only 6:00 a.m. The thought of going back to bed was tempting. But instead of catching another hour of sleep, she decided to hang up the cross that the girl at the soup kitchen had made them. Julienne was getting down from the chair when her phone rang. She dropped the hammer and picked up the call. It was Angelo; he was bringing coffee.

No, no no! I can't waste time today.

"Angelo, the Ice Queen was not thrilled with my sketches. She will kill me if I don't get my tail in the office asap," she said putting the hammer away.

"You don't understand; she is liable to cancel our honeymoon," she added firmly, taking sips of water to cool off her Java burned tongue. Julienne suggested they meet for lunch instead. They could walk together to the caterer to pay the last installment of the reception dinner.

"Honey, I have to perfect those designs before the wedding. My job depends on it," she stated, balancing the phone in her ear.

Her fiancé's voice was noticeably upset, but she had no time to spare. Julienne checked she had backed up all her work into her flash drive, then tossed it inside the zippered compartment of her attaché. She blew him a kiss through the phone, ending his cajoling.

Phew…thank God I am not standing in front of him. Those green eyes of his would do me in for sure.

Something was bothering her normally composed fiancé. Whatever it was could wait until lunchtime Today she would solely concentrate on getting Veronique's stamp of approval on her prototypes. Once that was accomplished, she could dedicate all her time to him. She would even tell him about the annoying emails.

Julienne retreated to her room to dress. She had to look sharp. After trying on a few outfits, she settled on her red sweater dress. She stepped into her black pumps and looked in the mirror. Adding a gel to her hands, she smoothed down the curls that reached down to her shoulders. Apart from her golden-brown eyes, her hair was her next best feature when she was able to tame it. She turned sideways, checking for imperfections. The last bout of IBS had left her bloated. From the basket on top of her closet, she pulled out an onyx sash with a gold clip and tied it around her waist. Women living in the hub of the fashion industry had no excuse for looking unfashionable. Even on a shoestring budget, she could turn a simple dress into a fashion statement with just the right accessories. Satisfied with the look, she sat back to enjoy another cup of coffee. At 7:30 she left her apartment in hopes of beating the morning rush hour at the subway station. She made it to the platform just in time to catch the train before it departed for the Garment District.

* * *

The elevator doors opened, and the large compartment was filled wall to wall with latte-carrying executives. Some nodded their hellos, recognizing the Junior Designer as Veronique's newest find. Others swallowed their liquid breakfast in haste. The elevator stopped mid-way, allowing some of the staff to shuffle in. Imperial Publishing owned the whole building, but when the economic crisis hit, they took on other tenants. Many were foreign companies who cornered the market with creativity and large bank accounts. Her stop was on the 25th floor. It was reserved for Imperial Design's top designers. The penthouse suite had several offices. It also housed large workrooms where the seamstresses and supporting staff worked.

37

Julienne pushed the large glass doors open. She stepped up to the reception desk. The platinum-haired receptionist led her past the wall of oil paintings depicting fashion from the late 1800s to the present. Behind her, two young interns rolled the mannequins Julienne would need for the runway presentation. They stopped in front of the last office to the left. The receptionist unlocked it. The helpers unloaded the mannequins. Julienne dusted them off making sure she had removed every speck of dirt that had accumulated while in storage. She was about done dressing the dummies when Veronique made her presence known.

"You still do not comprehend Haute Couture. I should demote you to the Prêt-a-porter department," she lectured.

In the middle of listening to why the hemline on the skirt needed to be half an inch shorter, her cell phone chirped. Julienne glanced at the text.

"Give *moi!*" Veronique commanded, thrusting out her upturned palm.

"I'm not answering it. You have my full attention."

"*Non,*" Veronique insisted, snatching the phone from her hand. "I will keep it, till you produce couture worth my time."

Julienne opened her mouth to protest, but the words all came out in a tangled mess.

"*Mon Cherie*, I am doing you a favor; they think you're worth keeping. Don't look so... what's the word? Shocked. I pitch ideas all the time to the PR department. If they like, I know I am not wasting my time." She removed a piece of lint from her blouse and tossed it into the air." Now get to work *tout suite*, before I don't give you time for honeymoon," Her amethyst eyes danced with amusement as she placed the

38

chirping phone in the pocket of her slacks and exited the room.

Julienne twirled her hair, rolled back and forth in her chair, and chewed on the back of her pencil, hoping inspiration would kick in. It took some time, but an idea flourished. She took pins and pinned back the stiff fabric until she had created an hourglass figure. Once the last pin had been placed, she looked at the clock on the wall and sighed. Soon her fiancé would be neck-deep in numbers wondering why the woman who claimed to love him was ignoring his texts.

***

A loud blast rattled the windows.

"The towers have been hit!" the platinum hair receptionist shrieked, bursting through the door.

Julienne flew from her swivel chair, "What? What are you talking about?" A nervous laugh caught at her throat. The wailing of sirens filled her ears. They looked out the window. Outside, people ran madly through the streets. Cabs were lined one behind the other caught by the unprecedented traffic jam. Dark smoke rose like a dragon devouring the top of buildings.

A pale Veronique joined them, her hands shaking. She held out the phone to her. "Here."

Julienne read the text that had just come in.

Juls, Pray! Tower on fire.
Ur the only real thing in my life.
I will always love you.
Angelo

It took a few seconds before the urgency of the message registered. At the moment it was as if the world had stopped. The only thing she could hear was the sound of her heart's thumping against her chest. She wanted to scream, to pray, but was paralyzed. Veronique took the cell phone from her. Dialed. No reply. Dialed again. Julienne tried for herself. She sent out a text. No answer. Loud voices were coming from down the hall. They followed the voices to the conference room.

Secretaries, Designers, and the janitorial staff huddled together in front of the mammoth, plasma tv screen, their mouths hung open as they watched desperate souls jumping from the burning building.

"Oh my God!" They screamed as the South Tower, like a set of blocks swipe sided by an angry toddler, collapses to the ground.

She couldn't take it anymore. Why wasn't anyone moving? In blind haste, she ran out into the hallway. It did not matter who she bumped against or what she knocked over; Angelo was dying!

Veronique cut her off at a corner and ran past her to the elevators.

"You can't go out there!" Veronique warned, blocking the metal doors.

"If he dies, it's your fault; he was calling me. He needed me!"

"They've stopped all the trains; the streets are closed. Even if you could walk, you can't get past the fire trucks and ambulances. *C'est impossible!*" She said, grabbing Julienne by the shoulders.

"Get out of the way! Move!" Julienne screamed shoving Veronique to set herself free.

The French woman shrieked. Julienne took a step back and took off running toward the west corridor where the emergency stairwell was. She pulled the door open and ran smack into the security guard.

"Woah, where do you think you are going? It is not safe. All hell has broken loose out there. We are on lockdown until we know what is going on."

He led her to the nearest office and got her some water before returning to monitor the halls. Someone shouted that the North Tower was falling. Julienne dropped the paper cup holding the water and ran back to the conference room. She arrived just as thousands of pounds of steel and concrete decimated on the screen. A sick feeling rose from the pit of her stomach. She leaned forward clutching her middle.

"Noooo!"

7

The lights that remained flickered on and off. Glass shattered as the ground gave way underneath frantic feet. Concrete flew like unguided missiles, smashing into those running to escape the madness. Awkward shapes of metal hedged in the plummeting bodies. Cries for mercy from tormenting pain echoed. He tried to move, to reach those hurting, but he could not. Fumes choked him. He took shallow breaths, listening to a hissing sound. He touched his hair. It was wet with blood that trickled down the side of his head. The hissing got louder. He forced his neck and looked up. From the ceiling, hanging like deadly snakes, two live wires crackled as sparks ignited from their ugly mouths. Lowering his eyes, he inspected the large chunk of concrete trapping his leg. He tried hoisting it up, but it was too heavy. He looked toward his phone lying on the ground next to him. The internal components had short-circuited. He took out the memory chip and with a rock he smashed it into tiny bits, pulverizing the sensitive information it carried. He couldn't afford to lose consciousness and his phone end up in civilian hands. A gush of blood dripped down his face, blurring his vision. He wiped the sticky substance on his torn shirt.

God help me. I don't want to die. Keep me alive, so I can help get the ones responsible for this. Lord, I need to return to Juls. I promise I will tell her the truth, even if I lose her. Give me a chance to set things right.

More ceiling caved in. He covered his head. A shard of dislodged roof hit his cheek. It hurt, but not as much as the gaping hole above his right ear that spewed blood like an active volcano. He started to shake; his teeth rattled inside his mouth. He was going into shock. Angelo ripped off one of his sleeves and made a tourniquet. He tied it tightly around his head. The shaking stopped. With his fingers he palpated the soreness on his cheek, checking for broken bones. He thirsted, his tongue sticking like sandpaper to the roof of his mouth. The structural foundation creaked and groaned. Sobs and screams of those whose hearts were still beating pierced the darkness.

"Stay awake! The pain you feel is keeping you alive!"

His advice ended in a coughing fit.

The building shifted causing an open can of soda to roll toward him. He stretched his body sideways. His muscles twitched. Like an overstretched rubber band, they obeyed, but not without excruciating pain. His fingers brushed against the can twice. He ignored the burning down his spine and tried again. This time an earthquake-like tremor moved the can closer. Most of the liquid had spilled, but the little that was left was enough to temporarily quench his thirst.

His eyelids were getting heavy, but he fought the desire to sleep by letting his mind wander back to the past.

43

***

It was all Julienne's fault. He had wanted to take her on a carriage ride through Central Park. But she insisted she had to finish her research paper on the fashion trends of the 20th century. That was the week she had been offered a paid internship with Imperial Designs. Angelo wanted to celebrate her accomplishment, but she dragged him to the library.

Julienne had busied herself perusing the non-fiction section of the NYU library. Though she had a stack of fashion magazines and books on the subject sitting on her table, she wanted more in-depth material. That studious spark did not last very long. Julienne was sidetracked by a book that was placed in the wrong section. It wasn't just any book. It was a brand-new espionage novel written by her favorite author. The reader brought the treasured find back to the table where Angelo sat reading a stock trading article. Julienne pushed the research books aside and started to inhale the novel. But every time she started on a new chapter, Angelo would make a funny face or comment and she would lose her place.

"The spy had a wife and kids back in Indiana. Do you think someone can live two separate lives like that?"

She had to go there. It was either that the other wives and girlfriends of his colleagues were dumb as rocks or she was more intuitive than most twenty-year-old. Then again, none of the other guys had gotten emotionally involved with a strong-willed designing major who was obsessed with the secret lives of spies. That's where he had to do some fancy footwork to convince her that it was all fiction and speculation.

44

She tapped her pencil on the table awaiting his response. He gave her a grin and shrugged his shoulders.

"The only secrets I know of are about corporate greed. It is hard to keep millionaires from investing in pipe dreams."

"Ooh, Angelo, check this out; they are introducing a new character. A love interest."

"Aren't you supposed to be reading up on *fashion*?"

"I can see him now," she said, moving her hands like a camera around his face, "he's cute like you but older and more mysterious."

Angelo lowered his eyes, pretending to read his magazine. The tiny beads of sweat on his hairline alerted him that his body was overreacting. He went to work regulating his breathing and his heartbeat.

"So, what happens to the poor Schmuck?"

She twirled her hair around her finger, "It's a secret."

It was time to change the conversation. A bribe always worked nicely in redirecting thought patterns. He offered to take her on the carriage ride but only if she concentrated on her research project for the next half hour, without any distractions. Julienne grumbled but eventually conceded.

***

Central Park was only a block away. He paid for the carriage and helped her up. He threw the thermal blanket over their legs and draped his arm around her. There was a nip in the air but not enough to be considered cold.

The horse's hoofs clicked and clacked down 5th street. Sturdy oaks dressed in bright orange and red regalia stood like soldiers ready to battle against the approaching winter. A group of competitive bicyclists whizzed past the horse-pulled carriage. The carriage continued down the scenic tour. He had paid extra so that the carriage would stop at romantic spots where they could get off and take pictures.

The carriage rolled deeper into the wooded areas of the park. Being a custom tour, the carriage took them down the private road that led them down 72nd to Cherry Hill. They were the only ones riding on the path when out of nowhere two teen boys appeared running alongside them. They climbed on each side of the carriage. One held a gun to the coachman, the other to the frightened couple. They forced the carriage to stop.

Angelo observed them. They were amateurs with no real experience to back up their big mouths. He wanted to smack the smirk off their faces, but unless they tried to shoot, he would not engage. The taller one with the multiple tattoos pushed him to the ground and took hold of Julienne. Angelo played the weakling, begging them not to hurt his girlfriend. The shorter one with the buzz cut and pierced eyebrow told him to shut up. He smacked Angelo across the head and bounced back to where Julienne and his accomplice stood. *Come on boys, stop messing with the pretty girl and come a little closer,* Angelo thought as he groveled. It was time for the waterworks. On command, Angelo's eyes welled with tears. Female agents were experts at using emotions to extract pity. Males, on the other hand, reacted with anger or disgust to another man's blubbering.

"I told you to shut the hell up!" the shorter one yelled making a fist. When Angelo did not shut up, he went for his face. Angelo awkwardly tried to protect his face with his hands, but the kid nailed him right under the eye. As the kid leaned in for the second punch, Angelo clumsily lifted his elbow jamming it into the kid's throat. The taller adolescent

46

with the skull tattoos watched his buddy lying on the ground weaponless and choking. Not sure what to do, he paced back and forth waving the gun in the air. He was cursing up a storm and bragging about all the things he would do to them. He stopped, pulled up his sagging pants, and pointed the gun at Julienne who was moving closer to Angelo.

"Freeze. Now throw me your purse," he said. After he had taken out her wallet, he threw the purse to the side and looked her over. "Get down on your knees."

Angelo grimaced and groaned, buying enough time for the snot-nosed kid to make his move. He would destroy the runt for even thinking of touching his girlfriend.

The plan changed when the coachman unexpectedly ducked under the carriage retrieving the gun the other kid had dropped.

"Patrick and James, you both have ten seconds to get your carcass out of this park!" the Coachman warned, aiming the weapon at the shorter kid. "Put that gun down and return the bag to the girl, before I shoot your head off!"

"Old man, you gonna do nothin," Patrick mouthed off.

The Coachman pulled the trigger. One of the small branches on the Elm tree fell to the right of the street punk.

"Next time it's your head!"

The kid knew the score. He put the gun on the floor and threw the wallet to Julienne. Then he took off running. The coachman fired two warning shots into the air. James who was still coughing on the ground stood up and ran hobbling behind his partner.

The coachman put a call into the office and went to calm the jittery horses. Once they were seated in the carriage, Julienne examined Angelo's face. It was purple where he had been punched. To anyone watching, the wimpy boyfriend had chickened out. Even his girlfriend had acted braver than he.

The coachman retrieved his top hat from the floor and dusted it off. He hoisted himself on the front and picked up the reins.

"I know those two. They have been in and out of Juvenile Corrections since they were old enough to walk. It is not the first time they tried to mug someone in Central Park," the coachman said, handing Julienne an ice pack from the first aid box under the carriage seat.

"That's some shiner you got. I know this is none of my business but you should take some self-defense classes. You don't want to get cornered in a dark alley, and those two, they don't forget a face. I have a friend at the Y..."

"You think they come after us?" Julienne interrupted.

"In case," he said handing Angelo a card, "tell him Rudy from the park sent you. He is a real nice guy. Teaches Martial Arts on Tuesday nights at the Y. Sorry your romantic ride was cut short. Next time you want a ride, it's on me. Ask for Rudy Thorn."

"We should call the police," Julienne suggested.

"You can press charges, but I already notified the Park Rangers. They will find them."

"Thank you," she replied, snuggling closer to Angelo.

"I would have popped a bullet in those two, but I know their Mother. She's a good Broad, works two jobs to make ends meet. Social Worker thinks they can be rehabilitated. So far nobody has been seriously hurt, but with the smart mouth they got, they're gonna end up on the bottom of the river, if you know what I mean?"

Julienne took the ice pack and held it to her boyfriend's cheek as they galloped back to the park's entrance. Angelo

48

thought about what Rudy had said. The young thugs had ruined his date. All the careful planning of surprises for his girl would have to be postponed. But there was no need to get the police involved. He would pay a visit to those juvenile delinquents and have a "little talk" with them. There was no doubt in his mind; that afterward, the boys would reconsider their criminal career.

***

Angelo's stomach grumbled. Patches of sunlight shone through the holes among the steel. Pipes that were underneath of what remained of the upper flooring exploded from the pressure. It sent cold showers to the incapacitated victim washing away caked-on blood and cooling his skin from the continual heat rising out of the spontaneous fires.

It was easy to become disoriented in situations like the one he was in. He took a thin rod he found lying on the ground and scraped the date on the slab imprisoning his leg. He knew the month and the year, but he was foggy on the day. Was it Tuesday? He counted back but he could not remember. He returned to the only source of comfort that was not fading.

"Can anybody hear me?" He yelled. "I don't know if you believe in God or not, but I am going to pray! God, I know you are sovereign overall. You are here with us. Please help us not give up or give in to fear. Keep us alive Lord, send us help. Amen."

A woman's scratchy voice responded from the darkness.

"Do you think God will forgive me? I slept with my husband's best friend. I was so mad at him!"

Angelo encouraged her to keep on talking. She told him the pain in her chest was unbearable. She had been faxing

49

some papers when the building began to move. The shelving unit that carried boxes of copy paper had fallen on her, pinning her under it. Angelo told her about Jesus and how no sin was unpardonable if you believed in Him and repented. With his guidance, she prayed for God to forgive her.

"Tell him I did love him," she said, taking her last breath.

He was alone again. Tears pricked his eyes. All the others had either fallen asleep or died. He heard the voice of his commanding officer. *Buck up soldier, real men don't cry.* At fifteen, he had bought into that lie. But he knew the truth; even Jesus had wept.

The tears cleared the ash from his eyes. He saw a light. In it was a beautiful woman with flowing brown hair and golden eyes. She smiled at him. He knew her, yet he could not register her name. He was growing more lethargic. Unable to keep his eyes open, he succumbed to the lure of sleep.

8

The announcement came over the loudspeaker around two-thirty. Like caged animals that had been freed, all the employees ran to the elevators. Fists flew after an argument broke out between two CEOs gambling for a spot on the next elevator. Julienne opted for the stairs. It was crowded, but people kept mostly to themselves. She was dizzy and out of breath, but she kept going. The wheezing made her stop on the fifteenth floor. She pressed herself against the wall to let the others pass. Inside the zippered compartment of her purse, she found her inhaler. She shook the canister and pressed the lever, dispensing two puffs into her mouth. The pressure in her chest started to diminish.

Only ten more floors to go.

She squeezed in between the space of people coming down. The rest of the way was easier. Before she knew it, she had reached the bottom floor.

Outside, a tidal wave of thick smog had swallowed the sunlight. People were running from one street to the next, looking for transportation. Julienne spotted a taxi driver leaning against the trunk of his car trying to light his cigarette. *Like there is not enough smoke choking us all!* she thought.

"Please take me to the towers! I...I was getting married. He texted me...He has to be alive!" Julienne blurted out.

The man took a long drag and stared at her unmoved. Julienne took a hundred-dollar bill from her wallet. The money was to pay the caterer, but she was willing to give it up if it meant she could get to Angelo.

"Look I have cash, it is all yours, just get me to the towers!." she said, flashing the money in front of his woeful face.

The man opened the cab door for her. Once they were both inside the cab, he addressed her.

"You were getting married huh? This whole thing is a joke. My ex-wife worked in the North. She has custody of my three kids. Hope she's not dead. I can't stay home to take care of a bunch of kids. They are all real spoiled too. She has them in that fancy school in Long Island. They won't like it with me, I work late, and my place is not kid-friendly. I can't take on any kids... I'll tell you what, I'm going to get you close, but you're gonna have to walk the rest of the way if it gets dicey, know what I'm saying?"

She climbed into the cab's backseat. Desperate people knocked on the windshield of the car shouting to let them in. If only she could fly! She punched in Angelo's number again and again on her cell phone. *Please answer!* Her bottom lip quivered, and tears puddled in her eyes. She had to find him. He had to be alive!

The cabbie turned the wheels away from the curve; they screeched pulling out in front of another car. The angered driver shot him the finger, to which the cabbie returned the favor adding a few obscenities of his own. As a comeback, the other driver drove his front fender as close as possible to the yellow cab's bumper. When he was inches away, he rested his palm on the horn. Julienne lowered her head. Between the smell of nicotine and the annoying noise coming from the car behind them, she was dizzy again. A fresh batch of tears poured out. *Get me out of here Lord, get me to Angelo... PLEASE!* After the fifth street, the revengeful driver let go of the horn. Julienne lifted her head and looked out the window.

"This is a conspiracy. The government is telling nothing, but we are at war. They are going to hit us with a nuclear bomb. We are sitting ducks," the driver commented as the news continued to blast through his car speaker.

"Can you please turn that off?"

He turned the volume down. "Lady, we are at war, you can't just stick your head in the sand and hope for the best...Some patriot you are."

They exited the bottleneck. The man with his non-stop blabbering was feeding her fears. A policeman directing traffic was blocking the turn lane. Julienne lowered the window and called out to him.

"Officer please, my fiancé is at the towers!"

"Sorry Ma'am you can't go in there. Authorized vehicles only."

"He texted me, He is in trouble. I have to get to him!" she shouted, opening the cab door.

"Stay in your car! "The cop placed his hand on his weapon, issuing her a silent warning. He turned his attention to the driver.

53

"Get her out of here!"

Julienne glared at the police but closed the car door. The driver clicked the child locks on and waited until the police signaled him to make the U-turn.

"Hey! Pipe down before you get us arrested," he said flashing her a dirty look. "I ain't got time for crazy. Where do I drop you off?"

Disheartened, she muttered her home address to the cabbie. He nodded his head and lifted the volume to hear the Presidential news conference already in progress.

Julienne sat back allowing the events of the day to unfold in her mind. She listened to what was being said from the Oval Office

Psalm 23, though I walk through the valley of death, I will fear no evil. She repeated the scripture President Bush had quoted. It was unreal. Evil as dark and sinister as this only happened in other countries. God had kept America in a bubble of protection. Wars were fought in distant lands where bombs and terrorist threats were part of the culture. Julienne used her inhaler again. *Why now Lord? Why have you taken your hand of protection from us?* Not only was Angelo gone, but the USA was under a terrorist attack! What would happen next? They had already hit the Pentagon and had tried for the White House. What other plans could they have to destroy North America? If only all those fictional spy novels were true and American spies could save the day.

The driver lit another cigarette. He found a spot a block from her apartment and let her out. Julienne paid him but he threw the money out the window.

"Take it, with your kind of crazy, you're gonna need it!"

She caught the flying bill and put it back in her purse and began her walk home.

God, I don't know why you have allowed this to happen to us. But if you are still listening, please help me find Angelo.

***

In front of the door of a neighboring Chinese restaurant, sat the owner and his wife. They were both crying. Julienne stopped. There were no words she could say to comfort the couple, but she had to try.

"Don't give up hope; he could have survived."

The thin man with elongated eyes cast them downward.

"He was a good son. Smart. Was in travel agency in the Twin when the plane hit. Getting a ticket to see sick grandmother in Japan."

"Kito was strong, like Angelo; they are survivors," she said giving them a comforting hug. She kept on walking until her apartment materialized in the haze. Some of the younger tenants stood on the top step, their eyes looking toward the fiery inferno glowing in the sky. A slew of women sat in a circle watching the news on a portable tv. Others discussed what they had witnessed. The doorman loosened the top button on his uniform. He sighed but made no effort to move. It looked like he had been glued to the same spot since the first plane had hit. Julienne pushed open the glass door and went into the building.

On her floor, there were no salutations from her neighboys who stood outside their apartments to get better reception on their phones. Not even a catcall from the fresh mouth in B13. Everyone was too involved with the recent happenings, to pay attention to the young woman struggling to fit the key in the lock.

***

Once inside, she threw the keys on the coffee table and went to bed. For a few minutes, she lay motionless. Fearful that if she moved the grief would crush her. But she couldn't just lay there while Angelo was trapped. Adrenaline ran through her like a circuit. She could feel the loud thumping of her heart in her eardrums. *How can I find you? They won't even let me near the place... God, I need a sign he is alive.* She sat up on the bed, panicking. Breathing hard, she continued her internal struggle. *What if he is dead? What if I can't ever see him again?* The poison of anger entangled her until she cried out with all her might.

"I HATE YOU, GOD!"

9

Day after day, like countless others, she dressed up walls, bulletin boards, and light posts with pictures of her missing fiancé. Mutual friends and co-workers helped, but the search was difficult because Angelo was an orphan and had no living relatives. Even Dream Chaser had no answers for her. It was as if the earth underneath those towers had swallowed him.

Full of confusion and grief, she paid a visit to her pastor. She found him among the blood and gore of the makeshift triage unit that now had taken over the soup kitchen. Seeing she was in a state of shock, he took off his examining gloves and spent some time counseling her. He prayed and shared stories about how God's goodness was still evident even amid such tragedy. He detailed how others had found their missing and that she needed to trust that God had a plan. He emphasized if God had taken Angelo home, he would be in heaven waiting for her. But the words sounded empty.

Julienne was making her way through the rows of occupied cots when a callous hand gripped her arm. She looked down and found a recognizable face. It was the man who had been at the soup kitchen. It seemed ages ago. The elderly man was covered in white ash; one of his eyes was swollen shut.

"Carrots," he said battling to breathe.

Anger burned inside her against the God who had allowed such an unspeakable act of horror to happen to innocent people. For what seemed endless hours, Julienne worked her fingers to the bone, easing some of the sufferings that surrounded her. While she helped clean and bandage the wounded, she kept the hope in her heart alive that someone was comforting Angelo in his hour of need.

***

Julienne kicked off her sneakers and ripped off the clothing she had worn all day. She threw it in the pile of dusty laundry lying unwashed in the middle of her room. Most of her casual wear had been impregnated with the particle-filled ash that covered a large part of the city. The smog at times was so thick, residents with respiratory issues had been warned to stay indoors. But nothing could deter Julienne. Armed with her inhaler she had continued her daily search, only to return to her home empty-handed.

She took a quick shower and half-dried herself. Her stomach grumbled; she made herself some cocoa and drank it in bed while watching the 11 o'clock news. When the first round of commercials came around, her eyelids began to flicker. Exhausted from the restless search, she fell into a deep sleep.

It was three o'clock in the morning when she woke up screaming. Sweat had soaked through her nightgown, Making her cold and sticky. She stumbled out of bed. Memories of the horrific nightmare still alive in her mind. Angelo was lying helplessly under a pile of rubble. A fire had erupted. Delirious from the pain, he called out her name. He was alone, scared, and dying. Her head swam in a muck of horrid. thoughts as she got dressed. Her head swam in a muck of horrid thoughts as she got dressed. Moonbeams slipped through the vertical blinds lighting her way. Underneath a pile of ash-covered jeans, she found her cell phone. Once again, she tried his number. This time she got a message that due to the high demand, no calls were being processed. The last text message from him, sat on her phone unanswered. Julienne dropped her Android. The man who had promised to never leave her was gone. The painful realization hit her, fragmenting her heart.

"Why God, why did you take him from me!" She sobbed inconsolably into the early hours of the morning.

**

A hard knock at the door caused her to jump out of bed. She padded half asleep and looked at the security camera. A delivery man stood holding a large parcel in his arms. A memory flashed across her mind. They had been arguing over a very expensive security system Angelo wanted to buy for their new home. She was fine with the extra locks he wanted to install, but the security system was over their budget. Julienne had thought the conversation was over until Angelo came home one afternoon smiling like a little kid on Christmas morning. His client, one of the top executives at

Microsoft, had offered to buy them the system as an early wedding gift. The Silicon Valley millionaire used the same advanced technology in his mansion and had ordered it to be installed at the engaged couple's new home. At some point, she would have to make decisions whether she was going to sell the house waiting for her in the outskirts of New York.

Julienne unlocked the chain and opened the bolt. She explained to the man holding the rectangular box that there must have been some kind of mistake. She had not ordered anything. The delivery man thrust the receipt pad at her, grumbling that it was not his problem. She stayed calm, understanding his misplaced anger. The terrorists had trespassed into their beloved Big Apple, and as a result, the residents were wound uptight. According to a mental health poll she had recently taken on her phone, New Yorkers were increasingly showing signs of depression and. The last thing she wanted was to deal with a stressed-out delivery guy throwing a fit on her doorstep.

Who had he lost in the towers? She wondered, signing for the package. She lifted the pen.

"Fifteenth of September," The delivery man barked.

Julienne's hand started to tremble. She checked the return address on the front of the package, scribbled the date, and handed him the clipboard. She took the heavy box and closed the door with her foot. Julienne dropped the box on the floor and ran to the bathroom. She was going to be sick.

***

60

She stared at her pallid reflection on the vanity mirror. Leaning in, she splashed cold water on her face and rinsed her mouth thoroughly before returning to the living room.

Imperial Designs, Paris, France was where her one-of-a-kind wedding dress originated from. With the terrorist attack, she had not remembered to cancel the order!

She broke the adhesive tape on the box with a pair of kitchen scissors and removed the protective plastic covering the dress. Julienne brought the snowy gown to her chest. Grief-stricken, she rocked back and forth, humming the wedding march. There was a second knock at her door. Then another. It took her some time to get up and check the security camera. A woman with her face half-covered by the Red Cross issued disposable mask, waited outside. Julienne rubbed her irritated eyes and tapped the key to turn on the voice recognition feature on the machine. The thick French accent hollering to let her in was easy to recognize.

Julienne scratched her unkempt hair and opened the door. The Ice Queen walked in; her elegant figure draped in Dior. Veronique inspected the wedding dress lying on the floor. She came with news about an old friend who worked for *Wake-Up New York*.

Veronique stared at the dead roses in the waterless vase. "I can get you an interview with him if you like."

"What good would that do?" Aggravated, Julienne picked up a stack of flyers and moved them to the dining room table. Veronique held one up. Julienne could have sworn she saw tears forming in her boss's eyes.

"You can ask for help on TV. *Monsieur* Locke wants an exclusive. *What it is Like to Lose a Fiancé in the Twin Towers.* He thinks it will make him, *Célèbre,* famous?"

61

"Angelo is not dead! He is somewhere in those towers!" Hot tears sprung from her eyes.

Veronique stepped closer, stiffly patting Julienne's shaky shoulders. "Um...There, there...I am here to help you."

Julienne watched her protégée rub the satin material of the gown against her wet cheek. The woman cleared her throat and pivoted on her overly priced shoes. "No tears, I will return the dress. A Parisian Mademoiselle might want to purchase it." Veronique took it from her and set it on the sofa. "But they won't take it back if it is...wet."

The French designer pressed down the delicate material with her hands, removing the small wrinkles Julienne's rough handling had caused.

"Return the dress, throw it away or burn it, I don't care. I will marry Angelo if it is the last thing I do! "She stomped off to the kitchen to collect her thoughts. "Tell your friend if he can get me into Ground Zero, I'll give him the stupid story!"

10

Though two weeks had passed from the catastrophic incident, the aftermath was still quite evident. Cars were piled up in a heap on the side of the paper-littered streets. The acidic smell of smoke became more pronounced, making her throat start to itch. A Red Cross volunteer handed her a mask. Her escort flashed a media badge to a group of policemen barricading the entrance. The interviewing area was cordoned off by a rope with signs that read, *News Coverage Personnel Only.*

Though they were a block away from Ground Zero, they could see on the monitors what was being filmed by the high-power lenses. Julienne blinked back tears, breathing into the mask. It was like watching a disaster movie while knowing that the noise, smell, and groan of the real human wreckage was a couple of streets over. No Hollywood created mayhem or fake fatalities. No director would say "Cut" and the people who were trapped would easily lift the weightless props, dust themselves off and be ready for the next shot.

She looked up into the hazy sunlight struggling to shine through the opaqueness. Minutes ago, she had been peering out the window of Veronique's Lexus. The sky had been clear blue, with sunlight beams passing through the clouds. Now a depressing canopy fell on the city, making everything different shades of gray. Her eyes diverted toward what appeared to be part of a wall with blown-out windows, leaning on two other walls.

The symbol of capitalism and financial success had vanished. In its place laid the crude reminder that someone had waged war right in her backyard. On the monitor, the camera surveyed the area. The dust-covered faces of the assembly line of Police, Marines, Firefighters, and Paramedics moving piles of rock and debris were being aired. Rescue dogs barked as machines whirled and power tools buzzed. Spontaneous fires erupted, sending shards of glass and debris falling to the ground and volunteers running for cover. The dramatic shot would be replayed over and over for 24 hours a day on every screen in America.

Someone had set up three folding chairs for them. Julienne was ushered to the chair directly across from the interviewer. Johnny Locke looked more like a surfer than a reporter. The pony-tailed journalist was dressed in a Hawaiian shirt and faded jeans. He bowed low and kissed Veronique's hand before introducing himself.

The wind had picked up. Julienne pressed the mask's metal, molding it tighter around her nose, hoping the ash floating around them would not enter her lungs. Veronique sat coughing next to the audio technician, who offered them bottled water as they waited till the dust bowl cleared so they could start filming.

The interview was long and draining. The unconventional interview was long and draining. The unconventional news hound pounced on every nuance of human frailty that could sensationalize the story. Julienne's eyes burned from holding back tears. The questions he threw at her, dug into her reservoir of hope draining it. She would not lose control. Johnny Locke may have been an opportunistic leech, but he had promised her a designated time after the interview to address the viewers. She was not going to blow that opportunity with viewers.

After the interview was over, Johnny Locke took them on a tour of the other streets where the impact had been felt. It was one thing to see it on the television or computer screen; it was another to walk among the ruins. The camera from time to time zoomed into her pensive face, but Julienne paid no attention. A shiny object partly covered by a pile of rubbish called her attention. She kicked the trash away with her work boot and bent down to pick up a gold-painted handle.

Attached to it was a chipped ceramic mug. She wiped it with her shirt, uncovering the outline of a dove. At the request of the reporter, she read the inscription written in fancy calligraphy for the camera.

"Peace comes to those who wait."

Just as if on cue, the reporter signaled it was time for her to address the viewers. Julienne removed the paper mask and gave an emotional plea to the public to contact the station if they had any news of her missing fiancé. The lens zoomed, capturing her fingers clutching the mug she had found. The journalist grinned wildly.

11

"Hey buddy, can you hear me?"

Angelo stirred.

"Hurt...hurt, I..." he stuttered.

What was happening? He sounded like a two-year-old. He tried to tell them to check the area for other survivors, but he could not remember how to say it. A sharp pain. His body began to convulse.

"Hey, over here! We are losing this guy!"

***

Edison, New Jersey

A halo of pain burst through his scalp. His body jerked underneath the sheets as the wheels of the gurney turned sharply into the examining room. The triage unit stabilized him and ran some tests. There had been notable damage to his brain which explained the confusion and the toddler-like speech. Those could be corrected with a comprehensive treatment plan. Then there was his amnesia. That was a profound problem that could alter the patient's life dramatically. But there was hope. Having been excavated out of that hellhole and brought directly to The Brain Trauma Center in New Jersey, had given him an advantage many 9/11 victims didn't get. Why the paramedics had brought him across state lines was still unclear to Dr. Patricia Healy, Head of Neurology. They had blamed it on triage units not equipped for the type of traumatic brain injury the man had suffered. It was a flimsy excuse, but they did have a bed available, and Dr. Healy didn't have the heart to turn anyone away.

"*Someone up there must like him,*" was the buzz around the nurses' lounge about the New York transfer. Most patients with brain injuries could become nasty and even threatening, but not their John *Doe.* He was always cooperative and polite. On difficult days the staff would often catch him quoting scripture to himself. Wagers on what his profession. was ranged from pastor to model and everything in between. The nurses gave him the nickname, *Mr. X*...mostly because they needed to identify him, but some carried it a step further saying he was *X-actly* the type of man women dreamed of marrying.

***

Mr. X's days were filled with long hours of intense speech and physical therapy. Guessing Angelo's identity became a game of sorts.

"Okay let's go through this again; the paramedics found you in the towers. Do you think you worked in an of-fice?" his

68

speech therapist said, sounding out the letters slowly. She showed him a picture of an office on her tablet and waited.

"I don't remem b...er...ifff... off..isss," he answered, slowly forming the letters. The therapist with the sunny disposition held his face, gently positioning his jaw and mouth to help him pronounce the word.

"Off i...ce," he repeated.

Dr. Healy walked in. The speech therapist gathered her materials. She mouthed a slow goodbye, which he obediently repeated before she disappeared to make her rounds.

"How are you feeling today?" Dr. Healy asked, disinfecting her hands with the sanitizer affixed to the wall.

"F... eel... g... ood."

Her *John Doe* was a very interesting case. The mystery patient exuded total control, even over painful examinations. Dr. Healy unwrapped the bandage on his head and pressed on the sensitive areas on his cranium, just a little harder than before. He didn't flinch. Other patients would at least moan or cry out. Then there was his body, physically traumatized from injuries. Some of his injuries pertained to the tower collapse, others were older. Surprisingly, his muscles were still as hard as layers of bricks. It was expected for bed-bound patients to lose some muscle tone. Yet he had washboard stomach and six-packs abs that could only come about by years of disciplined workouts.

"You are very fit," she commented, lightly tapping her tuning fork on the inside of his heel. Opening a safety pin, she pricked his feet. "Do you feel that?"

"Y... yes... pin... ch."

Dr. Healy ran her fingers through her loose ponytail and sat down.

The amnesiac didn't know who he was, but that did not stop him from being able to see that his Neurologist was a knock-out. She was perfectly shaped, with a lovely face and a cute upturned nose. When she spoke, the birthmark resembling a heart on her cheek moved up and down.

Dr. Patricia Healy looked down at her notes. "Hmm... you are still having some headaches, but you won't take pain medication."

Angelo shook his head. "No med... s."

"Why? We keep tight control of how we dispense our Oxycodone and we give you the minimal dose to keep you comfortable. There is no chance you can become addicted if that is what you are worried about."

"No... pa... in... k."

She cocked her head. "Are you a masochist? All kidding aside, you strike me as military. Were you a soldier?"

Angelo pressed his lips together into a horizontal line. His shoulders pulled back, separating from the pillow, and his chin shot up. Dr. Healy noticed the sudden changes in his posture. She had struck a nerve, possibly a memory.

"Air Force... Marine? ...Navy...Army?"

Angelo moved his upper arm horizontally and bent the elbow at a 45-degree angle. The tip of his finger lightly touched his bandaged forehead just to the right of his right eye.

Dr. Healy saluted back.

He dropped his arm hitting his chest distracted by the cleaning lady who hummed her way into the room.

"That's enough, you rest. We will continue our conversation later. I will keep on searching for your identity. Don't tell the other patients, but I am kind of an amateur sleuth. Haven't had a patient yet who leaves the hospital nameless."

70

12

The man wearing the noir Pierre Cardin suit with a flaming red tie, sat hands clasped, unsmiling. Dr. Healy was told he was there from Corporate to do an audit of the hospital. The man took out a financial report and began explaining the graphical data on it. Things began to take a negative turn when Mr. Roberts questioned her about the amnesic patient from the towers.

"I must be frank with you doctor; Corporate is not pleased when hospital resources are not being used wisely. Take the case of the patient in Room 307. There are notes from the physical therapist he will be walking within two weeks and the speech therapist is very pleased with his progress. Yet you still have him as an inpatient, occupying a bed, eating three square meals…do you see the fiscal deficit here?"

"What do you want me to do? Throw him into the street? The man is not ready to leave. He cannot follow multiple-step directions and he has nowhere to go."

"Dr. Healy, are you not familiar with the hospital patient coordinator?

"Yes, but..."

We need to stay competitive in this business. Corporate has just hired a new coordinator to help streamline the discharging process. She will be starting tomorrow. I heard she is quite resourceful. She can place your patient on disability, get him to qualify for a government-sponsored program, and find him temporary housing, all with a few clicks of a keyboard; isn't technology wonderful?"

"He is still in need of physical therapy, speech therapy, and will need some form of occupational therapy. I also want him to continue to see the psychiatrist. We almost had a breakthrough the other day. As a professional in the area of memory, I just can't see..."

"Doctor, the man can be treated on an outpatient basis. Patients like him are costing the hospital millions. Do you understand we have to keep this hospital running cost-effectively or they will shut us down?"

The doctor nodded her head.

He lifted the framed photo from her desk and smiled, "Dr. Healy, I read your publication on Mental Tics and Their Effect on the Tourette Brain. You have a personal connection with this disorder, don't you?

"Yes, my brother has Tourette Syndrome."

"You both have the market cornered on good looks," he said, looking at the picture of them parasailing in Hawaii.

Patricia and Joseph Healy were identical twins who shared the same blue eyes and fair blonde hair. They both were very tall with an athletic built that came from years of competitive running. They were known for humanitarian efforts and participating in races to support health-related causes. But even identical twins had their differences. The one that separated them started years earlier when Joseph began barking and stomping his foot for no apparent reason.

"Your twin brother has become quite the politician. It is a shame with all his lobbying efforts he could not convince the CDC to back up your research. But isn't it a fact, he has done quite well on the trial medication? I think you will agree that the hospital has been quite generous with their funding for your pet project, isn't that right Doctor?" He placed the picture back on the table.

"Mr. Roberts that trial has the potential to change the future of Tourette Syndrome. If the medication works, we could be looking at an actual cure for the disorder!"

"That's very philanthropic of you, but let's cut to the chase, for the drug to become marketable and get the FDA's approval, you need another grant, don't you?"

The young doctor nodded, feeling a chill on her skin.

"My dear Dr. Healy, you have nothing to worry about. The hospital appreciates all your hard work and dedication. You have always been a team player and if you continue to do so, I can guarantee you will get the funding you need. "

He waited until he saw the smile reach her eyes. "We have to trim the fat. Some jobs will be cut, but in the end, we will be more financially sound to help our neighbors to the North. Doesn't that sound like a win for everyone? We will be able to provide not only five beds in the rehab unit but possibly build on two new floors!"

Mr. Roberts painted a pretty picture, but she knew the numbers and no amount of cutting back would allow the hospital any kind of expansion. They had been closed to bankruptcy two years in a row and they were understaffed. The only reason they had agreed to fund her research was that they owed her. She was the only surgeon who had dared to operate on the wife of the Chairman of the Board after she had wrapped her Ferrari around a pole in the Poconos. But to hit him up for another grant, was as impossible as patient X seeing her as anything more than his doctor.

Mr. Roberts glanced at his phone, "I am afraid my time is being cut short. I leave you to your duties. Just make sure you read the memos coming from Corporate. We expect you to follow all the recommendations so you can correct these wasteful practices."

He handed her copies of the financial forms.

"I can see my visit has left you pained. I do apologize for that. I have every confidence you will do what is best for the hospital. It was a pleasure to meet you, Dr. Healy."

"Good day Mr. Roberts."

After Mr. Roberts left, Dr. Healy heard a beep coming from her computer. The search engine had found some reliable information on patient *X*. Excited, she turned her attention toward the monitor. The lights in the room flickered twice and the computer lost connection. A few seconds later, the Wi-Fi signal was restored, but the previous search results had been lost in cyberspace. She would have to start all over again.

***

"Is the situation at the hospital contained?" Javier Gutierrez asked, pressing the loudspeaker on his phone.

"Yes," the disembodied voice on the other end replied.

"And the doctor?"

"She won't be a problem."

"Good. Then let me know when you are ready for Phase Two. We need him back to full capacity. The situation in the Middle East is hot and we are losing too many agents. We don't have time to train anyone else. He is the one. If he knew who he was, he would be airborne by now. He was chosen for these perilous times; you just have to remind him."

13

Dr. Healy lifted the paperweight from her desk. It was a copy of the Hippocratic Oath. In her chest, she could feel the pressure building. So many times, she had sprung into a patient's room with a trigger for their memory. A song, a name, a place but with Patient X she had found nothing. Whatever little she had discovered was always somehow obliterated. A fire that destroyed valuable records, a missing roster of employees of the North and South tower, even the fingerprints sent to Washington had gone missing. And now she had been conveniently transferred to their sister hospital in Maryland, where she could continue her Tourette research if she left without a fuss. It was better this way. She didn't need to fall in love with a patient, especially one without a clue who he was or what his marital status might be.

There was some good news; Alice McGraw, the new patient liaison, had found him an apartment. He would still

76

be able to get all the therapies he needed through the Outpatient Services. The liaison even set him up with a visiting nurse to check on him. So why was she feeling like she had done nothing to help *Mr. X*?

Dr. Healy took a deep breath and looked around her office. It was time.

***

"Come on, just take a break man, you already done more in one day than most of my patients do in a month," said Mark, the physical therapist, wheeling the wheelchair closer to him. Angelo glanced at the chair with disdain. He had a new goal in mind. His hands gripped the rails tighter forcing his body to stay upright. The muscles in his legs twitched and cramped with each step. He groaned, pressing on until he had walked the full length of the parallel bars. The residents cheered. The nurses gave Mark high fives. Angelo let go of the bar and let his body free fall on the padded mat. Mark lifted him and dumped him unceremoniously in his chair.

"Bravo *Mr. X*. I have to hand it to you. You sure know how to work a room."

Angelo wiped his face with the handy wipe Mark had given him and fixed his eyes on the lady in the white coat entering the room

"I tol...d... you...I...coul..d walk."

She clapped," Good job *Mr. X*. You are the most stubborn and determined patient I have ever had," she told him, grabbing a stool and sitting down. "You will walk and even run. You will also regain your speech and one day if you work at it real hard, you will remember."

"You will see i...t." He said rolling the chair closer to her.

77

Dr. Healy looked down at her sensible flats. They had red hearts all over them. She bought them in her first year of residency to remind herself to always see her patients as human beings with feelings. Today she wished she had put on other shoes. It was one thing to feel for your patients and another to lose your heart to one of them. In the past few months, the interactions between her and Mr. X had become more personal. But he had a past. A man like him couldn't possibly be single. The transfer had come at the right time because if it hadn't, Patricia Healy was ready to ruin her career if it meant she could become Mrs. X someday.

"Too quiet...t," he stuttered, "What..what..i..ss wro...ng?"

Shifting her weight, she crossed her legs at the ankles and brought her hands together lacing her fingers. She moistened her lips, "I have been transferred to the Maryland Brain Institute. I leave this afternoon, but you don't have to worry. As we discussed, as soon as you can walk on your own, you will be discharged. Mrs. McGraw has a nice apartment lined up for you and there will be a nurse aide to assist you in bathing and other daily activities. The new Neurologist comes highly recommended. Award winner and all..."

It was subtle but he heard the strain in her voice.

"Do you wan...t...to go?"

Dr. Healy looked around the therapy suite. The room was empty, except for the two of them. The nurses had wheeled the other residents back to their rooms for their scheduled naps. Mark was in the supply closet taking inventory of what needed to be added to the purchasing list.

Her heart rate spiked when he touched her hand. "This is wrong and very complicated. You probably have a dozen women or at least one waiting for you."

"Don't... know." He leaned in taking in the smell of the lilac perfume she always wore. "I lik...e...you. Please...stay."

"I can't," she said, dropping his hand and walking away.

He wheeled himself to the entrance. He couldn't let her leave. She was the only one who gave him hope of a normal future.

Making sure her back was to the security camera, she bent down and kissed him on the cheek. "You need to go find your past, and I need to find my future."

"Fu..tu..re..wiss...you," he said angered with his lack of words.

"As much as I like you, I cannot take the place of your past, Mr. X."

"I can be your...fu.tu..re." He insisted.

Even with his speech impediment, the man had a way of wrapping her heart around his finger.

"I'm sorry *Mr. X,* but I don't date my patients."

Dr. Healy gave the wheelchair a slight push, moving him out of her way. Before he could catch up to her, she was back behind the plexiglass of the nurses' station.

14

Whom did that counselor Veronique had pushed her to see, think she was, telling her to leave New York? *If I leave, how am I going to find Angelo?* But even Dream Chaser agreed she needed the mental break. The interview she had done a month ago had resulted in a bunch of kooks posing as her missing fiancé.

Julienne added more detergent and closed the lid to her compact washer. It was not such a bad idea to get away from the reminders and the never-ending conversations revolving around 9/11. October was fast approaching and soon the winter months would bring snow; all the excavation would cease.

Julienne turned the knob and pushed the button for hot water. At least if she left, she wouldn't have to continue paying the astronomical water bill. She wouldn't have to disinfect her balcony furniture from the ash or wash down her bike every time she rode it. Breathing clean air would also help heal her sore throat and moisturize her dry skin. By the time she had completed the first load of laundry, Julienne was sure even New York's Health Department would side with her.

***

Julienne ran to her room, picking up the receiver on the last ring. "Ana, what's wrong?" she asked, hearing her sister's sorrowful voice.

"Tio Jose died. Some guy cut him off on I-95. His car was totaled."

"Oh no. When?"

"Yesterday. Tia is a mess. Julie, I can't go to that funeral alone...You have to come home. I will flip out!"

"Calm down. I always have your back, you know that."

"You mean you will come? *Gracias*. I just can't see him dead; it reminds me too much of *Papa'*."

Images of their past hit Julienne like lighting. She pushed them away. She loved Ana, and even though her lifestyle clashed with hers, she would never shut her out of her life. A month ago, she would have believed the call was God's perfect timing. But now her life was nothing more than random circumstances. If God did exist, she didn't feel his love. He had abandoned her just like Angelo had.

"I know. It will be hard, but we are strong women. We will get through it together. When is the funeral?"

"Tomorrow. It will be Cuban style so the viewing will last all night."

Julienne hung up with her sibling. When she was finished packing the closet was bare except for a couple of heavy sweaters, winter boots, and her ski jacket. She was not sure

81

how long she would be gone, but it was comforting to know she had everything she needed for any occasion. If her life could not fall in line with predictability, then at least her wardrobe would. But how was she going to manage Fashion Week from Miami?

She dialed Veronique's number and explained the unforeseen situation. Veronique was uncharacteristically accommodating. It helped that Imperial's show had been canceled along with all the other runway events. They would have to showcase their Spring line for 2002 in-house before launching out in Paris and Milan.

"You're serious? You are considering my designs for the Euro Tour?" Julienne asked, keeping the excitement out of her voice.

"I looked at your collection. You did *tres bie*n restructuring the bodices. I would like to see your work with the necklines and shoulders. We can do it when you return. I am jealous. *J'adore* Miami, the men, the music... *petite*, get sun, you look, blah. *bon voyage*."

Whether due to pity or guilt, the Ice Queen was thawing out. Julienne looked on the computer for flights leaving New York the same day. If she hurried, she could catch a flight to Miami in just a few hours. She copied her agenda into her flash drive and made her weekly call to the Missing Victims Center. There had been a D'Marco but he was a UPS worker who was delivering mail that morning to the towers. The odds were mounting against the possibility of Angelo ever being brought out alive. But she still had to hold on. As illogical as it was, the alternative was worse. She left a message for Dream Chaser and called for transportation.

Hurry up! I gotta leave before I lose my mind! Julienne paced back and forth waiting for her ride. From her window, she saw the familiar yellow dot and hurried downstairs. The symphony of cranes and bulldozers working in Ground Zero stung her ears. Julienne stared out the taxi's window. In the middle of the day, an empty New York skyline stood in quiet mourning.

***

The nasal voice of the flight attendant blared through the microphone detailing instructions. The monotonous step by step demonstration showed even the youngest of passengers how to open the life jackets and how to use the oxygen masks. Just what her flight phobic mind needed, a lengthy discourse on the possibilities of the plane crashing.

The flight was bumpy. Air turbulence made Julienne queasy. Her ears popped and her face felt as if it was being shocked by tiny electrodes. Her sinuses were acting up again. She should have taken the decongestant pre-flight. But she had been distracted by a message from Dream Chaser. He had not been able to trace the emails to the sender, but he would continue working on it while she was gone. During the flight, the weather cleared and the 747 stopped bucking the clouds. She fluffed up her travel pillow and as the stress melted from her body, she found herself dozing off.

***

A scared thirteen-year-old looked at the clock on the mantle. Her mother had not been feeling well. The baby in her belly was breached and the doctor wanted her to stay in bed. Her father was the hero that would save the day. He had an unshaven dimply face that would tickle and shoulders that were strong enough for her to sit on to watch the Three Reyes Magos Parade. At her age, it was impossible to understand the pressures of financial loss or endless job searches. All she knew was that her daddy would always make things right.

He was scheduled to take both girls to the dentist. They had been looking forward all week to show him the dance routine they had made up for the Miami Starlight Dancers competition. But that afternoon he came home, unusually angry. He started yelling about how unfair life was and how their mom needed to choose between girls with shiny teeth and living on the streets.

The pregnant woman had been vomiting and she was on the verge of dehydration. She begged her husband to get her Gatorade before taking the girls to their appointment.

Julienne and Ana watched him from their front steps. Their loving dad got inside his Firebird TransAm and blasted the stereo. They watched him speed out of the driveway; his hands banging the steering wheel to the sounds of Queen. That was the last time they ever saw him.

***

Julienne was jolted awake almost knocking over the other passenger's drink. He glared at her mumbling under his breath. But she was oblivious to the man's comments. It had been years since she had thought of her father. Now the unsolicited dream had ripped open the past leaving it festering in her mind.

The plane hit another air pocket and the sign for seat belts came on. She had never undone hers, but just in case, she pulled on the lap belt checking for an effective grip. The man next to her made a snide comment. As the plane began descending, she clutched the armrests with her fingers.

God, I begged you to find Angelo and you didn't come through for me... If you are still up there and care at all, you will land this thing safely.

He yanked up the shade that covered the window.

"Look, see over there? That's the Centrust Tower, lit up in red, white, and blue. God bless America. We are going to get those Terrorists!"

15

A mixture of Gucci bags, sturdy lightweights, and a pair of powder blue suitcases sluggishly circled on the conveyor belt. A boy fidgeted next to his mother. His sour disposition changed into smiles when his mother lifted his Transformer-themed bag and set it next to the pink Barbie overnighter. Julienne waited for her bag to loop around; her eyes shielded from the world behind a pair of round sunglasses.

The easy-to-spot, bright red Whitfield bag worked its way around to her. As it approached, Julienne lifted it off the belt and placed it on the floor next to her carry-on. She rolled her suitcase out of the airport to the passenger pick-up area. Her sister flagged her down, sticking her hand out of her Toyota Corolla's window. Julienne dumped her luggage in the trunk of the car and hopped in.

Ana shouted in Spanish at the car that had cut in front of her. Then she began a tirade about how all the Miami drivers had gotten their driver's license from cereal boxes. Julienne half-listened as she watched her sister take the ramp to the highway. It was always the same in South Florida. The blame-shifting that happened throughout every Hispanic-speaking generation was ridiculous.

"Oye Chica, now that you're here, you have to loosen up," Ana commented. "After the funeral, we can hang out like old times."

"I don't feel much like partying...our uncle just died; have a little respect."

Ana laid on the horn startling, the old woman crossing the intersection a cart full of groceries. "It's crazy, they take the cart home, park it in their backyard and use it when they need to go shopping. And you know what's crazier? Cops don't care."

They parked in the circular driveway. Apart from the coat of hunter green paint on the stucco walls, her childhood home remained the same. Ornamental black security bars blocked her entrance to the flat roof duplex. Ana stepped in front, opening the gate. Sweat poured down Julienne's neck down to her shirt. She dropped into the reupholstered chair with a heavy sigh. The native Floridian cranked up the air conditioning allowing the home to cool down. Julienne blotted her face with a handkerchief, grateful for the cold glass of lemonade her sister handed her.

After they reminisced about winters in Florida and palm trees decorated Christmases, she took a shower and dressed for the funeral. She chose a simple black dress, a string of pearls, and matching earrings. She used the hot iron to flatten her hair, then twisted it into a French twist. She applied her lipstick wondering what her family would think of her now that she was back. Would they bring up her leaving the nest after high school instead of staying until she was properly married like all good Cuban girls? Ana rapped on the door before entering the room. Julienne could not help but notice how short her sister's skirt was.

"You look like an old lady," Ana told her sitting on the bed.

"I don't want to make a bad impression."

She leaned back on her elbows and smirked, "Nah, they will be too busy shredding me to pieces. Did you know Aunt Teresa and Aunt Clara have dedicated a time to pray me into heaven every morning?"

"A Novena? I remember those. We counted Rosary beads while kneeling. Had sore knees for a week." Julienne added.

"Me too. You know I had a client at the hair salon tell me none of those rituals matter. The only important thing is that you believe in Jesus. Do you think that is true?"

Julienne thought for a moment. "I think people make it more complicated than it has to be. B.R.R."

"Bring your Rum Runner?"

"No Ana. It stands for Believe in Jesus. Repent of your sins. Release your life to him."

"Who told you that?" Ana asked, pulling down her mini skirt.

"Angelo."

"Err okay...Time to go see the fam," she told Julienne pushing her out the door.

***

Cervantes Funeral Home was a large, box-shaped building in the middle of what was commonly known as *Little Havana*. It was an area filled with establishments that had names dating back to the time when Cuba was a free country. Within walking distance was Versailles Restaurant. It was the gathering place for political conversations and well-known celebrities. Further down was Jose Marti Park where elderly men were known to play a mean game of Dominos. It was Cultural Friday. All the streets were filled with tourists and urbanites wanting to experience the ethnic flare. Art galleries displayed works of aspiring Cuban artists in their windows. The rhythm of the Island flowed out into the streets where people shopped and congregated.

Inside, Cervantes was filled wall to wall with friends and family. Julienne was greeted with clamorous voices and fierce hugs. Regardless of the reason, it was always a celebration when a family member came to visit. Aunt Teresa, the wife of the deceased, pinched her cheek,

"*Niña,* don't they feed you in New York? She's all skin and bones!" she commented to her sister Clara, who immediately offered a home-cooked meal. If you did not have voluptuous curves and meat in your thighs, you were not a real Cuban. Ana pushed her sister through the throng of family members so they could pay their respects to their uncle.

They knelt in front of the coffin. Julienne raised her head to see the man lying on the white satin. The resemblance to her father was uncanny. Roberto had the same straight-edged nose and oblong face. The protection she had built around her heart by years of indifference, started to crack.

Ana tapped her leg. "This is creepy. We should go."

On their way to the exit, Julienne was stopped by old family friends giving her their condolences. Julienne kept the conversation light but they kept mentioning Angelo's unprecedented death. Ana saw the tears start to flow. She took a hold of her younger sister's arm and pushed her way through the maze of people until they had reached outside.

"Let's get some food," Ana suggested, falling in line with the multitude crossing the intersection.

"I'm not hungry."

"Hurry up and don't let those *viejos* make you sad," she answered, putting out her hand to stop the traffic moving toward them. "How about some *café Cubano and pastellitos*? Later we'll do dinner. We can pig out all night. We can work it off at the beach tomorrow. You need a good tan. You are too white; you look like you're sick."

***

El Viejo Camaguey was an undiscovered jewel. A little hole in the wall, with plastic tablecloths and cheap plates. For a moderate price, you could eat the most authentic, homemade Cuban cuisine. On the wall across them hung photos of the chef's ancestors taken in different provinces of the island. A giant mural of the homeland was painted above the red faux leather booths.

"*Dos cafecitos, por favor,*" Ana ordered in Spanish. While they waited for the food, she shared memories of their Uncle Roberto. How he loved his espresso with a smidgen of milk and two spoonsful of sugar. She reminded her of the time they were little, and both their uncle Roberto and their father had taken them to the Dade County Auditorium to see Celia Cruz live in concert.

"Remember? *Papa'* was the best dancer around. He gave all the guys a run for their money,"

90

"I don't want to talk about him," Julienne answered looking over the menu.

"Why not? Yeah, he left us, but so what. While he was around, he was a good father and he loved us."

"He loved no one."

"They slit his throat in prison Julie, but what do you care. You never went to see him, not even once."

"He got what he deserved."

Ana looked over the menu at her sister. "I changed my mind, I want dinner. Their food is to die for."

Julienne agreed. Dinner would be a good way to keep Ana's mouth busy, plus she was getting a little hungry.

The waitress returned carrying their coffee. Ana advised her they needed some more time to look over the menu.

"Julie, "Ana said, stirring sugar into her ca*fé*, "Last time I saw *Papi,* he told me he knew Mami was cheating on him. That baby she lost when he left, was not his. She had been fooling around with Diego from the bank. *Papi* was heart-broken."

"Life is hard. You deal with it. You don't run out on your kids. He was a good mechanic; he could have found a job. He chose to become a junkie and a dealer."

"Saint *Juliana,* I thought living in New York would chill you out, but you are just as judgmental as ever. Why can't you remember the good times? He was not a total loser."

"I am far from a saint, but I am not going to approve of our father's decision to become a criminal either. Oh, and so you know, I am not *Juliana*, at least not anymore."

"What do you mean?"

"I changed my name to Julienne Juls."

"*Como,* are you *loca*? Ana asked, hot coffee sputtering out of her mouth. "Why did you do that?"

"I needed a name for my collections. Most designers use French monikers. I needed to stand out from them. "

Ana dragged her finger across the picture of Cuba on her placemat and stopped at *Camaguey. No* matter what you call yourself, you will always be a *Cubanita just* like me. We are loud and talk too much; our family is insanely overprotective, but *Papi* taught us to be proud of our heritage. I guess you forgot that."

"I haven't forgotten."

"The waitress took their orders. The sisters waited until she was out of hearing range to continue their discussion.

"You were named after *Papi*, and I was named after *Mami*. You can't erase it!"

"Ana, our father was a criminal. You think I want to be reminded of that?"

"So? You are still a Gutierrez. It is in *our* blood. Whatever you do, don't go telling the family...I don't want the cousins to talk smack that we gave their moms a *patatú.*"

Julienne raised her eyebrow, "A what?"

"Ugh, you are such an *arrepentida*! You are a Benedict Arnold, turning your back on your Cuban origin. *Patatú,* is slang for a conniption, a hissy fit. It is a lexicon of our native language, Miss NYU." Ana said placing the tiny cup back on top of the saucer. "And there is nothing like our perfectly brewed Cuban *cafecito!*"

"Can we drop this? Julienne asked, unrolling the silver-ware from the napkin.

"Not until you tell me how you came up with a stuck-up name like that?"

She pulled out a wipe from her purse and disinfected the utensils. "Veronique my boss suggested I go with a less ethnic first name. Since Angelo liked to call me Juls, J-U-L-S, I just added the E for emphasis and used it for my last name Ana, it is a great big world outside of Miami and unless you leave *Little Havana*, you won't understand."

Ana rolled her eyes, "You are still a germophobe? Whatever. Julienne Juls is not that bad. But can you add the Gutierrez back in? Do it for me. *Papi* wasn't always a dealer. Remember this song? It was one of his favorites."

The vintage, *Guajiro* music playing in the restaurant began to weave its magic, transporting Julienne to a lazy summer afternoon. She sat on her daddy's lap, curly pigtails moving in the wind. He strummed his old guitar, playing melancholic songs. Life was easy then.

Julienne blew into her coffee, cooling it down before taking a sip. The rich flavor of her heritage was filling her heart with sadness.

The waitress set down the heavy plates filled with rice and black beans, aromatic meats, and the customary fried plantains. Julienne's mouth watered; she mixed the beans and rice on her plate.

You are not perfect you need to forgive.

Where did that come from? She asked herself, chewing the shredded meat.

They busied themselves with the meal; neither one ready to speak of their past.

"What's bugging you?" Ana asked breaking the silence. She took a plantain from her sister's plate. "You are acting all plastic. Like you are too good for our family."

"You had it good after our father left. *Mami* hated me because of him," Julienne complained, feeling the acid of the meal rise to her throat.

The waitress returned, removed the plates, and brought out the desserts. She had ordered *Flan Diplomatico* while her sister went with her usual, *Tres Leches*. Every time Ana had a birthday their father would order a specialty *Tres Leches* cake for her. Julienne's parents never let her partake of her younger sibling's birthday cake. They didn't want another hospital bill due to her delicate stomach.

"I know. It wasn't fair the way *Mami* treated you. I think she went nuts after *Papi* was sent to prison," Ana said digging into her dessert.

"I don't want to talk about them, how is the hair salon doing?" Julienne asked, cracking the crystallized caramel on top of her flan with her spoon.

"Remember the owner of the gas station on Flagler? The one who used to always say how pretty we were?"

"He gave me the creeps; the way he always looked at us. Like he wanted to rape us or something."

"While *Papi* was locked up, she had a kid with him. We have a brother. Paquito has Autism. He is super smart. He wants to study Astrophysics."

"A brother? Why didn't you tell me?"

"A half-brother. I didn't want you to come back. You would have been stuck here, taking care of him. How do you think *Tia Isabel* found out you got kicked out and were living with *Abuela?*

Julienne let the caramel melt in her mouth before answering. "*Abuela* told me that *Mami* had called *Tia Isabel.*"

"Abuela didn't call her. I did."

"Why would you..."

"*Mami* was tripping on her psych meds... it was not your fault that rug got dirty. It was raining! Big whoop! She didn't have to kick you out of the house!" Ana responded before stuffing her mouth with the dessert again.

"But I thought..."

94

"*Papi* told me if we were ever in trouble to call *Tia Isabel* in New Jersey. So I called her and told her you were a real Fashionista, and how you were always making all these cool clothes. And how *Mami* had thrown you out."

Julienne put her spoon down; the heat from that day on her mind.

"If you are not going to finish your *flan*...."

"Ana when I left mom's house, there was a car with dark tinted windows following me. I cut through the backyards and got soaked by Mrs. Hernandez's sprinkler. It was parked at the curve when I got to grandma's block. It was weird, the minute it saw me, it took off."

"Probably a perv who got spooked," Ana said taking some of her sister's flan. "You don't eat much do you?"

"How did *Tia Isabel* know where to find me?" Julienne asked. She reached for a napkin, dunked it in her water, and cleaned off the stain on the tablecloth.

"Julie, it's plastic. They got people for that. I told *Tia* to check if you were with *Abuela*. I mean, where else would you have gone?"

"My boyfriend's house."

"His mother didn't like you that much ... It turned out for the best. You are living the dream, making tons of money. You got a lucky break."

Julienne sighed, "I don't know about luck. It was *Tia Isabel* who took my sloppy sketches and made me a decent portfolio. My first job was sewing buttons and hemming pants." Julienne lifted her hand to fan herself. *Was it always this hot at night in Florida?* "After High School, I applied for the Designing Program at NYU. To think it all began with me being homeless."

95

Ana laughed, "You are so dramatic...you were never homeless."

"Maybe not, but it was not easy to get to *Abuela's* house on foot. Once that car left, I got the spare key, you know the one she keeps under the Virgin Mary statue for emergencies? I didn't even get past the living room. I zonked out on the couch." Julienne watched Ana slurp the last of her soft drink.

"A*buela* found me. She didn't say a word, she just put on her *Telenovela.* We watched it and ate mashed malanga. The next day, *Tia Isabel* showed up. I told her I was fine living with *Abuela...*"

"Poor baby. You ever thought of writing a book about how you got your meager start?" her sister teased, chewing ice.

"What I don't get is why you had to call our father's sister in New Jersey instead of *Abuela*? We could have seen each other at school." Julienne handed the empty plates to the waitress clearing the table.

Ana unwrapped the mint the waitress had left with the check. "*Mami* would have guilted you into moving back. You would have never left to follow your dream on your own." Ana paused, sucking on the mint. "It bugged me that you always had to look out for me. Do you think Miami Dade Community College could have given you the kind of fashion design education you got at NYU? No way! I may not be the smartest or nicest, but I am the cutest and the oldest...it was my job to take care of you, not the other way around."

"Thank you," Julienne answered straightening out the salt and pepper shaker on the table. "Why did you move in with *Abuelita* when you turned sixteen?"

"That total scum bucket dumped *Mami*. She was so overwhelmed with Paquito. He would throw tantrums and break things. She was strung out of pills and beer most of the time. I tried helping her, but she turned on me."

"Why didn't you call me? *Tia Isabel* would have taken you in too." Julienne asked placing the empty napkin dispenser at the end of the table so the waiter would see it needed refilling. "I would have flown down to get you."

"Hey, chill out, *Mami* did me a favor. *Abuelita* was a saint. She took a lot of pain meds so I had time to hang and party with my friends. I didn't have to pick up after mom's hangovers or change dirty diapers...the best part was, I had nobody to nag me." Ana looked toward the male waiter carrying a pile of dirty plates to the kitchen. "Nice shoulders."

"Nag you? You mean supervise you. You moved in after high school with that two-timing loser. How long did that last? Two months?"

Ana thumbed through the few dollar bills in her wallet. "I can only cover the tip. My credit card is maxed out."

"Dinner is on me," Julienne said, taking out her Platinum card.

"Thanks...I will get it next time. I promise. Life is short. Yeah, I screwed up big time. But I wasn't gonna spend it like a nun," she said, smiling flirtatiously at the waiter who had purposely traveled past their table to serve the next guests. "Face it, you have always been the good one. You obeyed all the rules, you found a nice guy to settle down with and what did that get you? *Nada.* Cause when you least expect it, boom! Life hits you right between the eyes."

Julienne called for the check. She scribbled her signature on the bill while her sister exchanged phone numbers with the waiter.

Ana was right. She had done everything a good Christian girl should do, and what was her reward? A broken heart.

97

***

Outside, the hot breath of the sun was still lingering across the starless sky. They walked a few blocks, stopping to look over the paintings that leaned against the sidewalks on cheap wooden easels. They passed the "tourist trap" tent selling one size fits all beach dresses. In the next tent, Julienne haggled over the price of a leather bag her sister insisted on buying. The next block was filled with people dancing the night away. Ana entered the circle, her hips moving in every direction. Julienne found a quiet spot on a sidewalk bench. She took off her shoes, liberating her throbbing toes. The Jim Choy originals were a gift from Angelo. The pair had been set aside to wear for elegant nights during their European honeymoon.

Midnight rolled around but there was no sign Ana was ready to call it a night. Two teenagers sat on the edge of her bench throwing spitballs with a straw at each other. One fell on Julienne's hair. She put on her shoes and stepped into the middle of the arms and feet bouncing and swaying to the Latin music. She found Ana and dragged her to the sidewalk.

"My feet are killing me. Either you drive us home or I am getting a taxi."

Ana pouted, "Seriously?"

Julienne started walking toward the car. At twenty-five, she still felt like the parent of her Hyperactive Attention Deficit twenty-eight-year-old sister. Ana caught up with her sibling's quick steps. They returned to the empty funeral home and collected the car. As they were driving down Coconut Grove, Julienne opened the window letting the sounds of the party scene back in. Was she wasting her life playing it safe? She wondered, glancing over at her older sister. The streaks of blue in Ana's blonde hair blew back exposing a flower tattoo on the side of her neck. Her multi-ringed fingers tapped against her thigh. Her sister sang out the lyrics to the latest song on the radio. For a moment, Julienne envied her.

16

Angelo rubbed his head. *When will this miserable headache go away?* Clank. Clank. Clank! Hammer hitting an anvil. It bludgeoned his brain until he felt it might split in two. He popped two pills in his mouth and washed them down with a glass of water. Dr. Healy had told him the pain was a good sign. There was hope that the brief snippets of the amnesiac's life would eventually mesh forming a historic picture of his life before the Twins came down. But she could not give him an exact date when the excruciating pain would birth a real memory. While Angelo waited for the pain to subside, he leaned back on the second-hand recliner, remote in hand, surfing mindlessly through the channels.

The apartment the glorified social worker had gotten him was not half bad. It was not in the best part of town, but it was clean and recently fumigated. Angelo yawned. The new medication was making him sleepy. Dr. Healy would have never prescribed such a high dose. She was a firm believer in titrating medications. Angelo had texted her a few times to get her input on the new medication, but she had not responded. He stopped at a sports channel. The New York Giants had the ball.

A flash of light. The bewildered man found himself in another living room. Everything around him was covered by a dense fog. Then he saw a pair of honey-colored eyes...

A knock at the door interrupted the vision. He was not expecting anyone. Angrily, he threw the remote against the wall and got up to see who it was. He looked through the peephole. Two burly guys flashed their badges. Angelo eyed them suspiciously until they told him they were investigating the collision at the towers.

Angelo opened the door just a fraction, but they forced their way inside. One went for a headlock while the other tried to force his hands behind his back. Without giving it much thought, the amnesiac lifted his leg and kicked hard against the stranger's stomach, sending him flying against the wall. At the same time, he spun around, then jumped, missing the slashes of the knife wielded by the other guy. Taking a step back, Angelo sideswiped the man, causing him to lose his balance and fall. Just then, the guy from the wall smashed into him. They both fell to the floor.

Angelo's oxygen was dwindling as the hefty man sat on top of his chest. Instinctively, the amnesiac drove the palm of his right hand, straight into the bottom of the man's nose, breaking it. Adrenaline pumped through his veins as he pushed the man off him. Angelo found himself enjoying the challenge. He dealt a deadly chop to the larynx, leaving his aggressor withering in pain. That's when he felt a sharp prick in the back of his neck. Everything went black.

101

Voices, then the darkness began to fade...

Honey golden eyes under long black lashes called him to come closer. He struggled, reaching but never getting anywhere. A light pierced through the fog, bright and uncomfortable. It hurt his closed eyelids. The amnesiac opened one eye and then the other, trying to recognize his surroundings. He tried to move his arms but couldn't. Angelo pushed his wrist against the leather restraints but there was no way to break them. He followed the iv line to a pole with a hanging bag of clear liquid. He focused his eyes higher and found a human face staring down at him.

The man had a square jaw and wore an expression of disapproval. His eyes were two coals, that sat under bushy, gray eyebrows that rose when he spoke. His name was General Collins. He ran a covert Special Forces, Anti-terrorist unit of the CIA. They were the ghost agency, the ones that took on the jobs most agencies could only dream of handling. These agents would infiltrate enemy camps and go on rescue missions always with the knowledge that if anything went wrong, they were on their own. They were made up of forgotten children, taken from orphanages, boarding schools, and even the streets. A chip was inserted under the skin of their forearms; an invisible leash to keep them accounted for. They trained innocent eyes and dimples, molding them into fighting machines that would protect America at all costs. Angelo was one of those kids.

Angelo D'Marco was orphaned at birth. He was the product of two agents who had broken the cardinal rule and died in combat. At age five, he was taken from the orphanage and sent to live with Delilah, the woman who became his foster mother. For his tenth birthday, a recruiter handed his foster mother an envelope with cash. That was the last time young Angelo saw Delilah. He was placed in a special boarding school for exceptionally gifted children. It said in his file, that he was 'borderline genius' and 'a quick study.' A perfect soldier in the making. 'Smooth like butter' was a term used to describe the young rising star. By the age of twenty-two, he was running his own missions. He was the golden boy of the Agency. Nothing could touch him.

"Do you realize you put two of my best agents out of commission?" Collins smirked, rubbing the back of his neck. "No, of course, you don't! The doctor says you've forgotten who you are, where you came from. You probably don't even believe a word I have told you, yet..." he lifted his finger in the air, "...amazing how the mind works; while your memory is scrambled eggs, the survival instinct stays intact." He leaned on the gurney, his palms open, fingers spread out. "Then again, you always were a top-of-the-line model."

General Collins continued pontificating, "We had a few non-exciting years where the Agency became lax, allowing agents to live on the outside. If you ask me, it served no purpose but to make you weak, but I don't make the rules."

He poked Angelo in the chest. "That's where you got the bright idea to live in New York. You were still wet behind the ears, barely in your twenties...you thought you knew it all. You began to work directly for *him*. He thought you were a Master Spy, but you fell from grace, now you're all mine!"

Angelo wanted to punch the man Not only was he speaking in riddles, but he was giving him a migraine... hammer and the anvil, at it again. He shook his head violently, growling from the pain.

Shut up!

The amnesiac's eyes glazed over ...Yes sir. No sir, Pouring rain. Soldier, give me twenty more!...Eyes like fine liquid honey, shimmering in the distance.

"Ahhhhh!" he screamed, his body convulsing.

When he came to, Collins was gone. Sitting behind a computer was a thin man with a gaunt face and dead eyes.

"Agent 539, let's see what we can do about those headaches."

17

She slid through the water with ease, making her way through the demanding waves until she had reached the shore. The toasty sand felt good on her wet feet. Julienne plopped down beside Ana on the multicolored towel. Her hand dipped into the ice, retrieving a cold beverage from their cooler. The sun-burned New Yorker donned her straw hat and rearranged her towel closer to the umbrella's shade. A seagull skipped on by. Julienne threw a chip his way; he picked it up and flew back toward the wooden pathway that led to the beach.

Ana sat up and snatched the potato chips out of her sibling's hands.

A cruise ship sailed in the distance.

What I would give to be in one of those right now," Ana commented, tossing a handful of chips in her mouth.

If only... Julienne thought.

The Canary Islands was where they had planned to spend the first part of their honeymoon. Angelo had booked a villa bordering the Mediterranean ocean. They would spend three days frolicking in the crystal waters and climbing to see the majestic views from the Teide volcano. From Spain, they cruise all of Europe. Their trip would end in Austria, where Julienne's favorite musical, 'The Sound of Music' was filmed. It would have been a delightful way to start their lives together. Instead, she was stuck in Miami finding ways to forget.

Julienne frowned digging into the potato chip bag. "The last time I remember being on a boat, was when Angelo took me on the ferry. We had a picnic in Ellis Island."

"Hey," Ana elbowed her, "check out the guy by the net, he's looking at you."

Julienne scanned the volleyball players. Her eyes lingered on the muscular man spinning the ball in his left hand. He gave her a brief nod before returning his attention to the ongoing bantering between the teams. The girl in the pink striped bikini from the opposing team giggled. Someone shouted for her to stop fooling around and serve. The game went on. Julienne tried not to notice how his biceps flexed as he spiked the ball sending the other team diving into the sand for the retrieval.

"That's all I need, a steroid baboon coming onto me," she said picking up the reading material lying next to her. She opened the page where she had left off, "Anyways, I prefer some brain with the brawn."

"Would it make a difference if I told you I am a doctor?"

Startled, she met the stranger's eyes briefly, hiding her red cheeks behind the pages of her magazine.

106

"I'm Carlos Jose Hernandez," he said with a Spanish accent. "I work in the ER at Jackson Hospital. You girls like Salsa?"

Ana turned her torso adjusting her top, "Hola Carlos, I'm Ana, the one getting her foot out of her big mouth, is my sister, Juliana."

"Juliana, I promise not to hold it against you if you join me for Salsa Night at *Merenguitos* tonight."

"My name is Julienne, and thank you but I don't ..."

Ana stood up dusting the sand off her legs, "Sounds like a plan."

"I have to work," Julienne protested.

Carlos crouched on the sand dropping his elbows on his raised knees. "Till what time do you work tonight?"

Ana threw her chips to the seagulls. "Don't let her fool you. Juliana has a flexible schedule. She's a fashion designer visiting from New York."

"Then you have to go tonight. There is not a club in all of New York City like this one. You won't be sorry."

***

When evening came, South Beach took on a different light. Gone was the lotion lathered tourists flip-flopping through the stores in search of the perfect postcards and Mamey Ice Cream. The beach was transformed into the posh tropical paradise for all who sought open bars and heart-pumping music. The outside restaurants with their large parasols and plush seating attracted the curious palate. Julienne allowed Ana to take the lead through the narrow streets brimming with people. They stopped in front of large gates that opened to well-manicured gardens. They stepped inside. People were mingling and dancing around an Olympic-sized pool. Girls in puffy cream-colored skirts and shiny tops took orders for drinks and appetizers. Women and men in tropical attire sat on white lounge chaises drinking from their colorful straws.

Julienne was glad she had let her younger sister choose her outfit. Dressed in her flowered print sarong skirt and white halter top, she almost felt pretty. Ana in black silk shorts and a pair of knee-high white boots strutted across the garden like a model. Julienne sauntered behind her sister, avoiding eye contact with anyone.

It had been eons she had been in a nightclub. Angelo always had preferred home-cooked meals and quiet strolls through the city to dancing. On occasion, they did paint the town red with friends celebrating birthdays or promotions. They shared a mutual love for the arts, frequenting Broadway plays, famous exhibitions at the Metropolitan Museum, and Improv comedy. She missed the days when Angelo would surprise her with tickets for a show or whisk her off to the Atlantic City pier for Saltwater taffy.

Carlos caught up with them as they were headed to the bar. Ana ordered a Blue Margarita. Julienne settled for Seltzer Water.

"Isn't that for mixing drinks?" he taunted.

"I like mine straight up," she answered, trying to pry the cap off the bottle with her nail.

"Let me help."

He gave it a quick twist and handed it back to her.

Carlos asked her to dance. Julianne was rusty from years of not dancing Salsa. He was a skillful dancer who led her well and didn't mind when she stepped on his feet. The music slowed and couples filled the dance floor. Julienne went to check on her sister. Ana had taken a liking to a broad-shouldered, long-haired British man. They had disappeared behind some potted clay jars of pink Bougainvillea. Ana was an adult, even if she didn't act like one. Tired of playing chaperone, Julienne made her way to a cushioned divan overlooking the pool.

Carlos brought her a plate of desserts. "You have to try them. They are called *Merenguitos*. It's what this club is famous for. Guava, raspberry, chocolate, or pineapple filling, take your pick."

She picked up one and tasted it. Egg beaten to a mound of white toasted foam and stuffed with pineapple serenaded her taste buds. Two sets of attractive dimples appeared on his cheeks as he smiled. Carlos was of average height and blessed with brown eyes and long lashes that a woman would kill for. And as the night progressed Julienne found herself attracted to him.

By midnight he had sweet-talked her into trying the Blue Iguana Martini and other exotic drinks. Vodka shots came next. With alcohol swimming in her system, she laughed and cried, pouring her heart out to her new companion.

Carlos wasted no time in introducing her to his friends, the 'White Collar Partiers.' The group was made up of doctors, lawyers, CEO's and trust fund babies with multiple degrees. Their names and professions became a mix of syllables and sounds that tripped her tongue in the alcohol-induced daze. After they had enough of the ethnic vibe, they piled into a rented limousine and hopped from club to club. The night became a blur of activity and newfound freedoms that crashed into each other at warp speed.

18

Sweaty strands of hair spray were glued to her mascara-stained face. The taste of fermented alcohol stuck to her dry tongue. Tangled in the sheets, she tried to get loose, only to fall off the bed onto the tiled floor. What had she done? She didn't drink! Julienne untangled herself and went to take a shower. She scrubbed her face, hoping to exfoliate away the traces of the hangover. Then she brushed her teeth and tongue. The club-hopping experience flashed in her mind, bringing Julienne more shame. How could she have let herself act so irresponsibly? She put on a terry cloth pair of shorts and guided her soupy muscles into her NYU t-shirt. The nauseated woman gathered her wild hair between her two hands and tied it back with a clip.

In the kitchen, Ana was mechanically boiling a pot of Cuban coffee. Julienne heard snoring coming from the living room. A shirtless man lying face down on the sofa was the first thing she saw. On the floor, two women were asleep on her sister's rug. Carlos walked out of the guest bathroom, towel drying his hair. One of the girls leaped from the floor and ran past him, slamming the bathroom door behind her.

"Good morning, Sunshine," he greeted Julienne, sauntering toward the kitchen.

"What are all these people doing here?" Julienne asked, watching him find a spot at the kitchen table.

"They were too plastered to drive home. We had a sleep-over." Ana answered, refilling her new conquest's cup. She sat down, resting her feet on his hairy legs.

Julienne's eyes widened. She shot Carlos an accusatory look.

Ana grinned, "Oh relax, you crashed, and he helped me get you into bed. You have nothing to worry about. He slept in the office like a perfect gentleman."

Julienne mouthed an apology and poured some coffee for herself. She rummaged the cabinets for aspirin. Took two and returned to her bedroom. Minutes later, freshly shaven and dressed in blue scrubs, Carlos appeared at her doorway.

"Knock-knock," he said, pinning the hospital badge on his shirt.

"Sorry for earlier; I jumped to conclusions."

"Don't' worry. Drink tomato juice. It will stabilize your system."

It was stupid of me. I don't usually act like that."

"You mean the kiss?"

"I don't usually get drunk. I am never that forward...I'm engaged," Julienne said opening the gauzy curtains to let more light in the stuffy room.

"I know you told me about how 9/11 squashed all your

111

wedding plans and you think this guy is alive somewhere... that was before you threw up on my shoes."

"I...I am so sorry. Um, I'll buy you a new pair."

"Relax is just vomit. I have had worse happen."

A cardinal was perched upon a limb that almost touched her window. His robust feathers moved as he tweeted, calling to another cardinal sitting idle on the telephone wire. He happily swooped down and joined his mate.

Carlos strutted into the room, his heel-toe movements making a light thud on the carpet. Leaning up against the wall, he admired her long fingers as they tapped lightly the window to get the bird's attention. The creatures looked over to her, both coking their heads and opening their beaks as if to tell her to run.

was at Ground Zero. Remember? I told you I rode down with some firemen from Hialeah. Look, I don't mean to be insensitive, but if they haven't found him by now..."

"He got out. I won't accept that he is dead unless they show me his body!" She banged the window.

Spooked by the vibration, the cardinals took flight, their graceful bodies soaring.

Carlos squeezed her shoulder lightly, "I'm sorry. I just want you to know if you want to talk about it, we'll talk and if not, that's cool too." The doctor checked his watch. "I have got to get to the ER, but later on I will give you the royal tour of Miami."

"I was born here."

"*Sí*, but you've been gone what, fifteen years?"

"Seven."

"Everybody knows after five, your blood grows cold," he said, making a large circle with his hands. "You are from the Big Apple. We are the Big Orange, sweet and tangy."

112

"Is that your professional opinion?"

"I bet my license on it," he said with a wink before departing.

Julienne untied her hair and sprayed it with detangling spray. Carlos was a nice man, and after puking all over his shoes, the least she could do was let him take her out. She would enjoy what he had to offer, but her heart would forever belong to Angelo.

19

Angelo repeated the words that scrolled on the screen. Every time he fell asleep, a whistle would blow, and he would have to stand up and recite the slogan again. No sleep in over forty-eight hours, yet they expected him to stay awake. The sleep-deprived man forced his eyes open and screamed, "I am a sol..dier! Bor..n to ff..ight and defend my coun..tree!" Then he hit the wall with his fist until it bled. The whistle did not blow anymore. Concerned the amnesiac soldier would become suicidal, they allowed him a few hours of uninter-rupted sleep. The next day, was weapon training. Every time Angelo missed a target, he was placed in a dark room assembling and disassembling weapons as fast as he could. Then back to the range for more shooting practice. Angelo never missed the target again.

The soldier was transferred to an undisclosed facility for SEAL maneuver training and military drills. He had earned his bunk and more freedom. Angelo's favorite activity came after lunch, a game called "War." The first month it was all done in a simulation room. Fitted with special sensory magnets, he fought against virtual enemies. Different scenarios were played out, but the soldier seldom lost to the computer.

Angelo was excited. It was time to test his skills against other trainees. That quickly lost its luster when he beat them after the second day of defense training. On weekends he was expected to do book work and brushed up on profiling, survival skills, and memorizing agency rules. The soldier also worked tirelessly on improving his speech with a Speech Pathologist. Though he was still foggy about his past, absorbing what his brain perceived to be new information came easy.

Because of Angelo's quick progression through the Conditioning phase, Collins decided to accelerate his training. No longer would he compete against Newbies, but he would go up against the General's specialized Black Ops team, the Elites. Angelo relished the moment he could defeat them. He was tired of being harassed because of his lisp.

***

The Elites training field was as big as five football fields. It had three different types of landscapes. There was the fine dust of the desert, dense forest, and mountains. Caves filled with deadly snakes, piranha-infested lakes, and wild, roaming carnivores inhabited the land.

A deadly game of *Capture the Flag* was first on the agenda. No rules to follow. No rubber bullets. Real danger. If the soldier survived, he would graduate. The two-week battle was created to test everything he had learned in the sixty days he had spent in Recruit Island. But Angelo had a source that gave him an inner strength not found in the training manuals. God was his supreme commander.

As expected, in *Capture the Flag*, Angelo's team won. A celebration dinner lasted until 5 a.m., then he retired to his sleeping bag. The soldier was woken up with a beating. Barely awake he fought back. Accepting his new position as an endangered species, he escaped his back-stabbing team-mates and went into hiding. The battle ended with Angelo sending five men to the ICU. Some Elites chose to surrender instead of dealing with the lethal fighting machine. Hurting and dehydrated Angelo returned to his base camp on day eleven. The hunt was over. Two bullets had penetrated his shoulder, he had dislocated his arm and had been bitten by a spider, but he was alive.

***

Collins stamped COMPLETED on Angelo's file and closed it. He lifted the receiver and called on the secure line.

"Agent 539 is ready."

20

Julienne worked on fashion designs to send Veronique for the upcoming European show and spent all her free time with Carlos. They visited Vizcaya. He hired a photographer to take their pictures. He drove her to Bal Harbor and Miracle Mile to see what the wealthy Floridians deemed fashionable. They shopped at Bayside and all popular tourist destinations, rode in an airboat across the Everglades, and watched the Heat Game in the American Airlines Arena. The gallant Cuban even purchased VIP seating for the Mercedes Benz Fashion show as a birthday present for her.

Julienne put on her new outfit. She stopped to admire her creation in the mirror. It was a peach-off-the-shoulder dress with fabric cutouts. Julienne had strategically placed the geometric cutouts on the hem to give it a retro 80s look. Ana took a hair pick to her sister's hair giving it even more volume. Veronique had expressed mail her very own Designer ID. She wore it proudly around her neck, displaying the

Imperial Design House's impressive logo. The Junior Designer armed herself with a futuristic-looking clutch that discreetly held samples of her drawings.

Close to six o'clock, Carlos appeared in the driveway in the showroom Porsche they had been looking at the week before. He wore an Armani tuxedo and Italian shoes. He handed her a bouquet of roses and kissed her hand. The nerves in Julienne's stomach fluttered. She was used to seeing him in his scrubs or jeans. *Boy, the guy cleans up nice...accepting the tickets wasn't such a good idea. Come on Julienne, you got this...Just keep telling yourself, nothing serious, you are just having fun.* But she couldn't help feeling those butterflies in her stomach take wing when he winked at her. As they drove off, she sneaked another look. *What have I gotten myself into!*

***

Long-limbed models with hair tied back and minimal makeup worked the runway. The designer's intention to minimize the models' natural beauty so they could serve as live hangers, worked perfectly with the chic collection. The VIP seating was made up of the first two rows next to the stage. It made it convenient for Julienne to see the intricate stitching up close. She took out her pad and jotted down information for Imperial like she had promised Veronique. When the catwalk had been rolled up, they moved to the ballroom for cocktails.

The highlight of the evening came when a representative from Novo Stilo asked Julienne who designed what she was wearing. That was the ice breaker that permitted her to share her illustrative talent. Not only did the rep gush over her illustrations but called over other house reps to see Julienne's innovations. Shoptalk lasted late into the night. It pleased Julienne that the charismatic ER doctor didn't shy away from the discussions. Instead, with a megawatt smile, he voiced his opinions on the current fashion trends. As the night wore on Julienne caught herself stealing glances at the handsome doctor as he worked the room.

In between networking and dancing, Carlos stole a kiss from her. At first, she was angry, but how could she hold anything against Prince Charming who made her feel like Cinderella at the ball? After the event was over, they strolled on the beach. Shrouded by the darkness and lulled by the hypnotic sounds of the ocean waves, Julienne returned the kiss.

21

"I like you Carlos, but I don't want you to get your hopes up. Angelo one day will come back and when he does, this ends," Julienne warned, adding sugar to her *café con leche*. Since the night of their first kiss, the ER doctor stopped by every morning.

"Whatever you wish *Preciosa but* can you do me a favor?" Carlos asked, opening the bag of ham croquettes. He took one for himself and placed one on the plate in front of her.

"What favor?" Julienne asked, smothering the croquette with ketchup.

"Put the ring away."

"No," she answered firmly. Her eyes fell on the calendar. March 11.th Six months had passed since the towers had fallen. Tears threatened to spill. *Why am I still holding on to him?*

120

Carlos took her ring finger, rubbing it between his thumb and forefinger. "It's a nice rock. Expensive. But some of the prongs are loose. You'll lose the stone. I know an experienced jeweler."

"I don't trust anyone with my ring," Julienne answered, withdrawing her hand.

"Put it away. If the dude comes back, then he can get it fixed for you, what do you say?"

Unspoken pain was alive and glowing in her eyes. She picked up the wet sponge and cleaned the bits of food off their placemats.

Carlos touched her cheek in a wistful gesture. "Let him go, Julienne."

Loneliness crept in when she heard the door slam shut. She had to admit it. Carlos was right. The Missing Victims Center number had been taken over by a lifeless recorder that rattled off the same repetitive list of found survivors. Even Dream Chaser had stopped taking her calls.

Gulping back the tears, Julienne slid the engagement ring off her finger. Like a fallen star she carried it between cupped hands to her room. The heartbroken woman opened the jewelry box and placed it next to the necklace her father had given her for her First Communion. For a long time, she sat immobile staring at her naked finger.

***

Mindless doodles flowed from her pen to a sticky pad. She half-listened to her sister's chatter. Ana had always found a way to make simple meals into a major production.

"Write down Cuban bread, and butter, do you think we need more meat?"

"Go and get some paper plates from inside," Julienne answered, throwing the raw patties onto the grill. "I'll take care of the cooking."

"I made the stuffed zucchini recipe I saw on that cooking show. I'll bring it out. Duh, I forgot to pick up the shrimp. I'll get more mushrooms and green peppers for the Kebabs."

"Are we feeding all of Miami?"

"No, but this older sister is always prepared. Who got the candles and all the board games when we had the hurricanes parties, eh? Oh yeah, and the handy manual can opener. Who brought that to the safe room? Not you baby."

Younger sister lifted the tongs and waved her off. She picked up the corn and placed them on the top rack. The smell of the meat cooking made her hungry. Flipping the burgers over, the younger sister pondered if she should stay in Miami or return to her home state. Ana had volunteered to go with her to New York and move her down. That would not work. Ana would lose money if she took time off from the salon. Her older sister was not destitute, but she needed to budget herself. The weekend partying and shopping sprees ate up a lot of her paycheck. Ana expected Julienne to help her keep the house afloat. Angelo would have agreed it was financial suicide to pay rent for an apartment she was not using. Carlos was right. It was time for a new start. The first thing Julienne would do is let the landlord back in New York know she was moving to Florida. She would have all her belongings shipped to the storage facility.

Julienne tapped the bottom of the barbeque bottle with her palm. Brown liquid filled the glass bowl. She squeezed some lime and added three tablespoons of honey, whisking it together. Some would think it was crazy to leave the major fashion hub, but her plan did make sense. Unless Angelo was with her, the only thing left in New York was subfreezing temperatures. Julienne removed a cob from the grill. As she bit into the smoky kernels, the New York designer heard Carlos's sensual voice calling her.

"Hello, *Preciosa*..."

Looking at the man carrying two loaves of Cuban bread and a rose, she smiled. It was decided. Julienne Juls would make a name for herself in the tropical paradise. As a perk, she had a hot, Cuban boyfriend who spoiled her. What more could she need?

22

On his knees, he crawled through the stagnant water. The smell of sewage filled his nostrils until he thought he would throw up his protein bar. The further he went down the tunnel, the shorter the transmission in his communication unit would last. Not that he needed any orders. He could do what he came to do here in his sleep. He didn't want a babysitter, but he understood their concern. It was not standard procedure to send out an agent on the field who suffered from amnesia. Angelo could just see Collins, face beet red, steam blowing out of his ears. The General would be prowling around the compound demanding they get the system back up and running. He crawled ten more feet until he reached the manhole cover and slowly pulled it open. The mission objective was reconnaissance. The agent was not to engage. He was to stay invisible.

It had taken months of preparation and retraining, but

he was ready. The President wanted answers and he wanted them yesterday. Angelo had planted the bug, and now he had been instructed to leave the party. That just wouldn't do. It was not that he was cocky, or reckless. He knew the risks, but none of the other "Elites" had witnessed the devastation firsthand as he had. None of them had prayed to God for a quick death, trapped under pounds of solid concrete. His colleagues did not cough for hours or gasped for air, as the toxic gas and smoke stuck to their lungs like liquid glue. No, to them it was just another job. The agent removed his communication unit and smashed it with his boot. What did he have to lose? If he was to die on the mission field, he knew God would lift him to heaven in the arms of Jesus... could any of the others say the same?

The terrorist may have taken away part of his memory, but they could not touch the memory of a loving and faithful God. 9/11 had been his wake-up call. God didn't save him from death just to have him sit on the sidelines. Never had he felt so secure. He ditched his fatigues in the sewer and donned on the Middle Eastern *Dishdasha*. The undercover agent climbed out of the hole, careful not to be spotted. A few feet away, long beards with turbans congregated behind the clout of darkness.

Okay God, here we go again, straight into the lion's den. To you be the Glory.

Angelo approached the men, using the profile of an envoy from a well-known supplier. It was a plus he was a linguistic expert and that part of his brain had not broken. The undercover agent accompanied them to a desolated desert and made a trade for information. Then he went back into the city and contacted the Agency. Angelo assured them he had not turned rogue; he had just seized an opportunity that their algorithms and sophisticated profiling programs had missed.

* * *

General Collins let the air escape from between his teeth, as he paced back and forth. Part of him could not help admiring the kid's gutsy move. The other part of him wanted him bound, gagged, and court-martialed for disobeying his orders.

"Face it, Collins, I got you more useful Intel in two weeks than your pretty boys could have gotten in six months."

"You broke protocol boy!"

"You're right, but do we want to continue playing hide and seek with these fanatics, or do we want justice?"

"Let's just say hypothetically I can get your secondary objective authorized, and you succeed, what's in it for you, besides the satisfaction of seeing them squirm?"

The agent smiled to himself. "After the mission is over, you bring me back in. The same status as before the accident, no questions asked."

Collins laughed. "Not asking for the moon and stars, eh son?"

"The whole universe, if possible, Sir." Angelo returned the laugh. On the screen, the General appeared relaxed but that was the government-issued façade they all wore.

"Know, son, I didn't get where I am by being blind and dumb. You want clearance so you can look up your civilian profile... ain't that right?"

The agent ran his tongue through his teeth, keeping himself under control. The General took off his service cap

126

and placed one foot, then the other, on the desk, crossing them.

"You still can't remember anything about your civilian life, can you?" he said, in a smug tone.

Angelo closed his eyes for a moment then opened them. "No… part of my life is missing, and I can't shake the thought …"

"What thought?"

"I know it may sound corny but someone out there is waiting for me."

Collins hacked and sputtered, choking on his cigar. "Son, I can't promise the universe… but I will see what I can do about that moon."

23

"So it is true? This Novo Stilo is stealing you for Pumpkin Shwat designs?" Veronique quipped her accented words traveling through the phone.

"It's pronounced Punk-N-Swag. They want me to help with advertising," Julienne explained, feeling like she had been called into the principal's office.

"But you are a fashion designer, *ma petite.* What are those imbeciles thinking? Pff, don't they know designing and advertising are two different disciplines?"

"They like my ideas. They think it's just what today's teen Fashionistas are looking for," Julienne answered, rummaging through the stacks of magazines until she found the edition for last month's Miami Teen. She snapped her gum. "I am not quitting Imperial, but I am staying here. I can't go back and face..."

"You are moving to Florida? *C'est possible*? You would leave *moi* for this Novo Stilo, trash?"

"Veronique I am not leaving you. Been thinking of doing some short-term freelancing. I just need to know if it's legal since technically I am employed by Imperial."

Veronique asked her to hold on. There was some clicking and then she returned on the line.

"I spoke to Daphne in Accounting. You are paid out of a student fund. You have no contract, but you need to sign the Confidentiality and Non-competition agreement. Julienne, I expect you to finish all your work for *moi* before you do that Shwag fashion, *comprenez-vous*?"

"Have I ever let you down? Working remotely from Miami for Imperial is a good thing. I can be your eyes and ears for the Caribbean and South American markets. I can help you stay on top of the game."

"*Oui Cheri*, but remember you are still new to the business. Do not be fooled by big cash from these amateurs. They cannot offer you the prestige of the Imperial label."

"I know. That's why I want to continue learning from you. But having a chance to work on my stuff is important to me."

"Ah, *oui,* little bird wants to fly. You want independence, eh?"

"So, you understand?"

"I don't like, but... I was young once."

"I have a favor to ask you."

"Young people have no sense. Oh, just tell me before I hang up."

The Junior Designer asked if she could oversee how the moving company would pack her possessions. She was especially concerned with all the designing materials and all the unreplaceable gifts Angelo had given her through the years. An exaggerated breath could be heard over the line, but promptly the French woman threw her a smart remark about how the packing was so *blasé,* but she would sacrifice her tea with the mayor's wife to organize the blue collars.

"*Merci* Veronique. I don't care what they say; you are a softy deep inside."

Julienne flipped to the photos showing teens wearing the Novo Stilo label and made some notes.

"Petite, don't ever confuse my help with weakness. I will fire you the second you stop producing for Imperial and I will sleep like a *bébé!*" With a loud click, her boss ended the call.

Julienne, armed with the magazine, sketch pad, and colored pencils, moved to the porch for inspiration. She pushed her feet back to start the swing. The first drawing was of an average teenage girl with oversized untied sneakers bending down to pick up a flower. The initial draft was well-drawn, but it lacked depth. Her eyes wandered to the yard. The sunlight weaved saffron beams through the leaves of the fruit trees. Shadows of light and dark fought on the patio tiles. Two Sandhill cranes regally made their way across the lawn as a smaller one lagged.

Intrusive thoughts declared an all-out war on the present. The door of her heart opened wide encompassing both joy and pain. If Angelo was the past, could Carlos be her future?

The quandary became a tug of war between ambiguity and the backslash of repressed emotions. It flowed onto the paper, bringing a fresh new look to their advertising slogan. The addition of passive boldness and unrestrained rebellion was just what the Punk N Swag attire label had lacked.

130

24

Novo Stilo was created by a thirty-year-old Millennial Brazilian. Like most entrepreneurs, he had started his dream for success with an old sewing machine inside his parent's garage. Using CAD software and some fashion sense, he launched an affordable line of clothing geared toward teenagers and college students. Through social media, he had gathered a following that catapulted him into the pages of popular magazines.

Julienne met with him at Starbucks. He was down to earth. The designer took a liking to him right away. He was looking to hire someone who understood everyday wear. He was tired of *fake* fashion that only the rich and famous could afford. The urbanite pushed up his horn-rimmed glasses and whistled. A teenager with dark long pointy nails wearing saggy jeans and a navel-ring sauntered over to them. She placed three pieces of gum in her mouth. The girl flipped through the spiral notebook, boredom dominating her face.

Done, she lifted the sketch pad in the air and hooted. Half of the coffee shop patrons turned their heads from their frozen drinks and computer terminals. Paulo smiled as his assistant shouted urban phrases of approval.

Negotiations over the financials took place after both Paulo and the girl left to talk to the Barista at the front of the shop. A twenty-year-old, frizzy redhead took their place. He had barely sat down before he started spitting out numbers. The 'human calculator' not only had calculated her fee into the formula, but he had broken the cost of the project down to the last shiny penny. Paulo rejoined them, checked the spreadsheet, and handed Julienne the contract for her to sign.

For the next three months, Julienne ate, slept, and breathed only Punk N Swag designs. Julienne knew Carlos was not the type of man who would sit around and wait for anyone. He was into fun and living in the present. The young doctor had lots of female friends. Leggy blondes and flirty *Cubanitas* would throw themselves at him the minute her head would turn, so she ended it. But after the launch of Novo Stilo's new line, she found herself missing Carlos. Against her better judgment, she called him. Carlos admitted to having tried to forget her with the other girls, but he had found them shallow. None of them had the qualities Julienne had. He wanted to start where they had left off. The designer agreed to carve out more time to get reacquainted with the doctor. As perfect as he appeared, he was not flawless. When the novelty of his return wore off, she'd lose interest again. At least that's what she was counting on if she was to keep him out of her heart.

25

Angelo's request for government resources and personnel promptly arrived. Weeks later he received orders to meet with a new asset in Pakistan. He continued down the dusty path into the city square and met a fruit vendor selling melons. Angelo bought a melon and went over to the next merchant. The melon was exchanged for a Nile perch. The agent waited until he was alone. He cut a slit down the belly and dug his finger inside. He pulled out a silicon chip. He wiped off the fish guts and inserted the chip into his phone. A map lit up showing him his next destination. A woman covered from head to toe in a black *abaya* met him halfway. She led him through the back streets until they reached a river. He removed his shoes, tied the shoelaces together, and draped them on his neck. The agent went in waist-deep. He waddled near the edge of the river until he found a large rock hidden by the spiky reeds. Hidden in the cleft was an oxygen tank. He placed the mask on and submerged into the river. He swam the length of it until the tank ran out. Angelo held his breath and swam faster. He emerged inside a cavern. Old torches lit the ominous place.

"It's been a while. You probably don't remember who I am, but let's just say you are extremely valuable to me. My name is Javier. Did I ever tell you about the time I was held captive by a small weasel of a man in the Amazon Jungle?"

The agent's eyes adjusted to the darkness. The thin man with graying eyebrows and a pointy beard sat cross-legged next to a low table rambling away about his adventurous life. Guards stood with large swords ready to disembowel anyone who displeased their master. Javier gave a sign and one of the guards tossed Angelo a thin towel. He dried himself as best as he could. The man with a missing finger told him to sit. Angelo obliged, keeping an eye for any sudden movements from the. musclemen around him. Javier engaged the agent in a lengthy conversation filling in some details of his prior life.

"Why do you want to return to a boring civilian life? You are never happier than when you are in the front lines," Javier said, peeling an apple with a pocketknife. He poked the fruit and placed it in his mouth. The host broke off some pita and handed it to his guest. Hummus with crushed olives sat in an earthen bowl, tempting Angelo. He was famished. Praying there was no toxin, he scooped up the spread and ate.

"I want to return to America," Angelo told Javier.

"A woman! That is the only thing that can make a soldier as good as you leave the war," he chuckled.

Angelo raked his hair, "I have to know if she is an illusion fabricated by the neurons running amok in my brain or she exists."

134

"Oh, amnesia can be such a bother." Javier snapped his fingers. A servant handed Angelo another oxygen tank.

"You have signed up for a long mission my friend. You have months and perhaps years to give your decision to leave the field some thought."

"And if I can't get the woman out of my head? You said I saved your life. What if I can chop off the snake's head?" Angelo asked, referring to the terrorist organization they wanted to exterminate.

"Others will grow in its place."

"Not if we infect the wound," he answered.

"It is a noble quest and I have no doubt you will succeed. We can negotiate *after* you complete the mission."

Javier bid him farewell. Angelo strapped on the scuba tank and dove back into the murky water.

***

The mission proved to be more taxing than he had expected. There were victories where key players were questioned or detained. But he also had faith-testing moments. Captured and tortured. Rescued by his team just hours before Collins pulled the plug. Those experiences only served to make him more determined to win the fight. Win he did. There was a primal satisfaction being part of the team that ended the life of the evil man behind the plan to destroy America. But there would be no ticker-tape parade, no interviews, and no big producer would beg for the rights to his movie. It was a clandestine mission, one that would never see the light of day. Yet, two things kept him grounded as he lived as an undercover spy in the shifting sands of the Arabian

135

Desert: his growing faith in God and the golden honey eyes that never left his dreams.

26

Hues of light pink and gold painted the September sky. Sunlight glimmered on the waters, making the lake in Tropical Park sparkle. The trees rustled as the birds took flight.

Contented, she rested her head against her boyfriend's chest as the sun rays dried her hair. Though their canoe trip had ended with her falling into the lake, it had been a wonderful day. Even the gritty feeling of the sand that stuck to her wet arms and legs was not bothering her. The boyfriend at first had been nothing but a distraction from the pain leftover by Angelo's disappearance. Yet after the dance at the unveiling of the Punk N Swag Tween fashion line, she found herself craving his attention.

Carlos wrapped his arms around her waist and kissed her cheek. "I'm glad I took the day off from work."

"Glad you did too, otherwise I would be alligator meat for sure."

He laughed a boisterous laugh that lit up his face. Carlos had brought the fun back into her life. He was silly and boyish, full of pranks and fun. It was impossible to be around him without feeling thankful to be alive.

He craved adrenaline. He loved racing stock cars and jumping off planes. It was freeing yet terrifying to be spiraling down to earth, cheeks vibrating as the air slammed full force into her face. But when he kissed her in midair, her fear subsided. On the racetrack, her stomach jumped to her throat, as they reeled around the curves at 200 miles per hour. Not all dates were energy-driven. There were karaoke parties and movies as well.

They quarreled as any other couple did. Carlos had his share of flaws. He was impatient and had a jealous streak, that would show up now and then when another male paid her attention. But Ana was instrumental in getting her sister to see that those flaws were his way of showing Julienne that he cared. Julienne snuggled against him.

"I don't want this day to end."

"It doesn't have to ever end, *Preciosa*."

She toyed with the gold chain around his neck relishing the woodsy scent of his cologne.

"Julie, I never thought I'd be ready to settle down, but I can't think of any other woman I rather give up the party scene for. You and I... "

"I'm hungry," she interrupted.

"Okay Miss Romantic," he answered, helping her to her feet. "If I feed you will you let me continue my speech?"

They walked over to the checkered quilt spread out on the grass. Julienne opened the insulated basket and removed the pasta salad she had prepared earlier that morning. Carlos pulled out two chilled glasses and a bottle of red wine from his backpack. She made him a plate and then served herself.

"We make sense. Don't you get it? I love you."

"Yes, it's just... "

"Here, this will help you get your head on straight," he said. Julienne took the flute, brought it to her lips, and drank. Metal floated into her mouth. She spat it out on her hand. It was a ring with two smaller diamonds and a huge one in the middle.

"Carlos..."

"Can you stay quiet till I am done? Then you can give me every excuse in the book if you want."

He took the ring and slid it on her finger. "At first, I thought of asking you to move in with me, but I realize that's an easy way out in case things get ugly. I don't have a plan B anymore. I only want you."

"I can't."

"It's time you stop chasing ghosts. I have been asked to attend a 9/11 memorial in New York City. It has been a year. I want you to come with me and put Angelo to rest."

Julienne stared at the stone on her finger. She began to remove it, but he stopped her. "I cannot compete with a dead man. I want you to keep it on, so you can be reminded of what we've shared. Swear no matter how you feel, you will not take it off until we return to Miami."

She thought about it. She owed him at least that much. She kissed him on the cheek. "I promise I will keep it on."

***

The eventful day had opened the vault of suppressed emotions. She had gotten to be an expert on keeping Angelo out of her daily thoughts. She rarely mentioned him anymore. Wasn't that enough? She asked herself, taking out the cling wrap roll to wrap the leftovers from the picnic.

Ana, who was working on Mrs. Martinez's highlights, sauntered in from next door. The beauty school classes she had enrolled in after High School had paid off. Ana had saved enough money working as a cleaning lady to rescue the delinquent mortgage from their estranged mother. She had taken out a loan to remodel the other side of the duplex turning it into a hair salon.

She set the timer down on the coffee table, her expression tight with strain. "Someone has been stealing from the cash register."

"How much did they take?" Julienne asked covering the pasta.

"A thousand dollars! I am going to break some legs!" she yelled, producing a bat from behind the sofa. She began swinging it around until Carlos took it from her.

"Did your sis tell you I asked her to marry me?"

"For real? Oh man, you're going to be my bro-in-law!" she exclaimed, tackling him. Then she let go of him and speeded over to the kitchen and hugged her sister.

"It's not official yet. We are going to New York to the 9/11 Memorial," Julienne explained rinsing the glass flutes. "Carlos wants me to go and bury the memory of Angelo."

Ana walked over to the ticking timer and stopped it. "Have you got a date in mind? How about January? I will make some calls.

"But I haven't..."

"We can have the Engagement party here. I know the best DJ." Ana picked up the ticking timer and stopped it.

"I have two more perms and one cut and blow, then we can go dress shopping. This is going to be such a blast."

Julienne retreated to her mother's old sewing room; her temporary office. Organizing it would keep her mind from returning to her private hell. The first step was to open the mountain of mail piled on her desk.

"Wanna hand? I am pretty good at filing," Carlos said, grabbing a stack of paperwork and looking through it. "The nurses kiss my feet when I help them file the charts. They say there is nothing like a stud who can alphabetize."

"It's okay Don Juan, I can handle it."

"Can you?" he asked, flexing his muscle. He bumped his hip into hers. "I'm goofing around. I am not allowed to go in the filing room; I got banned three years ago. I was seeing this hot radiologist and we started using the filing room as our... ahem, break room. Now that you have turned me into a respectable man, they will probably let me file my patient charts again."

"Good for you," Julienne answered, stapling her bank statement.

"Where do these papers go? We have box seats for the Dolphin game. I want to get there before the tailgate party is over."

It was pointless to argue with Carlos. She handed him the file accordion where she kept her temporary files. In the Auto Insurance folder, he found a paper-back novel marked with a folded sheet of paper.

"What's this?" he asked, poking her with the eraser of a pencil to get her attention. Julienne took the book from him, but he held onto the paper.

'In my spare time, I like to read."

"And this note?"

"That's a copy of the weird emails that started arriving a few days before my wedding."

"You've never mentioned it."

"I haven't gotten any in a long time. I don't even know why I kept them."

"He is not who he claims to be. Lies come easily to those who are skilled? Hmm... sounds like someone had a beef with your Angelo. A jilted girlfriend or..." he surmised, handing her back the note.

"What preposterous theory have you invented now?" she asked, placing it inside the paperback before throwing it back in the accordion file.

"Have you stopped to think, the guy was into questionable stuff?"

Concern erased the calmness from her eyes. "Whether Angelo was a saint, or a demon is not important anymore. He's dead."

Carlos suddenly took hold of her lips with his own. He kissed her with unrestrained passion, leaving her breathless.

Julienne touched her sore lips. He had never kissed her like that before.

27

The bed felt lumpy. Angelo stretched his right arm over his face. The alarm on the night table continued to ring. His fingers found the shutoff button. He was bone-tired from staying up all-night chasing hallucinations again.

"Ask Neurologist to increase sleep medication," Angelo dictated into the high-tech, government-issued recorder on his cell phone. He swung his legs over the side of the bed and went to shower. While he dressed, the coverage of the 9/11 memorial played on the television. The History channel had been airing a documentary on its conception to birth all week, leading up to the historic event. The agent was ordered to stay away from Ground Zero, in case someone recognized him, but the voice inside him insisted he had to go.

Angelo dressed in a pair of casual jeans and a light blue button-down shirt. There was not a day he did not hear the voices of those who died crying out to him. What bothered the agent most was that he had been trained to deal with

143

emergencies, yet he had been incapable of bringing those innocent victims out. He took a swig of dark Espresso and left the apartment.

The agent drove over the speed limit until he caught up with the caravan of vehicles heading to the ceremony. Angelo found a parking spot, paid the meter, and walked two miles to the entrance. Behind dark glasses and a Yankees baseball cap, he blended with the crowd. Angelo had a fair view of the dusty circle where the towers had once stood. People bowed their heads out of respect. Women wiped their runny noses with tissues as men used their sleeves to dry their eyes. Everyone was affected in some way.

Angelo's thoughts turned to his profession. After he returned from the Afghanistan mission, there were discussions regarding his civilian profile. General Collins had proposed eradicating the profile to avoid any leaks to the public. Other high-ranking officers had disagreed. To General Collin's dismay, the final decision by the 'powers that be' had allowed for his civilian profile to remain active. As a precaution, medical records had been falsified to contain dates and times accounting for the time he was in Afghanistan. Agents had already been positioned in the Brain Institute as verifiable alibies Angelo amnesia and partial recovery would his real identity. The only thing not written in stone was *when* he would be free to continue with his civilian profile.

The President of the United States gave his speech One by one people shuffled closer to the circle's perimeter. Angelo stayed a few feet away, a leafy tree obscuring him from any cameras. But that would not help him avert the tongue-lashing waiting for him at the Agency. Angelo wondered if, before the amnesia, he had been as brazen as he was now.

144

As the sun was setting on the horizon, the agent turned his head toward the North fence. There was a break in the sea of people. In the far corner, he saw a woman. He moved the sunglasses down an inch. The woman's movements were slow and concentrated. Her hand faintly skimmed the flyers taped to the fence. She bent her head, respecting each person, perhaps praying for their families. The woman was meticulous covering each row with prayer. There was a glint of recognition when their eyes briefly met. Angelo shifted his glance toward his shoes. His brain needed time to process her image. But when he looked back up, she was gone.

The agent hit number two on his speed dial. "Need you to tap into the North end camera and zoom in. "

"Al-Qaeda?"

"No. I think I saw someone from my civilian life."

"Oh boy. I'll run a face recon. Call you as soon as I have a match".

28

The church had not changed at all. Sandalwood pews lined the two sides of the sanctuary. Two white screens were rolled down, ready for Sunday service. An American Flag and the Christian Flag both were proudly displayed by the pump organ. Though it was rarely played, it was a timeless piece dating back to the 1890s.

Pastor Cates stood in front of the lectern addressing the empty room. His eyes gleamed when he saw his young friend. Elated, he walked down the steps to greet her. The pastor twirled Julienne around. To anyone watching, that greeting would have been silly and out of place. But the peculiar greeting dated back to when she attended her first women's bible study. The twirl transported her back to the first time she had felt God's redeeming love.

***

It was the first snowfall of the season. Women from the streets and volunteers from different ministries were packed into the small classroom. Julienne's only reason for attending was to accompany a runaway teen who slept in a cardboard box behind the Chinese restaurant. The girl needed counsel. Julienne invited her to the study in hopes the pastor could convince the girl to return home. The runaway became bored with the study and returned to panhandling, but Julienne was deeply moved. The study focused on how females, no matter what they looked like or what they had done in the past, were considered Daughters of the King of the Universe. Worth was based on the unconditional love God has for everyone even those whose clothing came from the donation box. Julienne had never heard of that kind of love. The love her mother gave her was conditional. To receive that love she had to be the "perfect child." Young Julienne worked hard to keep that title, but it was never enough. The kind of love the pastor spoke about had brought her tight shoulders back down from her ears. She could relax, she didn't have to be perfect to be loved!

The young women were surprised with a celebration at the end of their study. Pastor Cates had transformed the Soup Kitchen into a royal ballroom, complete with chandeliers, linen tablecloths, and rose centerpieces. The pastor's wife had convinced Sally's Formals, to donate evening gowns and tiaras. That night the room buzzed with excited women awaiting their turn to have the pastor's wife affix the tiaras on their heads. Then every young woman was introduced to the rest of the congregation as Princess so and so. When it was Julienne's turn, Pastor Cates escorted her to the middle of the room, where he twirled the new princess around and around as the congregation clapped. Those had been happier times when she believed nothing could stop God from loving her.

***

"How is God's princess holding up? Today could not have been an easy day for you," Pastor Cates asked giving her one last twirl.

Julienne let go of his hand and bit her lip.

"You take all the time you need."

They sat on the steps of the altar. Pastor Cates caught her up on the special milestones in his life that had happened since she had been away. He and his wife had just celebrated their 50th wedding anniversary. Their youngest son had graduated from Harvard. Shortly after 9/11, they purchased a larger warehouse to use as a soup kitchen but also as a place for the homeless to sleep and bathe.

Julienne twisted the new engagement ring on her finger. The pastor listened intently while she unloaded her burdens. He understood her pain. He had lost his first wife when he was in his twenties.

"I was so mad at God for letting her die of cancer. We had a life ahead of us, and it was robbed from me," he said, the pain of loss still evident in his eyes.

"I made my peace with God," Julienne answered.

The pastor closed his eyes as if in prayer. "Julie, your problem isn't with God. It's with you."

She glanced at the back of the room, where they use to sit to hear the pastor preach on Sunday morning.

"If I would have met Angelo for coffee like he wanted, he wouldn't have been in the office... he...he wouldn't have died," she said, her voice laced with regret.

"Can you prove that? What about God's will?"

"Are you telling me 9/11 was God-ordained?" Julienne said, trying to control her temper.

"No, that attack was planned in the pit of hell. But have you stopped to think that if it was Angelo's time to go, nothing could have stopped God from taking him home? He could have been hit by a bus crossing the street or had a heart attack sitting with you drinking coffee."

"He should have just taken me!"

The pastor patted her hand. "It was not your time."

He handed her the tissue box.

She took the Kleenex, used it, and rolled it into a ball. "It was not his time either. Angelo is alive, I saw him!"

Julienne described what she had seen. How she was confused and hopeful all at the same time. She could not go back and marry Carlos knowing Angelo might be alive. Dream Chaser had not found evidence that supported his survival, yet his name was not mentioned in the memorial.

The pastor rubbed his bony hands, easing the arthritic pain.

"He is not the first person they miss. I don't want to be graphic but there are thousands of body parts in the Fresh Kill Landfill that haven't been identified. Julie, guilt can play havoc in a person's psyche. You keep punishing yourself. You are looking for a reason to refuse..." he lifted her ring finger exposing the glimmering diamond, "happiness and whole-ness."

"I know what I saw."

"Seeing Angelo allows you to continue playing God. You can be the judge, jury, and executioner all at the same time. You've spent a long time blaming yourself for your Pop

149

leaving; now you are doing the same thing with Angelo's death."

Call it divine wisdom, but Pastor Cates had always known her thoughts before she even verbalized them. He was one of the few people who knew about the abuse that her mother had inflicted on her.

But it is my fault...

"Let's say you are the judge. Where does that leave Jesus' sacrifice for you?" the pastor continued pointing to the silver cross hanging behind the altar. He didn't let her answer. "The absolution you seek is not in abstaining from happiness, but it is found on that cross. He died for *all* your sins."

She gave him a puzzled look. "I know Jesus died for me but that has nothing to do with this."

"If the God who made the universe can forgive you for whatever part you think you played in Angelo's death, then why can't you forgive yourself?"

The words scourged her debilitated soul. They stung and burned, exposing where the root of faith had been oppressed. Julienne turned around and knelt on the steps. The pastor prayed quietly alongside her. He prayed for the enemy to release her. Julienne stopped fighting the tears. She fell forward, the loud sobs echoing in the empty church.

"The devil is a liar; you were never meant to carry that guilt. Let it go baby girl. Give it to God."

Pastor Cates prayed silently as Julienne wrestled against her flesh.

God, I know I have been ignoring you. Please forgive me for being so weak. Oh God, I don't want to feel guilty anymore. Help me to know the truth.

The battle raged within her. The pastor called on the power of the Holy Spirit. When he felt that she was done doing business with God, and she had released all her business with God, and she had released all her culpability, he asked one more question.

"Do you love the man who gave you that ring?"

"I still love Angelo. I don't think I will ever stop loving him."

"I am not asking you about Angelo. What about this new guy, Carlos, right? How do you feel about him?"

"I guess I love him too if that makes any sense. But it's different."

"It will always be different until you stop comparing them. Now get out of here and let me get on with rehearsing my sermon, "he chuckled, helping her up. Pastor Cates wrapped his big burly arms around her and hugged her. "No matter what happens, I know you are going to be okay; cause God's Princesses always are. You need to get out of the way and let God work. Trust in His plan."

God's princess walked away from the church a lot lighter than she had come in.

***

Julienne sat in the back row of the train headed toward the garment district. Carlos had sent her a text telling her to meet him at LaGuardia Airport before 8 pm. They were short-staffed, and he was needed back in the ER. Julienne hustled, bumping elbows and arms against the people exiting. Turning left after the turnstile she climbed the stairs that led up to the street.

People carrying multiple shopping bags strained their necks to see if the light had turned red. As they waited, they left their purses opened to check their maps. Julienne removed the purse strap dangling from her shoulder and placed it over her head. Clutching the bag to the front of her body, she hastened her steps. The tourists were easy targets for pickpockets and purse-snatchers, but she was still a "smart" New Yorker. She briskly walked toward the glass and steel buildings reaching toward the clouds. Steps from her stood the yellow and green information kiosk with its giant needle and button. Adjacent to it was the famous eight-foot bronze Garment Worker sculpture.

She would have visited Imperial, but Veronique was in Europe and she didn't want to hear condolences from her colleagues. Another block down and Julienne found herself in the park where she and Angelo had their first date. She continued her bitter stroll past mutual places of enjoyment. The young woman stopped in front of the coffee shop where she had spilled coffee on Angelo's newspaper, the bookstore where he had bought her the wedding planner, and even the Calligraphy shop where their wedding invitations were printed. Turning the corner, she found Chachi's Philly Steak stand, where she learned of Angelo's love affair with onions. From there, Julienne hailed a taxi cab to take her to her next destination.

***

The block Angelo had lived on was deserted. Every New Yorker had left their neighborhoods to be at the Memorial. It was instinctual getting on the elevator of the George

152

Washington Apartments complex and exiting on the ninth floor. She walked past Monet's *Water Lilies* and turned left. A family of three with a jogging stroller was leaving the apartment. Julienne walked up behind the stroller, bend, and retrieve the teething ring the fussy baby had dropped. She handed it back to his mother, then introduced herself. The husband who was locking the front door told her they had just moved in a month ago. The wife added they had relocated from California due to her husband's job. In conversation, Julienne told the tenants about Angelo's untimely death. The mother whispered something to the father and had him reopen the front door. She invited Julienne in to tour the apartment.

The few eclectic pieces of living room furniture held Folded baby clothes and toys. A highchair with dancing elephants was part of the dining room décor. A changing table and crib took up most of the space in what used to be Angelo's home office. The ecru-colored walls had been splashed with nautical blue. Black and white photos of the young family hung on the ocean-themed walls. Everything was visually different, but Julienne 's heart mapped out vivid memories in every inch of the apartment.

The glass door to the balcony was stuck. Julienne twisted the round knob gently jiggling to the left, she gave it one quick pull and opened it. A gust of Autumn wind plowed into her. She lifted her foot over the track and stepped outside. Two bright pillars of light shot straight up into the darkening sky. Another visible reminder of everything she had lost.

The unsightly football fabric sofa welcomed Julienne like an old friend. A tear began to roll; she stopped it halfway. How many times had she tried to get rid of the hideous thing? But Angelo would not part from his ratty sofa. Gently, she

153

stroked the spaghetti stain on the seat. The tenant watching from inside turned away from the glass sensing the grieving guest wanted to be alone with her memories.

***

The sun dipped beneath the skyscrapers. Angelo had made his homemade Spaghetti Marinara in honor of the Superbowl. They sat on the green and yellow couch, carefully balancing a paper plate on their laps.

"Did you see that pass?" Julienne asked, hoping to get the conversation going. With his eyes glued to the television, Angelo mumbled if she could serve him another helping. He handed her his empty plate while yelling at the quarterback to throw the ball. Peeved by his lack of attention, she went inside to refill his plate. When Julienne returned, she noticed he had covered her plate with his napkin so that her pasta would not get cold. *That was sweet,* she thought taking back all the mean things that had gone through her mind in the kitchen.

While Angelo coached his team from the couch, she uncovered her food. Sitting on top of her spaghetti was an engagement ring. Angelo diverted his attention to the word-less woman. He picked up the ring from her plate, cleaned it off on his t-shirt, and slid the ring on Julienne's finger. When he leaned over to kiss her, he knocked over her plate on the couch. They would clean it up later. The crowd cheered from the television set, another touchdown.

***

154

Julienne sighed. Everything Pastor Cates had said made perfect sense. But sitting in Angelo's old apartment surrounded by the lure of his memory, she could not stop praying for a miracle.

An angry text came in, halting her prayers. She was late! Carlos was already at the airport. Julienne silenced her phone and ran her fingers across the stain one last time. *Good-bye Angelo.*

29

Angelo sat in the examining room of the Trauma Brain Center rubbing his temple. After reliving 9/11 he needed to get rid of the flashbacks and recurrent nightmares. The place smelled of antiseptic and the nurse had taken enough blood to fill a blood bank. It did not take long for the doctor to arrive. The babyface Neurologist was on the agency's payroll, so having bedside manners was secondary to obtaining results.

"I don't see a problem. Nightmares, flashbacks, PTSD symptoms are reported by half of my patients. They come with the territory. I have no interest in stopping the process by dulling your cognitive skills with unnecessary sedation."

"Why don't we just cut to the chase? I can live with the headaches, but I am not getting any restorative sleep. Not sleeping will also dull my cognitive abilities and slow down my reflexes, Dr. Kent. *Our* employer won't appreciate that."

"Irritability is another symptom. I can give you a mood stabilizer for that. The brain is a remarkable, complex machine. Yours as unevolved is doing its best to reconfigure and rewire new pathways. It may recalibrate from time to time as it tries to assimilate the past and the present."

What am I, a car? Angelo clenched his jaw. *Throw him out the window! The* voice he heard was tempting. But that was not the way to outsmart the scholarly Savant.

"Doc, you and I know there are many other neuro smart-alecs at the university that would kill to be in your shoes. So, I am asking nicely to please do your job and fix my brain," he said sporting a cunning smile.

"I will order some tests. Depending on the results we will revisit your..um...need for...um... sleep aids," Dr. Kent stuttered staring down at his notepad. He left without examining him.

Angelo hopped off the examining table. He missed Dr. Healy's tenderness. He had thought of showing up in Maryland and asking her out on a date. But his game plan had been squashed when he learned that while he was on active duty, Dr. Healy had married an Orthopedic Surgeon.

Dr. Kent put Angelo through a series of memory tests and another CAT scan. Results showed no notable change. The brain injury appeared to be permanent. Dr. Kent made it clear, it was not likely he would regain the memories of his past on his own. Anger filled him. Unless he could anchor the haunting golden eyes to his reality, he would never feel whole. He could feel it in his bones, the mystery woman in his dreams was connected to him in a very special way.

Dr. Elliot Kent ripped out three pharmaceutical orders from the prescription pad and handed them to him.

157

"You have never had a problem with addiction. So, I added Prazosin, to help with the nightmares along with your usual medicines. There are no refills unless you come in for a check-up. I will have Leslie schedule you for every three months. We are all done here."

As Angelo was buttoning his shirt, the untraceable phone vibrated in his pocket. It was a call from the agency's IT expert.

"So, what's the word on your memory chip?"

"It's fried."

"That's a bummer man. But don't worry; I've been working on a program..."

"We need to meet," Angelo said getting in his car.

"Umm... I guess. It will take time to fix some of the bugs."

"Work fast. I will be there in an hour."

30

    Chase Anderson, aka Dream Chaser, worked from a residential dwelling two hours away from where Angelo resided. Angelo made it in less than an hour. He parked the rented car in front of the brick-colored house. A young man in his twenties with a baseball cap and ripped jeans met him at the door. He led him past a sink full of breakfast dishes and a bedroom carpeted wall to wall with Superhero posters. A pile of empty pizza boxes aligned the hallway. They went down a flight of rickety stairs to the basement. There was a wall-sized television set hooked up to gaming systems and a couple of sofas. Chase led Angelo into the adjacent laundry room. He turned the knob and pushed the *delicate* setting on the washing machine panel. The wall slid open.

    "I don't do delicates," he said, stepping aside as Angelo entered the state-of-the-art computer station. Dream Chaser sat down and opened a bag of Twizzlers. With the gummy stick hanging between his teeth, he pulled up the program.

"I have compiled a bunch of videos that will take you through the years you spent as a civilian."

Angelo clicked on the start screen and began his walk down memory lane. The first surveillance video showed a girl wiping down a park bench, before sitting down to eat her lunch. Her back was to the camera, but he could hear the conversation they were having. The kid sucked on the waxy stick fast-forwarding the video. Angelo noted most of the time that he appeared on the video it was with that girl. The gears in his memory bank began to move. *Those eyes!* The swirls of golden caramel dancing in her irises...

"She's the one. I want everything you have on her," he said toning down the excitement he felt surging through him like a live current.

Dream Chaser grinned and cracked his knuckles. With a few keystrokes, the paper trail belonging to Juliana Gutierrez aka Julienne Juls appeared on the screen. He took his bag of goodies and disappeared to the gaming room.

After an hour, the hacker waltzed back in, his head covered by a simulation helmet.

"Is that the same girl you saw at the memorial?"

"It has to be her. Do you still have the footing from this morning?" Angelo asked enlarging her Sweet Fifteen photo.

"Sure do." He keyed in the date. The video showed the determined young woman pressing through the crowd. He zoomed in closer magnifying her face. It was unmistakable. Her golden eyes were fixated on the man leaning on a tree by the banner.

"She was looking straight at me," Angelo noted.

160

"Woah, today is September 15th. It would have been a year you would have been married to this chick," the computer geek commented throwing some peanuts into his mouth.

"No wonder I felt strange after I read my devotional this morning. It was 1st Corinthians 13."

"Isn't that, that archaic poem that religious people read at weddings?"

"Love is patient, love is kind..." Angelo said examining the video, frame by frame.

"Yeah, well whatever gets you through the day man, but you're running out of time. Unless that god of yours grants you a miracle, you got some heavy competition moving into your turf. There this ER doc from Miami and at first it was no big deal, now looks like she is falling hard for him."

Angelo's eyes turned into two lethal green slits.

"Get me his info NOW!"

***

The ER doctor was squeaky clean except for a couple of parking tickets. He was an upstanding citizen who voted and attended Jury Duty when summoned. The records showed he frequented certain dance clubs and was known as a 'Ladies' man. But within the last few months, his attendance at the bars and clubs had dwindled.

Dream Chaser turned from side to side on his chair. He rubbed his hands together and chose an Oreo from the half-eaten package.

161

"The guy used to be a real player, but she's got him hooked. The last recon record shows them at the Zoo, doing the family thing with his five-year-old niece."

Angelo rubbed his head. An aural migraine was threatening his concentration. He ignored the vertigo and continued viewing the files.

The young hacker drummed his fingers. "Can I be real with you?"

Angelo nodded his head slowly; wishing the room would stop spinning.

"When I was assigned to this case, I thought it would be boring. Keeping the civilians from learning your real identity was a no-brainer. Then you start working this Julienne babe."

Dream Chaser snapped his fingers, "Man! That girl kept me on my toes! Keeping her search results fictional was a challenge. You dubbed the operation, get this, 'Samson and Delilah.'"

"You knew who she was all along! Why did you keep me in the dark? I ought to break your neck!"

"Hey, you know how it works man, everybody has dirt on everybody. Let's just say that when I was in my angry stage I kind of hacked the Pentagon. It caused some serious problems with the servers. I could have ended up in Corrections or sent on a mission of no return. But hey, I guess your god likes me, or I was just lucky, that I am *that* good. So, I can't bite the hand that feeds me when they are watching. And they are always watching."

"Can you at least tell me who assigned her to me?"

"Sorry Dude, that is above my paygrade. The only thing I know is you were pulled from the field and sent to guard her."

"But why? Why is she so important? Any flags in her files?"

Dream Chaser searched the database. "Nah, she's your average Hispanic American girl. Oh, wait... looks like the Dad left them when she was a kid. He ended up serving time for drug trafficking. He committed suicide in jail."

"Do you have any files on my transfer? Who signed off on it?"

"It says 'Collins', but then the trail goes cold."

Angelo rubbed his eyes. The migraine was affecting his vision.

"You look like you are going to puke. You should take a break."

"Collins told me he did not want me on the outside. Someone higher up than Collins had to have given the order."

"There is another piece of intel you should know. Julienne, the one in the video, left me a message the other day. I don't know if anyone put you up to speed on my cover, but she and I met in college..."

Angelo held his head. It felt like an inflamed walnut and someone was trying to crack it open.

"It was in the...um... files," Dream Chaser answered. "She was ticked that I had no answer for her about your disappearance, so she hired a retired fed. He's been sniffing around but I got him chasing his own tail."

"Good. We don't need any interference."

"One more thing... I hope I don't get canned for this, but..."

Dream Chaser pulled up her emails. Angelo read the chilling notes written days before he was to marry the girl.

"Somebody was trying to blow my cover," he said, pinching the bridge of his nose. He dug in his pocket and found his prescription. He took the medication.

"Anywhere I can crash for a few minutes?"

Dream Chaser pointed to a whiteboard filled with algorithms and mathematical equations. "Behind the board, I got an awesome waterbed."

***

"Why did you let me sleep so long?" Angelo yawned, looking over the hacker's collection of graphic novels.

"You look like you needed it."

Dream Chaser crunched on some ice reading. "Oh crap, there is an update on her file."

"What is it?" Angelo asked thumbing through the pages of *Ultimate Spiderman*.

"Angelo you better sit down for this."

The agent put the novel back. "I only ask once."

"Julienne is getting married tomorrow!"

"You better not be pulling my chain," Angelo answered looking over his shoulder.

"Scouts honor." He said pointing to the message blinking on his monitor. "So, what do you plan to do about it?"

"Stop her."

"How?"

"Can you get me in the air in half an hour?"

The cocky hacker wiggled his fingers before placing them on the keyboard again. "That my friend, I can do."

31

The leather watch on her wrist alerted her that Carlos would be leaving his shift at Jackson Hospital. It also told her the date, September 15th. A year ago, she would have been walking down Emmanuel Church in NY, saying, "I do" to the man who had made her life complete. A year later she was in Miami, meeting a different man, in a different church to plan another wedding. Life was so ironic.

Saint Philemon Church was a cobblestone church situated in historical Coral Gables. It was the church Carlos had been baptized in as an infant and even though he had rarely laid foot in it as an adult, he had a sentimental attachment to it.

They were scheduled to meet his childhood priest at six-thirty. After the introductions, Julienne would ask the priest if he would consider co-officiating the wedding with her pastor from New York. Since she was early, she slipped into a pew at the back of the church and started to rehearse what she wanted to say, but her thoughts took her to forbidden territory.

Lord, should I go through with this? I know what Pastor Cates said back in NY but what if the man I saw was Angelo? What if he is alive? And what are you trying to tell me with that devotional this morning? Was that a sign to marry Carlos? I just want the truth.

A chubby man with a clergy collar and a black robe was headed in her direction. He knelt in front of the altar before continuing his careful steps toward the pew she was occupying. A couple of silver hairs gleamed on his bald head. His tiny blue eyes were framed by ruddy pudgy cheeks.

"You must be the bride," he said, the corners of his lips rising slightly.

She nodded her head, blinking away the moistness from her eyes.

He motioned if he could sit down. "I would say congrats but I don't think you want to hear that."

Julienne scooted over and rubbed her arms, trying to warm the chill of doubt that seeped into her.

"Excuse me?" she stammered.

"For years I have seen young ladies come and go from this place. Some are ready to be wives...others..."

"It's complicated."

"It always is when love is involved. I am a good listener."

Where could she begin? Today her heart was held together by a sliver of hope. It was so fragile that any mention of Angelo would cause it to break beyond repair. But she was tired of pretending and hiding the turmoil inside her soul. Her eyes met his soft gaze. There was a peace about the rotund servant of God that invited her to be transparent. Time had turned Angelo's story into an apathetic regurgitation of facts.

166

But during the retelling, the vault of details she had kept to herself, opened. She didn't shrink back from the memories or the feelings they brought. Julienne knelt; the raw burn of tears scraped the back of her throat until she allowed the floodgates to open. Sobs from deep within burst forth as the gentle stranger knelt beside her in reverent prayer.

"You have had a great loss. Your heart is still captured in the past. I don't know if that vision of yours was real. But I know, God is working to bring that chapter of your life to close one way or another," he whispered.

"I am a horrible person. Carlos is going to hate me. I should have just returned the ring when I got back from the memorial."

"If he truly loves you, he will understand. If you belong together, God will bring you back to him."

The priest helped her sit down again. He turned to face her.

"I knew it would take a special woman to trap Carlos. He must really love you. Young lady, it's only fair that when you marry him, you can give him all your heart, not just a part of it."

The doors of the sanctuary opened. Carlos hurried down the aisle. He wore a stethoscope around his neck and green scrubs. A hint of razor stubble accentuated his tanned complexion. He gave a hearty handshake to the short priest.

"Sorry I am late. Long shift. Two heart attacks and one old geezer who had too much to drink and thought he could fly."

"*Carlitos* is not nice to make fun of the elderly. Son, you are late, and *Señora* Josefina is waiting."

The priest quickly hurried to open the confessional. A widow with a dark veil and a rosary wrapped around her

167

hands waited till the light on the top of the boxed room lit up. She entered pulling the door closed, leaving Carlos and Julienne alone. Carlos plotted himself down next to Julienne and gave her a peck on the lips. "Sorry Babe, I didn't even have a chance to change. Between the flu and kids putting beads up their noses, it was insane. I'm sure he will get to us after he hears all her little dirty secrets." Carlos paused, noticing the puffiness around his girlfriend's eyes. "Please tell me you were crying happy tears."

Julienne looked down at her hands, lying motionlessly on her lap. "We have to talk."

He crossed one foot on top of his knee and leaned back on the pew. "Shoot."

Julienne looked toward the cross, gathering strength from the man hanging there. She clasped her hands and exhaled. "I can't do this. I don't want to lead you on. I think I saw Angelo at the memorial."

Carlos cocked his head and took the stethoscope off his neck. "Is that all *Preciosa*? You have a classic case of PTSD. It is common to see dead friends, family, etc. after they croak. It's just the mind trying to cope. I can prescribe you a little something to get you over the hump."

Julienne's chest rose and fell with each angry breath. She was tired of being thought of as a lunatic. The young woman had expected anger, sadness, and even some nasty remarks due to breaking off the engagement, but never ridicule.

"For your information, I am not making things up. They didn't even say his name at the memorial. You would have known that if you would have paid any attention."

Carlos shrugged his shoulders. "And? Do you know how many parts from different people are buried in that landfill? It's possible if they wanted to save the taxpayers some money

168

and not bother with his remains. He was an orphan, right? No next of kin. He wouldn't be missed."

Her eyes narrowed. Her nostrils flared. "That is the stupidest thing I have ever heard! Half of New York City knew we were getting married! He was a very successful financial consultant who had clients all over the world! I work for Imperial. One of the biggest fashion houses in all New York. We volunteered in a soup kitchen that served hundreds of homeless. Plenty of people miss him, especially me!"

Carlos impatiently tapped his stethoscope on his leg. "Can you please lower your voice? We are in a church."

"You're one to talk about reverence. You only come here for Christmas and Easter, Baptisms and weddings!" She argued back, her eyes wild with fury.

"You forgot funerals," he added in a condescending tone as he joined her in the center aisle.

Julienne ripped the ring off her finger. "I don't want to marry someone who can't take me seriously. I am not crazy!" She held the ring in her shaking palm. Carlos cupped his hand underneath hers. He bent her fingers upward until she had made a fist around the ring.

"We can postpone the wedding if you want to. But I am not giving up. I have never loved a woman the way I love you. We are good together and if you can't see that, then you *are* delusional."

Her eyes blinked back a tear; she opened her hand again. "I am not delusional. I can see you love me. You brought me back to life when I was dead inside, but I know in my gut he lives."

Carlos puckered his mouth. "So, if he was here right now, you'd forget about everything we have shared? That's cold."

She tried touching him, but he flinched, the pain readable in his eyes. She thought for a moment. What if Angelo was alive? What would be her first reaction? Would she kiss him, or would she slap him for leaving her? She would need answers, lots of them. In her mind, he had not changed at all, but time did strange things to people. Had another woman been comforting him? Would he even want to return to her? On the other hand, Carlos was alive. She knew of his insatiable desire to woo the opposite sex. She knew his need to excel at everything he did and his zest to squeeze every bit of flavor out of life. She knew Carlos' habit of rubbing his neck could only mean he was stressed and the way his brows knit together meant he was scheming. He was impossibly childish at times, but she saw past that to his kind heart. So big and so open, it could swallow her up, whole. If she was not careful, she could easily lose herself there and never look back.

"I won't make any life-altering decisions without concrete evidence that he is gone," she said.

"What more evidence do you need? Two experts you hired have told you he is D-E-A-D."

She smoothed out the wrinkles in her linen pantsuit. "A computer nerd and a retired cop? Not exactly top-of-the-line investigators."

Carlos threw his arms up in the air. "Fine, I'll join in your hunt for the elusive Mr. Angelo. I have a friend who works for the Missing Person's Bureau. I'll give him a call."

Julienne's eyes sparkled with renewed hope. She lifted the ring with her two fingers and brought it to his eye level.

"If he is dead, and your friend can prove it, I will marry you."

Carlos chuckled. "I have a better plan," he mused, taking the stethoscope off his neck and trapping it around hers. He pulled her closer. "If the dude is dead, it's your turn to propose. "

"Okay."

He kissed her. His finger pointed to the ground. "Like a man, down on one knee, asking ... no, better yet, *begging* me to marry you."

Julienne whacked him with her purse. "Don't push your luck."

"Ouch. Hey lady, we are in a sacred place. The nerve of you." He recovered his stethoscope from her neck and leaned on the railing of the pew. "Now who's going to tell my little buddy who was so excited to marry his favorite Altar Boy?"

"I think he already knows. Hold it. Didn't you get thrown out of the Altar Boys club for setting the altar on fire when you lit the candles on Christmas mass?"

Julienne recanted the information his older sister had shared with her on their last trip to the Metro Zoo.

"Mari!" he exclaimed. "That brat. I will have you know she was no saint either. You should hear some of the stories about her and the nuns."

Slowly, like dying embers, the laughter ceased. An uncomfortable silence followed. The lights of the candles burned underneath the graven images. Parishioners gathered in front of them to pray while they waited for the eight o'clock mass to begin. Julienne wrapped her arms around herself. It was suddenly cold in the sacred place. Carlos turned and walked toward the confessional to break the news to the little priest. There would be no wedding.

32

Carlos scratched his neck and sipped on the iced coffee. Julienne sat across from him; her hair freshly washed. Ana tapped the pedal lifting the salon chair until it had reached the desired height. Julienne's head was bent forward, her face practically touching the screen of her iPad. With her electronic pen, she moved the cursor, creating a vertical blue stripe down the center of the pants she was sketching. She had picked up another client from the Miami Beach Fashion Show. The word of her unique design style was spreading fast.

"Do you want to ruin the cut? Sit up and stay still. You're worse than a *niñá.*"

"How long does it take to pick up the phone and dial a number?" Julienne complained, glaring at Carlos.

Earlier in the day, Carlos had received a call from his buddy at the Missing Person's Bureau. He had found a clue as to the disappearance of Julienne's missing ex-fiancé. Before he could go into detail, he was interrupted by an urgent situation. Carlos received an apology text stating he would call them back in the afternoon.

"Why hasn't he called? You said he had some news."

Carlos lifted his sleeve that had unrolled. It had been sprinkled with coffee. He cursed trying to blot out the stain. Ever since he had agreed to help her find Angelo, she had not given him a moment's peace. The woman was a nag, but her looks made up for it.

"He will call. Relax and let your sister do her job." He told her watching her unconsciously use her short-jagged nail to scrape off the polish of her other fingernails. Julienne usually kept her nails manicured, healthy and long, but lately, she had taken to biting them until her fingers bled.

Carlos hated to see his fiancée all worked up. Once they got married, he would make sure her fascination with the late Angelo D'Marco would stop. He was sick of the ghost. He scrolled through his phone. *You are going down, Angelo,* he thought, clicking the save button on a picture of the Ritz-Carlton Royal Honeymoon Suite.

"*Preciosa,* let's play devil's advocate for a moment."

Julienne continued picking at her nails.

"If it's lopsided, it's all on you," Ana huffed, picking up the scissors to fix the uneven side.

"Sorry, Ana. What do you want, Carlos?" The annoyance in her voice was palpable.

"Let's pretend the dude was not in the towers when the planes hit. For argument's sake, let's say he is alive. What reason could he have for not contacting you?"

Ana pushed Julienne's head down. She lifted a section of her sister's hair and cut it into long layers.

"Hear me out before you start yelling. What if the dude is not dead but is happily married to some woman or has a

173

girlfriend? What if he never died, he just needed a way to, you know...get the noose off his neck? It's not that far-fetched. Didn't you tell me he was desperate to meet you for coffee that day?

"You're unbelievable. He loved me. Angelo was a die-hard patriot. He would never use a national tragedy to leave me!"

Ana stopped cutting. "Carlos *ya*! Drop-it! This is the second time I almost cut her head off!"

"I am not heartless. But you have to wonder," he said, ignoring his soon-to-be sister-in-law.

"Leave her alone! You are playing with fire. When Julie gets angry, she's a real..."

"What about those emails? Have you gotten any more?" he interjected.

"No more emails, if you must know."

Ana squeezed a dollop of hair mousse in her hands and worked it into her sister's hair. She poked Carlos with the tip of her styling pick.

"Oww!" he yelled, almost dropping the yogurt he had taken from the mini-fridge.

"*Preciosa*, could it the *muchacho* was already married and was keeping you on the side? The emails stopped because the jealous wife had no reason to worry anymore. You said he traveled a lot. You see where I am going with this?"

"I swear, the next time you open your mouth, I am using the scissors to shut you up!"

"It's okay Ana, he doesn't know Angelo. My friend said that the emails were coming from places like New Zealand, and Tokyo. The signal jumped around through multiple places on all the continents. Only a person with extensive computer knowledge could have made that happen."

Carlos waved a brush around. "A young wife with lots of computer experience." Holding the handle, he clocked Ana on the head. The two ran around Julienne's chair armed with hair products. Ana tried poking Carlos's arm with the pick, but Carlos used the blow dryer's hot air to keep her in line. They chased each other around the salon, ducking behind furniture.

"Will you two act your age?" Julienne said picking up her iPad to finish her design.

Their horse-playing came to an end when Ana inadvertently spritzed hair volumizer into his face

"*Carlitos,* sorry *chico*...I know it hurts," Ana apologized, holding his eyelid open while shoving his head under the open faucet.

"Let me do it, you're going to drown me!"

"ER doctor my foot! You're a big baby!"

Eventually, the squabbling died down as hush tones took over their conversation. Julienne strained to hear, but the water masked their words.

"What are you two whispering about?" She asked, looking at the back of her head with a handheld mirror.

"Hold up, there is a text coming in," Carlos said, trying to see through his burning pupils. Ana threw a towel at him. "Dry up you fool."

"Well?" Julienne asked, starting to remove her cape.

Carlos tossed her the phone so she could see the incoming text. The message was from Detective Morales. It stated he had to leave the country on a special assignment. He would pass their case to Detective Andrews.

175

God, why are you making it so difficult to find Angelo? Is this your way of telling me that he is dead, and I should stop looking for him?"

"I'm sorry, *Preciosa*. We have to wait till the new guy calls us."

"I am fine Carlos. You don't need to stick around and babysit me. When we finish here, we are going to the spa. Call me as soon as you hear from him."

"You will be the first to know." He said grabbing his keys.

33

Carlos ran along the shoreline. His feisty bulldog ran alongside him, his paws wet by the small waves coming in. The dog tugged on his collar, wanting to go play. His owner removed his leash, allowing the animal the freedom he Craved. He dabbed the sweat line on his brow with his tank top and surveyed the beach. It was dotted with groups sporadically spread out enjoying the sun. Two boys tossed a Frisbee. Parents sat under an umbrella cooing at a chubby cheek baby looking up from her playpen.

Carlos picked up a shell and threw it far into the ocean. A few months ago, it would have been impossible to picture himself as a husband and a father. But as he watched the man gently lift the infant girl and give her a bottle, he felt a longing in his heart he had never felt before. It was not just a wife he wanted. He wanted to be a part of a wholesome family who could love him for more than what he could do for them. He stretched out his taut muscles, clearing some of the cobwebs from his brain. It was his day off and though he longed to spend it with Julienne, yet a spa day for the ladies always seemed to work in his favor. He hoped those mud baths and algae wraps would not only purify the toxins from her body but rejuvenate her thoughts about their future together.

The techno dance music blaring from Eden Rock Hotel made the happy bulldog run back to his master. Carlos unclasped the clip that attached the back to the happy bull-dog run back to his master. Carlos unclasped the clip that attached the buzzing cell phone to his waist and brought it to his ear.

"Dr. Hernandez, this is Detective Andrews. I am calling about the Angelo D'Marco case."

"I'm listening."

"The preliminary report stated Angelo D'Marco was nowhere to be found. All evidence pointed to him dying at the towers."

"Any tangible proof?"

"No, but I did find some conflicting information in the report that was handed to me. So, I decided to do some digging on my own."

"Go on," Carlos muttered watching the dog run in circles around him.

"Morales was concentrating on the US. I went a step further." There was some rustling of papers. "Here it is. One of our contacts found a picture of a traffic camera. At first, I was not sure it was the MIA but then I ran a face recognition and Bingo."

"Where is he?" Carlos asked crushing the plastic bottle he had finished in his fist. He smiled at the pretty lifeguard and threw it in the trash.

"He was in Afghanistan."

178

"Patriotic moron," he mumbled, kicking the trash can making a dent in it. The lifeguard stood from her perch. calling out a reprimand. He waved an apology and flew up the stairs of the wooden walkway with his dog running behind him.

"Hello, Dr? Are you still there?"

"Yeah. Hold on a minute. Let me just get in my car," he answered as he deactivated the alarm of his Mazda Miata. He ushered the dog inside the steaming car. "Sorry *Papo*, I forgot the sunshade," he told the distressed animal, opening the sunroof.

"So, you're telling me, the dude never died," he said, picking up the phone again. "Pity."

"The guy vanished from the grid but looks like he is back on US soil."

Carlos slammed the steering wheel. "Where is he?"

"The last report states he has been in New York for a while. Don't worry sir, I have alerted Homeland Security."

"*Gracias amigo*, you've done well. Let me know if you hear anything else. And Andrews? Let's keep this info Between us. It would cause a big scandal if your lawyer's wife finds out about that underage Korean girl you got holed up in Liberty City. Do we understand each other?"

"How do you? ... Um... yeah sure we never spoke."

The bulldog whined, his tongue lolling out one side of his mouth. Carlos quieted his dog and peeled out of the parking space. He had come too far to lose her now.

179

34

Julienne ran down the steps. She wanted to hear it was all a big mistake. But in Carlos' hand was the proof. She snatched the envelope from him and tore it open. She read across the lines, her eyes blurring. The contact they had in the Missing Person's Bureau had found a DNA match in the Fresh Kill graveyard. It was kept in the data bank that the government had compiled for the unidentified remains. It went on to say that the reason his name was not read had been a clerical error. They should have contacted her but because he had no family listed for emergencies, the person in charge of the calls did not investigate further. There was an eyewitness account of Angelo D'Marco leaving the building to buy coffee that morning. But he had returned before the planes hit. Julienne sat on the steps, the report slipping from her fingers. Carlos bent down retrieving it. She could feel her breakfast churning. She leaned forward, clutching her stom-

180

ach. He sat next to her, rubbing her back. She placed her wet cheek on his t-shirt. A mixture of relief and grief overshadowed her. A small giggle escaped her lips. Mortified by the noise she had made, she tried to control it, but the next cackle was louder. *Am I going crazy?* she wondered as more uncontrollable laughter bubbled out of her. The peals of laughter quickly turned into loud wails. The noise brought out curious neighbors which Carlos shooed away. After some time, she pulled herself together and accepted his hug. Breaking the hold of his embrace, she dropped to one knee on the second step.

"You don't have to do this. I was joking."

"I know. But we had a deal. Angelo is... Will you marry me?"

"Are you sure that is what you want?"

She nodded, the smile not reaching her eyes.

Carlos scooped her up into his arms. "Okay, *Preciosa*. I don't want to have to wait another minute. How about next weekend?"

Julienne bit her nail. "Um, I can't plan a wedding in a week."

"Yes, we can. I know you want a church wedding, but if the date is taken, we can have Father Ignacio marry us at the beach. Right where we met; wouldn't that be romantic?"

***

They broke the news to her sister. She called together all their mutual friends. After work, everyone gathered for a celebratory toast. Those who were able to show up to the last-minute party came with food platters, liquor, and gift cards. They took turns speaking into a microphone as Ana

181

videotaped the event. Some of the men told jokes while the women bombarded her with questions about how she had won over the confirmed bachelor.

The noise of clinking champagne glasses and festive music grated Julienne's nerves. Without anyone noticing, she slipped out of the back door and stepped into the yard leaving the commotion behind. Dark clouds covered the moon. Only a splinter of light guided her to the firepit.

The bench was made from weathered wood. Both sisters had rescued it from the neighbor's trash. They had sanded and varnished it until it looked like new. Julienne sat down, careful not to spill the champagne on her dress. She swirled around the golden liquid and stared at an iguana as it made its way up a limb of a mango tree. She downed the glass. A dull ache radiated from inside talking the place of the numbness. False hope, and wishful thinking; that is all it was, she reminded her retrieving the photograph from her cardigan. Julienne lit the logs. Extending her hand, she opened her fingers, letting the photo fall into the pit. Billows of smoke rose upward toward the cloudy sky. The innocence of their first kiss, the urgency of the last, and everything in-between became fresh in her mind's eye.

"I have to let you go," she whispered. Julienne watched the flames sing the corners of the brittle paper. She ripped the skin around her nail with her teeth until it bled. Carlos had shown her studies where small cuts from nail-biting could lead to painful infections, but she didn't care. She would welcome physical pain if it took away the relentless heartache that torched her every breath. Thunder rumbled in the distance. The angry clouds burst open drowning out the fire. Angelo's wet picture lain intact on the ashen logs.

She looked up raising her fist to the heavens. "Why are you doing this to me? Haven't I continued to serve you? You won. I've accepted you took him from me. I don't deserve this!"

Carlos came from the porch carrying an umbrella and a drink. He looked down at the photo floating on the shallow pool of water that had formed in the pit. He took one of the roasting sticks and stabbed the photo against a wet piece of log submerging it underneath.

"Let's get you dried up. Ana wants us to take some more engagement pictures."

She stood up from the bench slick with heaven's tears.

"I am going to make you so happy you won't have time to miss him," he murmured, kissing her ear. Julienne shivered as a gust of wind pelted nails of rain into her skin.

"*Preciosa,* your skin is like ice. Drink this. It will warm you up," he said, lifting the cocktail he was holding with his free hand up to her lips. The alcohol burned her throat as it went down but she continued to guzzle it. She coughed, her eyes tearing up.

"Man, that's strong."

The shivering stopped. The rainstorm stilled; wayward drops fell silently to the ground.

Woozy and lightheaded, she hung on his neck.

"I love you Carli-*toes.*"

He let her go first up the stairs. She climbed, tripping over her own feet and almost falling backward.

"Oops, I think I'm a little tipsy." She said as he helped her the rest of the way.

The loud boom of the music playing inside poured out of the open windows.

"How about if tonight you take off your halo and we can have some real fun," he whispered to her as they danced their way back into the house leaving the past behind.

Julienne giggled.

I am not that drunk.

35

It was not long before Julienne was elbow deep in potting soil. Her small hands cupped dirt from the bag and placed it around the stem of the daffodils. She patted it down then picked up another one and planted it. *Not bad,* she thought. The flowers had been purchased from a reputable garden store; the owner had assured her she would have lovely blossoms by summertime. She was watching a lizard with a dash across the lawn when she heard the faint voices. The retired old man that lived next door always listened to talk radio in the afternoons. Today they were discussing the future liberation of Cuba from Castro's regime. Julienne pulled the weeds from the garden bed and listened. The voices were not spewing the usual political jargon in Spanish. They were speaking English. The retiree turned off his radio and closed his garage door, but the voices continued. She stopped gardening. Her sister was arguing with someone.

***

"I heard rumors you were alive. But I didn't believe them. Ana turned on the dishwasher. "Is it true? You can't remember your name?"

"Angelo D'Marco. You're Ana, Julienne's older sister, is that good enough for you?"

"You are not supposed to be here." Ana opened the fridge and took out a beer. "You want one?"

"No. Where is Julienne?"

She sipped slowly. "So, what's the plan? You are going to run off with her into the sunset and live happily ever after?" she chuckled, shaking her head. "Why are you here?"

Angelo looked around the kitchen wondering if he had ever been there before. "To stop her from marrying that doctor."

The blonde woman finished the beer and opened the package of uncooked chicken breast. She picked up a knife and started cutting it into strips. "You are too late."

"I need her to know what happened."

"Don't make this about you. It was never about you!" she said, slamming the knife down.

"Ana, I need to see her!"

Ana picked up the knife again. "Over my dead body."

***

Julienne cleaned off her hands with the garden hose and quickly showered the thirsty plants. Intrigued by the continual argument, she turned off the running water and placed her ear closer to the kitchen window. Knowing Ana, she was probably telling off the beauty supplier who had mixed up her order again. But the voice

again. But the voice answering her sister's angry outburst sounded disturbingly familiar. She ran around to the back. She dusted off her shorts and removed her wet flip-flops, leaving them drying by the swing. She opened the screen door. Her heart raced faster as the voice continued to get stronger. When she entered, she saw a tall man, his back to her. Ana's eyes widened as big as golf balls noticing her sweaty sibling.

"What's going on here? Is this guy bothering you?" Julienne asked, holding the bat she had picked up on her way in.

"Hello, Julienne," he said, turning around to greet Ana's defender. Flecks of gold stared at him from underneath the fringe of her long lashes. It took less than a second before the cells in his injured brain reconstructed the missing timeline. It was not the first time his eyes had taken notice of the curvature of her sun-kissed cheeks or the pale button nose that sat just above her symmetrical lips. Her hair was a glorious tempest of clay-colored ripples. He noticed she had gained a few pounds just in the right places to compliment her slender figure. Her legs long and lean ran down to meet her slim ankles.

He envied the tiny droplets of water glistening contently on her polished toenails. This was *his* Julienne, the woman he was destined to marry!

Julienne gasped, the air leaving her lungs. The blood in her face plummeted to her feet. Pale and shaken, she leaned against the countertop, dropping the bat. She tried to speak, her mouth forming words that were not audible. It was not possible. He was dead! She had seen his death certificate, yet

187

he stood there, his deep green eyes glimmering with life. She tried to catch her breath. *You're hallucinating,* she told herself. Everything around her started to spin. she gripped the edge of the counter; her knuckles turning white. He moved in slow motion; the outline of his broad shoulders blurring with each step.

"It can't be. You're dead!" A stab of pain penetrated her chest. She doubled over unable to breathe. Her legs buckled, giving way. She collapsed into his arms. The last thing she heard was the screams of her sister calling out her name.

***

Carlos felt the tension leave his shoulders. It was perfect that he was the only ER doctor available when the ambulance had brought her in. Watching Angelo helplessly stand by as he took over her care was priceless. Sure, there would be some explaining to do. After all, the hospital was very strict on ethics, and providing emergency care to his fiancée, was a conflict of interest. But he was a smooth talker and being drinking buddies with the president of the hospital did have its perks.

Angelo watched her from behind the slightly opened curtain. It had happened instantaneously. The minute he had seen her, he knew. But it became much more real when he held her collapsed frame in his arms. All the history along with the love that connected them came flooding back into his memory like a tidal wave. It washed over his brain making the final synaptic connections that brought even minuscule details of his past back to life.

She was so small and fragile, like a wounded bird in a nest of hospital sheets. She was even more beautiful than he remembered her.

"Why did you have to come back? Why didn't you stay in Afghanistan or wherever the hell they sent you to? You were home free. I had it all under control," Carlos complained as he looked over her test results.

"Really? Since when was marrying my fiancé part of the plan?"

"You are not the only one who loves her. I can give her more I can be satisfied with a civilian job and give her stability. A chance at a normal life."

"She belongs with me," Angelo answered firmly, studying the conceited agent who had taken over his life.

"You should have stayed dead."

Ana pointed her finger at the curtain. "You are both idiots. Angelo welcome back to the land of the living. But what matters now is my sister's health. So, focus!"

The woman stirred and coughed. Carlos opened the curtain and glanced at the frail young woman lying on the bed. Her breathing was a bit labored, but the heart monitor showed improvement. He closed it again and continued arguing with Angelo. Ana's phone chirped. She picked up her leather bag sitting on top of the unoccupied hospital bed and stepped into the hallway.

"You coming back from the dead did not cause her to pass out. She has a weak heart," Carlos said, flipping through the pages of the chart to access the CAT scans results.

Angelo demanded to see Julienne's medical information. Carlos handed him the patient's file.

"Cardiomyopathy." The word left a bad taste on Angelo's tongue. He stuffed down the distrust overtaking him,

189

scratched his chin, and asked for her prognosis. Carlos explained that with the right medication she could live a normal life. But if she was to avoid having further complications, she would need to remain as stress-free as possible.

"If you go now, I can convince her that she was hallucinating due to insufficient blood flow. Ana would back me up."

"I could take her to the best hospitals. She would never be without medical care." Angelo countered.

"Coming back was a huge mistake. If you marry her, she will become a target, a liability. Can you live with yourself if harm comes to her because of your selfishness? Come on man, do the right thing, for once play by the rules!"

"Like you have?" Angelo asked handing the file back to him.

"I can't help it if she is a cut above the rest."

Ana's return put a halt to their bickering. On the blank canvas of her face, sat two cold emotionless eyes. Carlos could only guess what was on her mind. Irritated, he began firing questions at her. Ana stared straight through him.

"She is in operational mode. The only thing you are going to get from her is her name, rank, and serial number." Angelo mused.

"Now what am I supposed to tell Julienne when she wakes up that her sister is MIA?" Carlos asked, annoyed by the inconvenience dawning on him.

"We'll handle it. Ana, go and stay safe."

Ana casts one last look at her sister. "Please take care of her. She's all I have left."

36

The nurse slid the curtain open. The ache inside Angelo grew as he approached her bedside. He was counting the hours when he could tell her how sorry he was for staying away so long. Carlos checked her drip line and with a grim look, wrote some notes down on her chart. Warnings about her health kept replaying in Angelo's head. He started to leave. Julienne's eyes fluttered then opened. She held out her hand in a feeble attempt to grab a hold of the vision of her beloved.

"Angelo!" she whimpered.

Carlos looked over to the heart monitor. Her arrhythmia was getting worse. He glared at the man halfway between his patient's bed and the entrance. He motioned for him to go.

"Angelo! Don't leave me!" The alarm on the monitor beeped faster. Her eyes rolled to the back of her head; her body jerked with convulsions.

"She's crashing!" Carlos started barking orders at the nurses running into the room with the crash cart. Not wasting any time, they all went to work. Like a well-choreographed dance, they all knew their part. One added medication into her IV, while the other threaded a tube down her throat.

"Get him out of here!" the doctor hollered as he placed the paddles on her chest.

The nurse tried to push Angelo out of the room, but it was like trying to move a brick wall. She threatened to call security but gave up as Carlos demanded that she get back to work. Angelo found a spot away from the medical personnel. He closed his eyes and prayed feverishly for God to intervene.

"Yeah, you pray; I'll do the real work," Carlos growled, sending another surge of electricity into the young woman's heart. Her small chest rose but no heartbeat could be felt.

"Clear!" he yelled out keeping his eyes on the monitor. Another shock was sent into her. "Come on, baby, nobody dies on my watch... you have to live!"

Both men watched as the flat line hiccupped, giving them a sign of hope. Angelo thanked God. Joy returned to his soul. The line on the monitor continued to rise and fall, as the relieved medical staff slowed down their frenzied work. The tired doctor sat at the foot of the bed. He was shaking. It was not every day he saved the life of the woman he loved. Angelo went over to him and offered him his hand.

"Thank you."

A smug smile appeared on his tanned face. "As I said, no one dies on my watch."

"You and I both know the man upstairs was not ready to call her home. But I'll let you gloat this time." Angelo patted him on the back. Carlos lifted Julienne's limp finger showing him the ring he had bought her and kissed the unconscious woman on the lips.

Great job saving my girl. You're all invited to the wedding!" he shouted out to the medical team that was dispersing.

Angelo mused. Dr. Hernandez would make an interesting opponent.

***

Dr. Hernandez called upstairs and had his fiancée admitted to the Cardiac Unit. When he was done updating her records, he leaned back on his chair and placed his hands behind his head. It was good Ana was out of the picture. He could fast forward the wedding plans without her butting in. With a spring in his step, he took the elevator to the ground floor and made his way to the cafeteria. It was time to send Angelo packing for good.

He found him sitting alone in the area overlooking the parking lot. His face was downcast. His forehead wrinkled as he read the information on his phone. Carlos ordered the black beans and rice special and joined the troubled man. He removed his stethoscope and set it on the table. He told the sullen agent how Julienne had it engraved as a birthday gift for him. When Angelo did not comment, he added that Julienne was resting comfortably in a private suite with a spectacular view of the Intercoastal.

"Only the best for my future wife," Carlos bragged.

Angelo stabbed the steak in front of him. "Julienne is not as gullible as you think. If I leave, she will continue to look for me. She won't have any closure. How is that going to benefit her heart condition?"

Carlos placed his forearms on the table and leaned forward. "Rumor at Agency is you have Retrograde amnesia. So, in case you are not connecting the dots, let me clear this up for you. The moment you went dark, I was called to take your place. My orders were very clear, keep her safe, and help her forget. I have accomplished the first objective by saving her life and once we are married, I *will* accomplish the second."

Angelo dumped the whole packet of sugar into his coffee and stirred it.

"I am not leaving. I am going to tell her the truth. If she chooses to stay with you, I will honor that. But if she chooses me, do I have your word you will back off?"

"In my professional opinion, honesty is overrated. You're playing with her health."

"Do I have your word or not?"

"It's your funeral. But I would not drop the bomb until she is fully recovered."

Both men threw their leftovers away and headed to the elevators. When they were inside, Carlos informed him that Dr. Milagros Pratts was the Cardiologist who would oversee her care. The doors to the 1st floor opened, reluctantly Carlos walked through them. He had six more hours left in his shift before he could be free to check up on Julienne's progress. Seeing a room full of emergency patients, he sighed curling his fingers inside the pocket of his white coat.

***

The insistent beeping on the monitor awoke Julienne. She opened one eye, then the other. Her throat hurt from the tube that had been removed. A hand brushed away the hair from her face and caressed her cheek. As her eyes began to focus, he came into view. Julienne's heart pump harder in her chest. The man she had dreamed about was in the room.

"Are you a ghost?" she asked, struggling to stay awake.

"No sweetheart, it's me. I am here and I am not going anywhere."

The medicine the nurse had put in her IV was taking effect. She mumbled his name and fell back asleep.

***

During the time she was hospitalized, both men catered to her every whim. When she asked the whereabouts of her sister, they both agreed to tell her that Ana had gone to Cuba to see their grandmother who was dying. What was harder to explain was that Angelo was alive. Since Julienne was only awake for short periods, it was easy for Angelo to skirt the issue. But once she was fully alert, the conversations between them grew more challenging. Not wanting to worsen her arrhythmia, Angelo's visits became sporadic, blaming it on having to go back and forth to New York for work-related meetings.

***

"He probably had a wife and kids all along," Carlos Commented feeding her a spoonful of Jell-O.

"So why did he come back?" she asked, refusing the red blob wobbling on the spoon.

"He couldn't keep juggling both you and the other woman, so he faked his death. With all that traveling he does; he probably has mistresses all around the world."

Julienne moved her arm, making sure the IV line had not kinked, and picked up the spoon, "I can feed myself."

"Don't take it out on me, *Preciosa*. I have been here since day one taking care of you," he said taking a brush from the drawer so he could brush out the knots in Julienne's hair. "The man cannot be trusted, my love. "

"Angelo is not the cheating type."

Dr. Hernandez laughed, "Julie, every male on the planet is the cheating type. It just takes a special woman to keep us interested. Maybe Saint Angelo found her but after squeezing a few kids, the sexy went out the window and he got tired of coming home to the depressed whale sitting on the couch with morning breath."

"You have such a way with words...so if we have kids and I get a little overweight...."

"*Olvidate,* Vanish the thought *Preciosa.* Your heart is too weak for childbirth. Even if you could have a C-Section, the stress of a newborn would put you at risk of another heart attack."

"I want to have children someday. I don't care what the risks are."

"*Si*, there is a way we can have some rug rats. Adoption. Then you can keep that knock-out figure and be the envy of every mommy on the playground."

Who says I am having kids with you? "Dr. Hernandez just keep brushing and leave the family planning to me," she answered. Julianne closed her eyes enjoying the feel of the coarse bristles on her rebellious curls. It did not matter what the Cuban Neanderthal said...Angelo was back and that was all that mattered.

37

It was a blistering summer day. It was the type of day in South Florida where Floridians craved the coolness of a body of water. The air condition was having trouble removing the steaming breath of the sun shining through the blinds. Dr. Milagros Pratt patted the sheen from her forehead looking over the test results. Then she concentrated on the steady rhythm of blood rushing through the chambers of the patient's heart. For someone who had suffered a heart attack, Julienne's heart was working remarkably well. Removing the instrument from her ears, the Cardiologist gave Julienne a thumbs up and left to sign her discharge papers.

The short curls on the nurse bounced as she pulled and tugged at the stubborn adhesive on the patient's arm. Her meaty fingers gripped the tip of the thin plastic tube and pulled it out. She chatted gaily covering the tiny hole with a band-aid. The floor nurse, Yvette was known as the gossip machine of the cardiac unit. It was when she mentioned Dr. Hernandez that Julienne's ears perked up. According to the hospital rumors he was preparing for an administrative hearing. Julienne pressed the woman removing the heart leads from her body for more information.

"Dr. Hernandez likes to play with fire. This time he got burned. Somebody snitched on him. The board is scared that if your health declined while he was treating you, your family would sue the hospital," Ivette explained.

"They wouldn't do that."

The chatty nurse turned off the vital signs monitor, placed her hand on her hips, and laughed, "Oh no? Everybody is nice until you accidentally kill their family. But don't worry; your boyfriend is a real flirt. The old ladies on the Board of Trustees like them young. He could easily convince them to vote against disciplinary action, but you didn't hear that from me." Yvette brought down the railing on the patient's bed. "Between you and me, I like the model with the sexy green eyes better. He's not only hot, he seems like he cares about you." She took Julienne's pulse and wrote it on the chart. "You can go ahead and get dressed. I will call down for transport once your ride arrives."

"Carlos was my ride," Julienne replied taking off her hospital socks.

"Let me give the guy next door his med and I will let your caseworker know we have a problem."

As the nurse was exiting the room, she met Angelo in the hallway. After speaking with him for a few moments, she peeked back into the room, "Hey, the nice one is here. I think you just got your ride."

Angelo entered the hospital room with a bouquet of roses in hand. Julienne sat on the recliner. Her normally tight-fitting jeans and t-shirt hung loosely on her thin frame. Yet he was relieved when he saw the pallid cheekbones had regained their healthy glow.

"You remembered."

"How could I not? You are one of the few women I know who prefer purple roses to red ones."

While they spoke, Angelo placed the roses on the ledge of the window and gathered the get-well cards stuffing them into the overnight bag he had found in the closet. Nurse Yvette came back with the discharge papers. Once the forms were signed, Angelo guided her to the attendee waiting with a wheelchair and went to get the car. He was more than bring happy to drive her home.

38

Angelo added garlic and stirred the soup simmering on the stove. He picked up the sea salt but stopped himself; she was on a strict low salt diet. He poured the steaming Quinoa and chicken soup into a bowl and set it on the wooden tray. He took it to the woman he had missed more than he cared to admit. As he placed the tray upon her lap, he saw the questions were only a syllable away. The agent told her to eat then quietly returned to the kitchen.

Wiping the kitchen counter, he watched her. She dug in her bowl with the spoon. Her intensity surpassed hunger. She was angry and rightly so. He put down the spray bottle and turned on the faucet. Angelo squeezed the dish soap and dunked the pot and cutting board inside the soapy water. Later, when she was resting, he would return and clean her kitchen. *Think of it like a mission,* he sighed, wiping his hands on the rag hanging from the stove before returning to her.

He was in total control until he saw those golden eyes questioning his every move. *What irony*, he thought. He had been interrogated by the most ruthless villains on the planet. Back at the agency, they referred to him as *Mr. Indestructible*. Ha, if they only knew that his throat knotted at the mere thought of confronting the harmless woman.

The agent took the tray from her lap and casually placed it on the coffee table. "Juls, there are things about me you need to know,"

The young woman tucked her bare feet back under the quilted blanket and brought it to her chest.

"That night after the soup kitchen I wanted to come clean, but you were so determined about getting your job done. I didn't sleep that night. I spend it praying that God would give me the strength to tell you the truth. The next morning, I called you, remember?"

"I had worked all night. You wanted to bring me coffee," she said, revisiting the past. With the pads of her fingers, Julienne pressed down on the quilt flattening down every wrinkle.

"You didn't want coffee. All you wanted was to finish your mockups. You said we could meet for lunch," he added sitting down across from her.

Julienne found the jagged end of a cuticle and began to pick at it with her other nail.

"I tried to reason with you, but you wouldn't budge," the agent said placing his palms together under his chin. "I figured I had time, but..."

"There was no time," she finished his sentence.

Angelo rubbed his unshaven chin and looked away. "I still don't recall much of it, except it was hard to breathe and something hit me on the head. I was told firemen dug me out. They rushed me to the Brain Institute in Edison. The area hospitals were full, and they only were doing triage."

He told her how the traumatic brain injury had altered his life. He took her through the first months in the hospital where he had no clue who he was. How he had to learn to walk and talk again. He shared the frustration of having her lost somewhere in the recesses of his mind.

"When did you get your memory back?" Julienne asked. *If only I would have stopped and listened to you, things would have turned out differently.*

The agent stopped pacing. He shoved his hands in his pant pockets and sighed. "I was released from the hospital in October. But it wasn't until I saw you at your sister's house that all my memories returned."

The cottonmouth and clammy hands didn't belong to a seasoned agent. Angelo raked his hair with his fingers and cranked up the volume on the TV's music station. The jazzy tune drowned out any other sound. Julienne sat up, propping herself on the decorative pillows. With petal-soft whispers, he confessed the real story behind his disappearance.

Julienne's eyes flashed with indignation. "So, being a financial consultant was a cover? Everything you ever told me was a lie!"

"No, you are wrong! You were the only real thing I cared about. A week before the blast, I called my superior and told him I wanted out. He said if I wanted to marry you to go ahead, I could take some time off, but he wouldn't accept my resignation."

She laid back down feeling faint. He had drilled the truth into her like a dentist repairing a cavity without Novocain.

Tears ran down Julienne's cheeks. Angelo clenched his jaw, worry lines forming in his forehead.

"I'm sorry. I was going to tell you the truth. I wanted you to have the option to stay or leave. But then the explosion...I love you, Julienne. I always have."

"Do you think that matters? We were together for five years! I can't believe you never said anything. I don't even know who you are."

He rubbed his shoulder, the wounds of the past haunting him. "I've done things I am not proud of... I don't expect you to understand. All I want you to know is I never meant to hurt you."

" No wonder you hated my spy novels... I bet you are not even a klutz, are you?"

Angelo shook his head and grinned. "No Juls, I am very coordinated."

"I've been such a fool!"

"Don't blame yourself; I am very good at my job. After my head injury, I was reprogrammed and sent to Afghanistan. It's classified. What I can tell you is the minute I arrived back in New York, I started searching for you."

"I'm getting married," she blurted, biting another piece of dead skin off her cuticle.

He placed his hand over her fingers. "You promised you would stop biting your nails."

"And you promised you would never leave me."

The wall she had built up broke down, eliciting pain. "I nearly lost my mind, searching for you all over New York. Everyone kept telling me you were gone!"

Angelo stroked her back, her wet tears staining his oxford shirt. He allowed her pent-up anger to flow freely, absorbing the impact of her small fists beating against his chest.

"You lied to me! I trusted you!"

"I know... I am so sorry. I'm here now," he murmured, kissing the top of her head.

Julienne withdrew from his embrace. "It doesn't matter anymore. I'm getting married."

"I heard your boyfriend is in a lot of trouble with the hospital., he said walking over to the wall unit. He picked up her laptop and set it on the coffee table.

"He was trying to save my life. I'm sure they will cut him some slack," she retorted.

Angelo sat cross-legged on the floor and opened the laptop. Julienne waited for his clumsy hen and peck typing to begin, but once he touched the keys, it was as if someone else was in the room. She stilled her breath, watching at the skillful way his fingers flew across the keyboard.

"Carlos is not the good Samaritan you think he is. I took the liberty of reviewing all your medical records. I contacted your pediatrician, your primary, and every doctor you have ever seen. All of them agreed apart from your average cold and your Irritable Bowel, you are the picture of health. They are willing to testify under oath you have never had a heart condition."

Julienne's flesh grew cold. "How... how is that possible?"

He forged those records, just like the death certificate."

"You are lying!"

"See for yourself," he said, showing her the incriminating surveillance video. "In his own twisted way, he fell in love with you. When I came back..." Angelo paused, then let out a breath, "...he was threatened. He knew the only way he could keep you was to make you completely dependent on him. He gave you drugs to cause your heart attack. Then he did the superhero thing and saved you."

"Why?"

"He figured the Florence Nightingale syndrome would kick in, and it would buy him some time to woo you."

"No...it can't be."

"This guy sees you as a possession and he is willing to do anything to keep you. But he was sloppy and now he has a lot of explaining to do."

Julienne turned her face towards the window Though it was only three-thirty in the afternoon, the sky was dark, storm clouds had kidnapped the sun. The palm fronds in the front yard bent, oppressed by the intensifying winds and the lashes of rain. Ana's empty recycle bin rolled across the street and kept on rolling. Outside, the world seemed to be engaged in a fight of its own.

Angelo's phone lit up. The National Weather Center in South Florida had issued a warning of tornadic activity due to the heavy summer thunderstorms sweeping across the state.

"Juls, do you have a room with no windows?"

***

Julienne held his arm leading him to the staircase behind a wall at the end of the hall. Most families in Miami shied away from building underground. Oddly enough, the Gutierrez family had paid good money to hire engineers who claimed to be experts in waterproofing basements. However, extensive repairs had to be made after *Hurricane Andrew* flooded the house.

The underground room was their father's secret room. A *man cave* where not even their mother was allowed. When asked, he would mutter that it was the only place where he found peace from all the "estrogen" in his house. Their father eventually stopped using the room when a pipe burst. All that remained of the basement was hard cement walls encasing empty space.

After the room was dried and the wall paper damage was removed, he gifted the room to his daughters. He had left a nice fat check to redecorate the room and add children's furniture that included a large dollhouse for the girls to play in. But instead, their mother had used the money to pay a gardener to tend to her rose bushes and what was left was used to pay an art teacher to teach her to paint.

Little Ana was broken-hearted but fueled by Julienne's imagination, the discolored walls were transformed into a make-believe world. The girls attended royal balls in lavish castles, they pretended to be teachers who taught reading and writing to their stuff animals and they held mermaid races across the ocean floor.

Adult Ana had turned the magical room into a catch-all. The walls were lined with shelves where her sister stored their childhood keepsakes. Old chairs and furniture were stacked up in a corner. A twin mattress was propped up against a blue painted wall. Her visitor's muscles flexed under his polo shirt. He lifted the mattress moving it away from the basement window. Exhaling slowly, he brought it back down to the floor with a thump. Angelo had her sit on the mattress before he went upstairs for emergency supplies. While he was gone, Julienne rehashed the unbelievable conversation they had upstairs. Was their relationship nothing but a cover?

Angelo returned with a flashlight and a cooler. Just as he was positioning the cooler next to them, the lights went out. Julienne sucked in a breath. The sturdy house creaked and

206

groaned as the wind's velocity increased. Above them, they could hear debris hitting against the steel bars protecting the windows and doors. Julienne trembled, covering her ears. She did not protest when he pulled her into his arms.

"It's okay. God is with us," Angelo reminded her.

Through the egress window, they could see the unrestrained fury of the storm. Lightning illuminated the sky. Her neighbor's patio umbrella flew across the yard.

Angelo tugged playfully at one of her curls. "Juls, God's kept me alive through situations most men died in. And he is going to keep us safe tonight."

"Yeah, well you should let me go. He wouldn't like it."

"Why not?" he chuckled turning on the flashlight.

"Because I'm taken," she answered, squinting to see his face in the darkness.

"By a nut job."

Julienne elbowed him. "At least he loves me enough to do something crazy to keep me."

"Oh really? I can be just as romantic. I can put a bullet through your leg then patch you up if that's what you're into," he teased, loosening his grip but not creating any real space between them. She knew it was wrong, yet it felt so right to be in his arms. Thunder clapped. Lightning briefly lit the room.

"Do you love him?" he asked, inhaling the scent of her strawberry shampoo.

She wanted to lie. She wanted to hurt him as much as he had hurt her. But he would see right through her.

"I'm still hungry," she answered, changing the subject.

Angelo unwrapped one of the sandwiches he had made and handed it to her. The unusual taste of peanut butter and ham flooded her taste buds.

"Wow. I haven't had a sandwich like this since..."

207

"Your second day at the Soup Kitchen? Do you remember when that clumsy volunteer dumped the peanut butter all over the ham? I wanted the Pastor to fire him, but you took a taste and said it was delicious."

Julienne took another bite. "Yeah, then the next day you invited me to lunch at the park. You brought peanut butter and ham sandwiches. I laughed so hard I almost choked."

"The truth is I prefer peanut butter and jelly," he commented, his stomach growling. With all the commotion, he had left his sandwich sitting on the counter.

"You're not hungry?" he asked when Julienne set down the sandwich she was eating.

"Why me Angelo?"

"I can't answer that without disclosing information that I have been sworn to keep. Think of your life as a tapestry. It has many different color threads, but if you pull one, it could potentially unravel the whole thing."

She scooted to the edge of the mattress. "What is that supposed to mean? Stop speaking in riddles. Just spit it out!"

Angelo covered half of her uneaten sandwich and tossed it back in the cooler. Then he pointed the flashlight toward her direction so he could see her face. It was time to detonate the other bomb.

"It was not a coincidence you met Carlos," he began. "He works for the same agency I work for. He was assigned to you when they sent me on the mission. I can show you the surveillance video from when you met at the beach to the present. But he has created a huge problem for the agency by the stunt he pulled."

"That's not possible! You are lying!"

"I wish I was." Angelo turned off the flashlight leaving them in darkness. "Sorry but I have to ration the light, the batteries are at thirty percent."

Julienne counted her breaths trying to slow down her heart. Confusion plagued her. Why was Carlos planted in her life? Was her reality nothing but a slippery road paved by lies?

The storm lost its punch. The ferocious winds died down leaving the steady tapping of the rain to keep them company. Angelo checked the weather report on his phone.

"Danger is over. The wind probably did some damage, but the tornado never touched down. We can go upstairs if you want."

"You didn't answer my question: why me? Why was I chosen? I don't have ties to the government. Or do they just randomly pick people and ruin their lives?" she asked, raising her voice to compete with the lingering thunder.

Angelo turned the flashlight back on. "It's not random You're more important than you think, but it is classified, and I have not been given the green light to tell you more at this time."

"You sound like a stupid robot! I am so sick and tired of your platitudes!" Furiously, she made a ball of the cellophane paper and threw it at him.

He popped open the tab on a ginger ale can and offered it to her. She ignored him. He scooted himself closer to her and forced her hand around the can.

"You have to stay hydrated." He held the can in place till he was certain she would not drop it. Julienne took two sips and placed the soda between them.

"I know this is not fair. But keep in mind everything we have done has been to protect you."

"We? Who are *we*?"

209

Angelo turned his attention back to his phone ignoring Julienne's unending questions. Anger sparked in her like a firecracker. She raised her hand, but he caught her wrist before she could slap him. He was caught off guard by her aggressiveness that he missed catching the soda before it spilled on the mattress. The lights turned on. He swore under his breath and let her wrist go. She jumped off the mattress, avoiding the sticky mess. Grabbing her by the arm, he spun her around and forcefully kissed her. Then just as abruptly, he let her go. She stumbled a little but quickly regained her balance.

"How dare you? You have no right!" she screamed, her eyes turning into two slits.

"Would you prefer if I let them kill you?"

Julienne started climbing the stairs. "You're living in this sick twisted fantasy your messed-up brain came up with. I'm not playing your stupid spy game anymore!"

Angelo blotted his pants with a napkin and climbed after her. When they reached the top, they found Ana supporting herself against the wall. Her wet torn garments hung oddly on her lopsided frame.

"Help me."

39

Angelo lifted Ana and carried her to the closest room.

"We're compromised," Ana moaned as he deposited her wounded body on the bed in the guest room.

Angelo ripped open her running jacket and applied firm pressure to the gaping hole. Blood continued to flow soaking through the fabric of her blouse. The pulsating wound kept its pace draining her of the life she was clinging to.

"We have to call an ambulance!" Julienne shrieked in horror. A gush of blood poured out of her sister's body. She panted for air like a tired swimmer.

"I don't wanna die alone." Ana gasped, sucking wind. The talons of death were slowly draining her face of color.

"You can't die. Just hold on! Angelo call now!" Julienne screamed.

"It's too late Juls. They won't make it in time." Ana dug her nails caked with blood into Julienne's soft palm as a wave of internal pain traveled through her like a hot poker

"I am so scared Julie, I have done...bad things, will God forgive me?" she asked panting. Julienne brushed back the wisps of hair sticking to the side of her sister's face.

"Anita, remember how *Abuelita* use to tell you that God sent Jesus to pay for your sins?"

Ana nodded her head, A tiny smile parted her bluish-gray lips, "Yes, I remem...ber."

"Ana, you have done the hard stuff already," Angelo told her placing a pillow under her neck. "This is the easy part. Jesus loves you so much and he is waiting for you right now. All you need to do is ask him to forgive you and ask him to take you home."

"Ang... does He love me after all the stuff...?" she asked, remembering the dark alleys and seedy motel rooms. She had become a pro at excusing her behavior as being just a part of the job; but with nothing to gain from the lie, she could be honest with herself. Her promiscuity had started back in high school along with heavy drinking and partying. Praying the rosary and going to church with her grandmother was done out of obligation. Most of the time her attention was solely consumed with planning her next escape out of her bedroom window. She had always been good at pretending. But not even the colorful wigs, costumes, and exotic locations she had traveled to could exonerate her.

Ana squeezed both of their hands with the little strength she had left. "Jesus please forgive...me..." she groaned; her eyes opened wide as a second wave of pain shot through her body. "I am so tired...Jesus I need...you," she said as a different kind of exhaustion sapped all the strength in her bones. Each heartbeat was lethargically slower. A coldness traveled through her capillaries and tissues as the blood started to pull away from the vital organs. Her eyelids fluttered. She breathed in one last time the oxygen of life and whispered, "Trust Angelo."

There was no pain now. Warmth and dampness enveloped Ana as if floating in the water, but the darkness enveloping her was not frightening her any longer. Light brighter than any human eye had ever seen burst all around her. A robed figure she recognized from her First Communion coloring book extended his nail-pierced hands out to her. She was going home, and it was going to be okay.

***

Angelo pulled Julienne away from the lifeless body. What he would give for her to allow him to hold her. He wanted to let her cry and mourn like any other person. Luxury like that only existed for those who didn't have a price on their head, and Julienne's price had just gone up. He was not insensitive he would also miss Ana, but he had been taught to hold his feelings hostage. Their ransom would come, stealing his sleep, then he would lay his soul bare and weep like men rarely did.

"Juls, there is nothing you can do for her. She is with Jesus now." Angelo said, then placed a call to the agency.

"I have never seen anyone die in front of me. It is strange. She looks peaceful." Julienne said cleaning off the blood from her sister's fingers with the bedspread.

"We have to go," Angelo announced tossing in a trash bag the leftover sandwiches and sodas they had been eating downstairs.

"We just can't leave her here."

213

"I don't have time to argue with you. The authorities will find her body at the parking lot of Dadeland Mall. She was attacked and robbed on the way to her car. It was stormy and she tried to fight them off, but they shot her."

"What about all this blood?"

He put his hand on her shoulder, "Juls the people I work for will take care of all the evidence. Please trust me," he said taking the laptop from the coffee table.

Trust Angelo. Why would her sister's last dying wish be for her to trust somebody Ana barely knew? Someone who had been presumed dead. Nevertheless; her sister had never steered her wrong when it came to important things

"What did Ana mean we are compromised?" she asked, watching Angelo open her sister's phone.

"It means those who killed your sister are on their way to kill you."

"Why would anybody want to kill me? What did Ana do? Did she give you a reason?"

"There is no time for explanations. You have to do as Ana said and trust me." The agent removed a chip from Ana's cell phone. "Give me your phone."

He opened her phone and swapped the computer chip for her sister's. "I'll get you another phone you can use. This one stays with me."

"I'm not stupid Angelo. I know my sister did cocaine. She went to Liberty City a lot. Supposedly it was to buy the hair supplies cheaper, but I know she was using. She probably owed money."

"Julienne knowing the why, is not going to matter when they blow your head off! Focus!"

As they hurried through the hallway, Julienne's eyes

picked up random details. The baseboards were scratched. The paint was peeling off one of the walls and her sister had reframed the picture of them wearing matching sundresses. No one looking at the picture could tell, but Ana hid an ice cream stain between the pleats of her Sunday dress. Julienne had taken the blame for her sister's mishap. The belt marks hurt, but she knew it was one less beating her baby sister would get. Angelo stepped in front of her and snapped a picture of her childhood memory with his phone.

"We have to go!"

"I don't have any place to go, this is my home."

"Not anymore."

***

They left Julienne's childhood home through the back porch. The streetlight had been struck by lightning, making them invisible. He put the car in reverse and pulled out of the driveway. After they had passed the stop sign at the end of the block, an unmarked vehicle pulled out after them. Angelo zigzagged through the traffic picking up speed as he entered the Interstate. On the lane next to him, there was a caravan of semi-trucks. He squeezed himself between the massive vehicles and rode between them for three exits. When the Semi's broke formation, he veered to the right and exited the highway. Angelo kept his foot on the gas pedal as he hugged the curve. He checked the rearview mirror, slowed down, and adjusted his speed to the pace of the other drivers. They drove past broken-down homes with tires and trash strewn all over the yard. He turned into an unpaved road; bumped and bounced through the rough terrain, until they stopped in front of a grassy field. The dark brooding clouds had parted, and a bright full moon hung in the midnight sky. Julienne got out of the car and looked around.

"Now what?"

Angelo took her hand. "We fly."

40

The white sleek body of the Cessna 172 was partially hidden from view by the tall blades of grass. Angelo flipped the corresponding switches and checked the gauges on the instrument panel. He slowly taxied down the empty field, accelerating to reach the maximum speed for takeoff. Steadily he applied pressure on the yoke and the plane lifted off the ground. Julienne's heartbeat settled into a normal rhythm.

They stopped to refuel at the Flying Baron. Julienne went to buy a snack and use the restroom. He almost had to break the Ladies' restroom door to get his reluctant passenger to back come out. He explained to the busybodies at the Flying Baron Cafe that she was working on conquering her phobia of flying. Once she was back in the co-pilot's seat, the aerial escape took them to Georgia. Angelo ditched the plane in an aircraft graveyard, then they were picked up by Angelo's old friend, Demetrius Jones.

Mr and Mrs Jones owned a diner in Chattahoochee Hills. An African American woman with bony arms and protruding front teeth gave the escapees a warm welcome. From the backroom, she brought out a freshly plucked chicken. She dredged it in buttermilk and an egg wash. A salt and pepper seasoning were rubbed on the chicken's flour-covered body before it was thrown into a cast-iron skillet. The bird was fried to a nice golden brown and served with homemade mash, collard greens, and cornbread muffins. As they ate, the hosts shared harvest stories, and how excited they were because the grandkids were visiting in a few weeks. When supper ended, the rail-thin man with a large beard that stretched to his belly asked Angelo to join him in his work shed. His wife, Mama Jones, prepared the guest room and ran a bath for her guest.

As Julienne soaked in the old-fashioned porcelain bath-tub, her life flashed through her mind at warp speed. Who was she? Why were people trying to kill her? Her sister was dead, and she was alone, running for her life. She had been lied to and betrayed by two men who claimed to love her. Now she had to rely on one of them to keep her alive. Fear and confusion played tug of war in her mind. She couldn't stand any more of the madness. She slid under the water. The palms of her hands touched the bottom of the tub. It was better this way. All she had ever been to him was an assign-ment, that's all she would ever be... The burn inside her chest spread quickly to her throat.

Just a few more minutes and it will be over... She thought.

A pair of rough hands lifted her out of the water and threw her on the floor mat. She sputtered and coughed trying to clear the water from her lungs.

"You a crazy girl, if you think you gonna end your life in my tub," Mama Jones said, giving Julienne's back a few hard whacks and covering her with a towel. "Now what is so awful, child, that you go do this dumb thing?"

Julienne wrapped the towel around her body and sat up. Forlorn, she leaned against the side of the tub.

"Angelo is a good man. If you are in a heap of trouble, he'll get you out. He's gotten others out of their hard times. You have to trust him and the good Lord who watches over all his children."

"My sister is dead. I have no family left I can trust. I don't even know who I am anymore!" Julienne bawled.

"Well, I do. You're a child of the King and that is the only identity you need. Angelo said you are a believer; was he fibbing?"

"I don't know what I believe, it was all lies," she said squeezing the excess water from her hair before standing up.

The older woman with jet black eyes smiled. "Child, that doesn't surprise the good Lord. He's known you since you were in the belly of your mama. I can see it in your eyes. You're a strong young woman, you will be alright." Mama Jones gathered her dirty clothes and placed them in a bag.

"Angelo said it be best if we change your hair color," she commented opening a bottle of hair dye. "Just lean your head on the sink and let me do the rest."

Julienne tucked the end of the towel into her cleavage fastening the towel tighter around her wet body and bent her head into the sink. The old woman poured the dark black color and rubbed it into her hair. She added extra by the ears and around her forehead making sure it concealed her natural color. Mama Jones rinsed out the excess and towel-dried it.

219

"Now you go on getting dressed. We aren't wealthy, but we can spare for folks in need."

Julienne finger-combed her hair. The red plaid dress fit her perfectly with the Cowboy boots Mama Jones had given her. Julienne stared at her reflection on the bathroom door's mirror. A country girl with shockingly dark curls smiled back.

***

The two women sat back against wooden rockers sipping from mugs of hot tea. The night displayed a twinkle fest of stars that spread out like diamonds on black velvet. The shed light was on and through the small window, Julienne could catch a glimpse of her protector holding an AR-57 automatic rifle.

"How do you know Angelo?" Julienne asked, setting in motion her rocking chair.

The wrinkly cheeks on Mama Jones became taut with tension recalling the fateful night. She was the daughter of a US ambassador and their family was in Colombia helping negotiate a peace treaty. One night two men forced the limousine they were traveling into a ditch. They shot her mother. They took her father to an alligator-infested swamp and executed him. They threw his body in the swamp and went back for her. Just as they were getting ready to rape her, Angelo with a team of agents descended on the drug cartel's henchmen.

Mama Jones straightened her curved spine and brought her hand to her mouth. Opening it she took a hold of her yellowing buck teeth and pulled them out. Beneath the veneer, her real teeth were white and very straight. She placed the fake teeth in her pocket and pulled off the silvery wig. Mama Jones fluffed up her afro and smiled.

"Life as you know it will never be the same," she said, removing her glasses and a bulky sweater. Within seconds the old woman had shed thirty years and dropped entirely her Southern drawl. With a steady hand, she poured some more tea into Julienne's empty cup.

"After that night I was taken to the agency. I was offered the witness protection program or to enter a training program to become a field agent. I chose the latter."

"Will that happen to me?" Julienne asked stopping the rocking chair with her feet.

Mama Jones sipped on her tea. "Every scenario is different. I was an orphan, still young enough to be molded into one of them. I was angry and resentful. I lived for revenge, and they knew how to exploit that."

"How long were you...?"

"We have to go," Angelo cut in.

"There is a word the location has been leaked. We need to prepare for any unwelcome visitors," Demetrius added, stroking his beard.

Mama Jones inserted her teeth back in her mouth and removed a small handgun from under her long, peasant skirt. She twirled the wig on her finger. "I reckon these folks need to get a move on, Papa. Angelo, don't cha think yer girl looks purdy?" she asked, adding bullets to the chamber. "Well go on girl, stand up, and let's give 'em a look-see."

Julienne stood up.

"She's perfect, thank you, Mama."

221

The overall-clad man whistled. "Man, I wish I had your job." The voice of the bearded man had also morphed. It was deeper with no noticeable twang. He winked at her and turned to shake Angelo's hand. "Take this pretty little thing and follow the unmarked road to Willow's Creek. The truck is in the barn. It is all gassed up and ready to go."

Mama Jones gave Julienne a fierce hug. "Stay strong. Follow *his* directions and you will be okay."

41

Angelo closed his cell phone and took a sharp left back unto the asphalt. He nudged his sleeping passenger. For a second, Julienne thought she was back in her bed, but that notion quickly passed as she saw the river of cars entering the airport. She yawned, "What time is it?"

"Six-thirty. There has been a change in plans. The people who wanted you and your sister dead have been taken care of. You're free to go home. We will set up a plan to explain your absence and you will be home in time to bury your sister as it should be. If anybody asks, you were visiting your old Pastor at the Soup Kitchen in New York. It is all being set up as we speak. All you have to do is follow the script and you will be fine."

"You thought of everything didn't you." Julienne frowned. Though she could not imagine spending months on the run, part of her was not ready to leave the excitement

223

that associating with the real Angelo had brought. She looked down at her half-bitten nails and scowled.

"What's the matter? I thought you wanted your old life back. I am giving you a chance to go back to your love ones and put all this behind you. Isn't that what you wanted?"

"Yes of course. Thank you," she replied, bringing down the mirror on the visor.

"You look good with dark hair. Then again, you would look beautiful without a single hair on your head."

Julienne could feel the thumping of her heart. *Don't get your hopes up, he does not want you.*

"Where are you going?" she asked reapplying her lipstick.

"New York. I have to debrief. They will probably reassign me. Afghanistan still is unstable but so are other parts of the world."

"So now that this nightmare is over, tell me ...why me?"

Angelo hit a pothole in the street; the truck bounced. He placed his hand protectively in front of his charge.

"It is not my intention to frustrate you, but I am not authorized."

"Angelo, who's responsible for my life being turned upside down? You owe me a name!"

The agent entered the airport parking garage and parked. He ran his hand through his hair and turned off the headlights. His greenish eyes focused on her like two laser beams.

"Javier Gutierrez."

"That is a sick joke. My father died in prison."

"Your dad is alive. In the early 60's he became the director of a black OPS unit of the CIA. After you were born, someone sent an anonymous letter threatening your family."

224

"He faked his death."

"And left us alone...coward." Julienne surmised.

"Let me explain. Javier indoctrinated Ana into the agency hoping the training could keep her safe. You were next, but when Ana was kidnapped, he decided he didn't want both of his daughters working for the government. He made Ana swear not to ever tell you. It was calm until you turned thirteen. An old enemy resurfaced. Your father had no choice but to go underground to flush him out."

"I remember the kidnapping. My mom got distracted when I fell off the monkey bars...Everyone blamed me for leaving Ana alone on the swings. My father never treated me the same after that. She should have told me the truth."

"She would have been signing your death sentence."

"Fascinating! Now do tell, when did Agent D'Marco come on the scene?" Raw hurt glittered in her eyes. She flashed him a scornful smile.

"When you moved out of your aunt's house in NY, Javier put me in charge of your safety. I broke the rules. I fell in love with you. I asked for his blessing. He gave me a flat-out *no*. I was not good enough for his little Juliana."

She felt the air drain from her lungs. An overwhelming wave of dread ran through her body. She opened the truck door.

Angelo stood on the driver's side, his fingers rapping lightly on the hood.

"I eventually proved him wrong. He gave me his blessing, but 9/11 changed all that. Can I trust you with this information? If any of it gets out..."

"My whole life has been a setup." She heaved, as the last digested meal came up.

"Juls!"

225

"Don't you dare touch me!"

He extended a bottle of water to her. She swished the water in her mouth and spit it out on his boots.

"Don't worry, I will keep your stupid secret. Where is my father now? "She asked, wiping her mouth with her wrist.

"We haven't heard from him in a while. Ana was the last to see him but if they got to her, perhaps they got to him too. When people are so high up in the chain, it is hard to authenticate their death.

Angelo's heart cried out in protest, but he silenced it. "Whatever the case, it won't be made public. Julienne, you need to go back to Miami and forget this ever happened." He removed the one-way ticket from his pocket. A woman dressed in a grey suit approached them. She had flawless milk chocolate skin and very straight teeth.

"Mama Jones," Julienne ascertained. "What are you doing here?"

"I have been reassigned. I am your bodyguard for the next few weeks."

"You met Grace in New York. You both lost someone in the towers. Grace can sell it. You just follow her lead." Angelo said, laying out the scenario.

Julienne looked down at the ticket. "Looks like you have it all figured out. What do I say when my family asks about you? Do I tell them what a jerk you really are, or do I continue pretending you are dead?"

Angelo grabbed his laptop case from the back of the pickup, "you've gotten really good at blaming me. So, go with that." He handed her the ticket. Julienne hurled the box of mints she had taken from her purse at him. "I hate you!"

He caught the box and threw a couple in his mouth before he returned to the truck. Agent Grace locked arms

226

with Julienne and walked her into the airport before the pair could start to argue again. They handed their tickets to the ticket agent and boarded the plane. Once seated, Julienne let the fury out of its cage.

"I don't even recognize him. He's so pig-headed and obnoxious. He is nothing like the man I knew!"

Grace let her speak her mind but did not contribute to the hateful rant. It was not that long ago that she and her handler, aka, husband, had been at odds over the silliest

aka, husband, had been at odds over the silliest things. The over-protection and commands could get old. Being a spy was not a democracy and one's pride could create havoc if left unchecked. Would Julienne ever see past the pain Angelo had cost her? Only time would tell.

***

Streaks of sunlight broke through the clouds as the plane cruised closer to Florida. Julienne turned slightly toward the window and pulled down the shade. She wanted to escape, even if it was only through sleep. There was a dull ache in her chest. She twisted and turned trying to find a comfortable spot in the small seat, but sleep would not come.

When the seat belt sign came on, Julienne had a hard time buckling herself in for the landing. Earlier she had been challenged by the complimentary peanut bag that would not open until Grace assisted her. *It's all Angelo's fault, why did he have to come back only to leave again?*

They landed on the tarmac. Julienne unbuckled herself and dusted off the mess of scattered nuts all over her country girl dress. Her cell phone rang. It was aunt Clara notifying her that Ana had been shot leaving the mall parking lot. Julienne tried to gather her thoughts. She was a designer, not an actress. Feigning a believable combination of surprise and grief would take energy she didn't have. Grace speedily typed a message on her phone and showed it to her.

ANGELO IS GONE FOREVER...HE IS NOT COMING BACK.

The words knifed her. The hope of sharing a life with him, crumbled. A wail from deep within rose to her lips convincing Aunt Clara that her niece was unable to speak due to being extremely affected by the tragic news of her sister's murder. The woman with the crying infant sitting in the row beside them called the flight attendant. She was convinced Julienne needed medical attention and fast! Grace assured everyone on the plane her friend was fine and all she needed was a few minutes to process the bad news she had received.

Julienne drank the warm tea the stewardess brought her while they waited for the tarmac delay to disembark.

"I can't believe he didn't come back with me."

"He can't. By staying away, he thinks he is doing you a favor."

"With time I could have forgiven him. We could have worked it out," Julienne answered with a twinge of longing.

Grace picked off a stranded peanut from the crease of her skirt.

"Angelo is hard as a rock on the outside, but he loves very deeply. He shared with me how happy you made him. How he dreamed of getting away from the agency, marrying you, and starting a family. You anchored him." The agent had always liked when she was sent to warmer climates. Balmy palm trees and surf-worthy beaches awaited her.

228

"Obviously, I did not anchor him enough," Julienne answered, her mood veering back to anger.

"He's drifting. It scares me to think he could drift so far away; he will never find himself again." Grace replied, noting how large was the sea that surrounded the gun-shaped state.

42

Grace won the Gutierrez family over with her upbeat, quirky personality. Julianne's new "best friend," Grace, was a breath of fresh air. The aunts agreed she was sent by Ana from the great beyond to help Julienne heal from the loss of her older sister. Agent Grace did her job so well, that when she left back to New York, the aunts did not stop gushing about *Gracielita*.

After the burial, against the family's wishes, Julianne sold their childhood home and moved into a more affordable apartment. They thought she was being cold-hearted, but they weren't the ones suffering from PTSD and constant flashbacks. Ana's last will named Julienne as the sole heir to the hair salon. With the profits she made from selling the house, she opened a fashion design studio. To pay the bills, she took on more freelancing jobs while continuing to work for Imperial Designs.

As the weeks passed, Julienne spent more time in her little studio and less time in the apartment. She took on multiple jobs, trading sleep for work. The need to be working became so vital, that she began to forgo all outings except for buying food and necessities. In the beginning, her hard work paid off with satisfied clients and nice fat paychecks. But Julienne's anxiety intensified when all the work projects ended.

With nothing to do she had no barrier to keep her from the ache of loneliness. It was in those moments of solitude when her heart began to beat to the dreadful rhythm of the *"What ifs."* What if Angelo had stayed with her? What if she had gone back to New York with him? Night after night, the doubts kicked her out of bed. When her clients returned from their hiatus, they found the talented designer in the middle of a nervous breakdown. Paulo the owner of Novo Stilo gave her a stern ultimatum: "Get your head on straight or we can't use you."

Julienne lost the desire to eat. When she did eat, it gave her terrible stomach aches. The IBS medicines the doctor prescribed did little to stop the bathroom runs and the anxiety medicine was making her into a zombie. When she cried out to God, she found no peace in prayer. It was as if her Heavenly Father had shut her out. Her designs for Imperial began to suffer as well. Convinced there was no other way to end the torture, Julienne packed an overnight bag and booked a flight back to New York.

*

43

The Nor'easter chilled her to the bone. She paid the taxi driver and got off in front of the Brownstone that Grace had confirmed he had moved into. The staircase led to a large glass etched wooden door. She had been reading online about the remodeling that had been done to these dilapidated buildings. The door creaked; she opened it. The original handcrafted wooden arches led up to a large vestibule. She climbed the grand staircase to the third floor and walked past the ornate spindles to apartment C-4.

You've got this, she told herself, rocking on her heels back and forth as she worked up the nerve to knock.

Suddenly the door opened.

"Hi," she greeted him, her hand frozen in mid-air.

His eyes were heavy with displeasure. "This is not a good time."

"I'm sorry; I probably should have called."

Angelo stepped aside making room for her to come in. White bare walls, functionally efficient furniture, and a wall-sized tv screen decorated the sterile room.

"I have a meeting downtown." He glanced at his watch. "There is Chinese takeout in the fridge if you are hungry."

Julienne placed her carry-on bag on the floor and looked around. "When will you be back?"

He answered by slamming the door behind him. Julienne removed her wool hat and coat. What was she thinking? It was a mistake to come. A bookshelf caught her eye. It only held technical books and computer manuals. The man she knew had devotionals and sports magazines scattered around his apartment. She sauntered to the kitchen. It was pristine. The Angelo she knew was a typical bachelor, with messy counters and grease-stained burners. *He must have hired a cleaning lady,* she told herself opening the stainless-steel fridge. It was empty except for the expired milk and the quart size of Chinese takeout. No soda, no eggs, not even a hint of the peanut butter they both loved so much.

The bedroom was not any better. A simple gray bedspread covered the mattress. One lonely metal chair sat by the bay window. She pulled up the shades to let some light into the morose room. She opened the drawers. They were empty. I the closet, only a pair of black jeans and a black non-descript shirt hung on a wire hanger. A pair of hiking boots with a heavy thread sat on the empty closet floor. She searched in the bathroom cabinet. Hotel toiletries sat undisturbed inside a small travel bag. Had he just moved in? There was no sign of a suitcase or packing boxes anywhere. Behind the door was a towel. She brought it to her nose, hoping to find his scent. There was no indication he had even used it. Not one picture, not one knickknack, not even a fake

233

plant. A troublesome thought flashed like a warning sign across her mind. *Is that what it takes to be a spy? Did he detach himself from anything real? From me?* Julienne sat on the corner of his bed digging into the flesh around her nail until it hurt.

God, please don't let him disappear again.

***

It was midnight when she finished the Vegetable Lo Mein. She threw the container in the trash along with the plastic fork and went to the living room. She curled up on the couch and closed her eyes waiting for sleep to come.

"You're still here."

She jumped, startled by his deep voice resonating from the darkness.

"I didn't hear you come in," she stammered, turning on the lamp. "You sent me away when there were things we needed to talk about."

He removed his gun from the back of his jacket. "There is no '*we*' anymore. He removed the clip and cleared the chamber, "this is who I am." He placed the gun on the coffee table. "The Angelo you knew is dead."

"All this neutrality... it's all an act. You may be a spy, but you are still human, and humans feel and react." She sat up waiting for his rebuttal.

He went around the back of the couch and rested his hands on her shoulders. His fingers moved gently squeezing and kneading the tight knots. "Like this?"

Julienne felt her heart skip a beat. "Um...yeah."

"Do you trust me?" he whispered, his warm breath on her ear.

234

"If I didn't, I wouldn't be here."

He removed an opaque scarf from his pocket and placed it over her eyes. Julienne 's heart sped up.

"What are you doing?"

He pulled her to a standing position. She lifted her hands to remove the scarf.

"Please don't. We are going out."

He guided her arms into the sleeves of her coat. Her heart flutter beneath the checkered wool. "How am I going to get down the stairs?"

"I'll carry you."

The next thing she knew, she was holding on to his neck as he quickly descended the four flights of stairs. The noise of the city let her know they were outside the building.

"Can you give me a hint where we are going?" she asked, the woodsy smell of his aftershave overpowering her senses as he helped her sit. She felt the material of the seatbelt when he strapped her in.

"Come on Angelo, a little hint?"

"No, but I do need your hands, "Julienne 's pulse quickened as she felt metal graze against her skin. But it was not until she heard the defining click that the excitement turned into panic.

"Take these off!" she demanded, straining against the handcuffs.

"Don't make me have to silence you," he warned starting the engine.

"Where are you taking me?"

"Behave yourself or I will put you in the trunk."

The car swerved thrusting her from side to side like a rag doll being shaken.

"You are driving like a maniac! Why are you doing this?"

235

All the response she got was his steady, rhythmic breathing. The agent made an unexpected turn and then a sudden stop that jostled her bones. Thoughts raced through her head. She knew Angelo D'Marco. She knew of his preferences, his secret longings, and even what made him angry. But what did she know of his stranger who had taken her captive? She knew nothing! Her breathing caught up with her thumping heart. Her hands trembled against the cold steel imprisoning them. Muscles tightened. The adrenaline coursing through her veins quickened. *Oh God, what if he has orders to kill me! What if he is a mole and wants information? I... I don't have any information! What will he do to me?*

"Breathe, it would be a shame if you arrived unconscious," he told her. His voice was velvet yet edged with steel.

"Tell me where we are going. Please," she pleaded, in a suffocated whisper.

Again, total silence. Her head filled with horrible thoughts. She had to get a hold of herself. *Pray, my child. Okay, God, I don't know if he has snapped, but please keep me safe. Give me the supernatural peace I need to think clearly.* Like clockwork, her mind slowed down. Rational thinking replaced the anxious thoughts. *He left the gun. He is not armed, or he could be carrying another weapon. I don't think he wants to hurt me.*

She took a deep steady breath. "Angelo, I love you. I came back to be with you. I never loved Carlos... it's always been you."

The vehicle stopped moving. A small square object was dropped into her two cuffed hands.

"That's my cell phone. It's voice-activated. You have a choice, you can tell it to call the police or you can trust me."

She thought it over. It would be simpler to call the police and end the terrifying charade, but deep inside, her heart ached to understand the man he had become. With her cuffed hands, she dropped the phone back on the cup holder and stared straight ahead. Her captor didn't speak, but even in the darkness of her blindfold, she sensed he was smiling. "I trust you; don't make me regret it," she said trying to scratch an itch in her nose with her palms.

Angelo stifled a laugh, "Sit back and relax; we are almost there."

The rest of the ride was smoother. Julienne estimated the trip had lasted about half an hour before she heard the ignition turn off.

***

Her boots crunched the dry leaves on the path. The cool wind slapped the back of her coat pushing her along. Her captor maneuvered her in front of him, his strong hand on her shoulder and the other like a protective vice on her thin arm. She took slow, unsteady steps in the disorienting darkness. All she could do was move forward relying on his direction. He didn't acknowledge her during their walk except to bark, "Be careful. Slow down. Turn here." Julienne wondered just how much longer before she could rest her aching feet. High heel ankle boots were not the right footwear for long treks through nature. Her legs itched as the dew-covered foliage snapped back against them.

You could have warned me we were going on a hike. I would have dressed accordingly."

"Watch your head," he said, pushing her head down. She heard leaves rustling and then the creaking of a door being opened.

44

Angelo led her inside, the light of his flashlight guiding them to the nearest chair. He moved to the window and looked through the opening between the opaque curtains. The scenery was undisturbed except by the trees moving in unison to the frigid wind. He closed the curtains making sure not a sliver of light was sneaking through. He did a quick sweep of the room, then returned to his guest carrying the gas lantern he had taken from the supply closet. After lighting it, he removed her blindfold.

Julienne's eyes blinked, gradually adjusting to the light. He opened the cuffs, setting her hands free.

"What is this place?" she asked, rubbing her wrists.

"Why didn't you call for help when you had a chance?" Angelo tossed the logs into the wood-burning stove.

She walked around the cabin, taking in her surroundings. The rustic walls were dingy, and a lattice of cobwebs hung from the beams on the ceiling. The kitchen area was made up of a metal sink and a mildew-stained refrigerator. Two rolled-up sleeping bags were lined up against the wall. Her eyes stopped briefly on a picture of an American flag tattered and broken flying high above a battlefield.

"I trust you," she answered moistening her chapped lips.

Angelo's eyes softened a fraction. He closed the door to the stove.

"This is a safe house. After tomorrow, Angelo D'Marco will no longer exist. Things like 9/11 aren't supposed to happen but in my world, they happen every day."

The incandescent light of the wood-burning stove bathed Julienne's cold cheeks, giving them a rosy glow. Gold flecks sparkled from her almond eyes reminding him of his dream in Afghanistan. She rubbed her hands together to get warm.

God, she is so beautiful. Angelo ran his tongue over his front teeth. He hated the duality of their relationship. Even if she had his heart wrapped around her little finger, he couldn't afford to act like a lovesick schoolboy. From the moment she had walked into his apartment she had unwittingly become his mission again. Settled comfortably on the wooden chair, he crossed his legs at the ankles.

"Tell me did it frighten you to be blind and unable to use your hands?"

She let out a sigh. "Yes, I was scared, but anybody in that circumstance would be."

"Are you afraid now?"

"No."

Angelo rose fluidly. In slow, deliberate steps he circled her chair.

"Most people don't encounter danger on a regular basis. They like to think they are in control when they seldom are. My job is to keep that illusion going."

"Fine, so you fight crime. Why all the theatrics?"

"Juls, I was testing you. Being able to stay in control even when you are being held against your will is vitally important. It could make the difference between living and dying one day."

Julienne's forehead creased; she cocked her head. "Did I pass your test?"

"You tell me. You said you love me. You want us to be together, but are you willing to step out of your comfort zone?"

Julienne held her palm up. "Stop right there. I have a question too. Are you a Christian, or was that part of the act?"

His lips parted into a joyful smile. "God is not a profile. God is my life. I rely on Him to protect me and sustain me. I know agents who are Atheists and honestly, I don't know how they do it." He sat forward, his face full of strength, shining with steadfast faith. "You must believe in someone bigger than yourself to fight the enemy head-on as we do. I know this may sound crazy, but like David, God has called me to be a warrior."

Julienne resisted the urge to hug him. Instead, she circled his chair, copying his slow intentional steps.

He laughed, "So now I am the one in the hot seat, huh?"

"Something like that," she replied clasping her hands behind her back. "So, tell me, Mr. Spy ... how is this devious plan of yours going to work?"

He imprisoned her hand and pulled her onto his lap. "Well, for starters, I am looking for a wife."

"Really? Please go on."

241

He toyed with her hair, capturing the curls in between his fingers. "She must be willing to follow me to the ends of the earth, no questions asked. She will have privy to some information, but some will remain classified for her safety. In return, she will have all my love and devotion. Do you want to search me? I could be wired you know," he jested, lifting his arms.

Julienne played along sliding her hands down the sides of his jacket until she reached the pockets. One felt bumpier than the other. She reached in the left pocket and took out a small velvet bag. She raised her eyebrow untying the string. She tipped it over. The engagement ring he had given her fell into her hand.

"I never thought...I had to sell it. I had to move on," she said her brown eyes clouding with tears. "How did you find it?"

He lifted it from her palm and slid it on her ring finger.

"I got the address where you pawned it. From there I tracked it down to a couple in Hialeah. I offered them a nice chunk of change for it."

"Oh, Angelo... I..."

He turned his face suddenly, distracted by the subtle noise outside the window.

"Shh..." He covered her mouth with one hand and dragged her to the floor. "It's not a game; we have company."

Julienne's eyes opened like giant saucers.

"Just point and shoot at anything that comes through that door." He told her handing her the gun that he kept in his ankle holster.

Angelo reached up, trying not to make a sound, and removed the shotgun from the wall. The chamber was empty. There was no time. It would have to do. The sound of leaves crackling became more decipherable. The gun trembled as Julienne held it in both of her hands. Angelo pulled the blanket off the rope that separated the bathroom area from the rest of the room and threw it over his terrified fiancée.

"Don't worry about shooting! Just stay down!"

His attention swayed from her to the potential danger outside. "You should have never come looking for me."

"Are we going to d...d...die?" she asked, trying to stand up again.

"Not if I can help it," he said pushing her back down.

Hinges and wood exploded; a masked man blasted through the front door. He was a beast of a man, large and muscular but extremely fast. The scream caught in her throat, as he threw the blanket off her. He lifted her by her hair. She tried fighting him off, but he yanked her head back until all she could see was his hatred-filled eyes. She dropped the gun and he kicked it under the table. He yanked her hair harder, "I don't like guns, dead too fast. No fun."

He looked back up locking eyes with the agent.

"Your woman is very pretty. Beautiful eyes; they will pay good money for her," he said, removing his mask. A grotesque scar covered his right cheek.

"Viktor let her go. She has nothing to do with this."

The man's meaty fingers squeezed Julienne's chin, "Sasha will like her."

"Let her go and I will go easy on you. I will even let you throw the first punch."

The tip of his knife pricked the soft flesh covering her jugular vein. "You will pay for what you did! I swear on my brother's life!"

"What are you waiting for? Come and get me you piece of garbage!" Angelo shouted, sliding the unloaded rifle to the floor.

***

Viktor's nostrils flared. He brought the knife down and snarled, giving Julienne a vengeful push. She stumbled and fell, hitting her head on the floorboards. Viktor laughed, readying himself for the fight. Before he could make the first move, Angelo was on him, a blur of fist and knuckles. Viktor growled but did not drop the blade. It cut through Angelo's leather jacket, nicking his chest. Angelo jumped back to avoid a slash to his stomach, but it caught him on the way up, slicing his elbow. The agent continued to move backward, dodging the relentless thrashing and jabbing of Viktor's blade. Viktor was not an ordinary opponent. The man was well trained, not to mention twice Angelo's size. Tiring him out was not an option.

"You owe me a new jacket, dirtbag!" Angelo shouted, warm blood running down his forearm. He jerked back deflecting the blade's newest trajectory. Two more rounds and it was the agent's upper thigh that sustained a nasty gash. Prayers for wisdom and guidance tumbled through his head. He needed a way to distance himself from the oversized cheetah. Angelo darted a glance at Julienne. The sight of her lying like a discarded doll on the floor pierced his heart. He prayed she had just passed out.

Viktor's mind was racing as he grappled with his prey. He could almost taste the victory. A few punches to the major organs would weaken his competitor further. Then Viktor could slice his throat and leave him choking on his blood. But that was a generous death, one reserved only for honorable opponents. Knowing his massive frame was consuming all of Angelo's strength, he pulled back. Angelo took the bait, nailing him in the jaw.

"Is that all you have? You disappoint me, Comrade!" Viktor mocked, spitting blood into Angelo's face.

I can't let him get in my head or I'm as good as dead, Angelo thought as he felt the sting from the slap. He wasn't sure how much more he could take. The man was a tank. Angelo's knuckles were swollen from punching, but he was not making a dent in his adversary. *Lord! I need super strength!*

Viktor was giddy thinking of ways he would make Angelo pay. First, he would beat Angelo until he was half dead and then torture his woman in front of him. The American pig would cry out for mercy, but there would be no mercy for either of them.

The next blow sent Angelo flying into the refrigerator. His whole back throbbed. Wracked with pain, he limped to the sink. From the corner of his eye, he saw Viktor wielding the knife in the air like a crazed Samurai warrior.

"I am going to cut you into little pieces and feed you to Sasha!" Viktor shouted, running toward Angelo in a murderous rage.

"You still keep that decrepit cat around? Let me put you both out of your misery!" Angelo grabbed the mugs and plates from the shelf and hurled them with all his might at his attacker. One plate hit the side of Viktor's bald head, cutting him. Another hit his right eye. His feet skidded to an abrupt stop. He held his injured eye, yelling profanities.

His boisterous threats brought Julienne out of unconsiousness. She rubbed the throbbing bump on her forehead, trying to remember how it got there. It took a few minutes for the confusion to clear. She slowly lifted her head off the floor and looked up at the backside of the man who had thrown her down.

Angelo was still in danger! Julienne crawled across the wooden floor to where the gun had fallen. Holding on to the stove, she stood up and pointed the gun toward Viktor. Her heart raced like a wild stallion. She would not lose Angelo again!

"Stay where you are, or I'll shoot!" she croaked.

The man whipped around, cupping his bloody eye with his free hand. "You stupid girl! I sent you emails, you didn't listen. Ask him what he did to my little brother! He is not a good man. He is evil!"

She shook her head, steadying the weapon.

"Your man and I had a deal. I had good information. I gave it to him. He swore he would protect baby brother… and then he let him die alone in that rat hole!"

Terror-filled, she broke out in a cold sweat. *Angelo would never purposely leave someone to die… this is a tactical simulation, a test to see if I have what it takes to marry an agent. They want to see where my loyalties lie.* But there was nothing fictitious about the blood dripping like a leaky faucet from Angelo's eyebrow. Julienne moved the trembling gun toward the vicinity of Viktor's heart.

"If you don't put that gun down, you will wish you were never born! You will feel what it is like to have flesh torn off your body. Sasha my beautiful tigress will make you hate him like I do. You will curse his name too!"

Viktor turned his head to the side, sizing up his brother's killer. The fool was leaning against the sink, struggling to stay upright. The mighty American agent looked pathetically weak by the beating Viktor had given him.

Julienne's breathing came in gasps. Her throat was raw with unuttered shouts. She couldn't kill anyone in cold blood. Thoughts of her dead sister raced through her adrenaline-drenched mind. Could the dragon with the bloodied eye be her sister's killer? She had to know.

"Did you kill...?"

Viktor pounced on her like a hungry lion, ripping the gun from her hand. His iron fingers tightened around her throat. The knife glinted, inches from her eye. Her teeth rattled as he slammed her against the wall, pinning her there. She gagged repulsed by the odor of sweat and grime. Her heart pounded in her compressed chest. The blood roared in her ears. Her stomach knotted and stiffened as his rough hands tugged at her coat buttons popping them off.

Angelo could hear her cries as he scanned the kitchen for a suitable weapon. It was a long shot, but if he timed it just right, the next move might buy them some time to getaway.

Viktor brandished the knife aiming for her Adam's apple. "Don't worry, girl; I show you a real man!" he gloated. His maniacal laughter bounced off the walls.

"Get off me!" she shrieked. The blade cut through her turtleneck, nicking the skin underneath. Her ear piercing screams turned into helpless whimpers.

Angelo calculated the distance and prayed. *God, please give me the aim of David so I can defeat this Goliath!* He pulled the carving knife out of the knife block on the counter and flung it. It sailed like a bullet, penetrating the fleshy part of Viktor's neck slicing into his spinal cord. Viktor's cav-

247

ernous mouth opened as his eyes bulged from their socket. Julienne watched in horror as the blood slowly drained from his face. Her tormentor's punishing hands slid off her body. His trusty weapon clanged with finality as it hit the floor.

Angelo ran to her; his pain forgotten as he pushed the dead weight off his fiancée. "It's over; you're safe. Juls, he can't hurt you anymore," he murmured, kissing her forehead between sentences. He pressed on her collarbone with his index finger, stopping the crimson line seeping through her tattered turtleneck. Julienne stared at the body lying on the floor, unable to speak. She saw the knife moving closer. The knife cut into her, drawing a river of blood. She let out a chilling scream piercing the quiet. His arms created a protective cocoon around her trembling body. With his boot, he kicked his Goliath.

"See? He's dead."

Julienne flinched. Voices were coming from the dead man's fatigues. Angelo bent down and unzipped the pocket. Someone was trying to communicate with the dead man. The agent stomped on the walkie-talkie with the heel of his boot, crushing it.

"We need to get out of here," Angelo mumbled through his swollen bottom lip, but Julienne would not move.

"Juls, I know you are scared. But shake it off! They are coming for us!" he snapped.

***

Julienne threw her hand up, to cover her face from twigs and leaves smacking into her as they ran. Her ankle hit a rock. The pain traveled up her leg and her knee gave out. Angelo heard them coming. He gritted his teeth as he lifted her by her midsection and swung her over his shoulder. A hot poker of pain ran down his hips as he stretched the distance between themselves and the moonlit silhouettes. Angelo pumped his legs harder and increased his strides, dodging bullets as he reached the targeted exit.

In the clearing, two dark SUVs waited for them. Purple spots hindered the agent's vision. He felt for the car handle and yanked it open. He dropped Julienne's body on the back seat and fired two rounds before closing the door. Four agents scurried out of the other vehicle weapons drawn.

Angelo held his side and groaned, "She needs medical attention, get us out of here!"

45

The light of the day broke through the blinds. The images of the night before filtered through the hazy patch of drug-induced sleep. Julienne blinked and opened her eyes. She carefully moved her legs. A burning pain shot through her ankle as she positioned her injured foot back on the pillow. Her head turned sideways; her eyes connecting with the unfamiliar scenery. High ceilings covered in Frescoes depicted angelic wars. Louis XV sitting room furnishings were arranged in the middle of thick marble pillars. Large vases with fresh yellow roses brought cheerfulness to the room. A blonde woman in a tailored suit placed a silver tray on the night table and returned to her post.

"Where am I? "Julienne asked groggily.

The double doors opened. Angelo stood between them.

"The doctor says you have a fractured ankle. Apart from muscle strain, you are in good health." He said sitting on the edge of her bed. The agent's face was an assortment of purple and blue marks on his expressionless face. He turned his attention to the untouched food. "You need to be eating and drinking before you can leave."

He started to get up, but she stopped him laying her hand gently on his bandaged wrist. She ran her fingers across the bruises on his cheek. "That animal worked you over good, huh?"

He gave her a faint smile.

"I was afraid he would kill you." She added.

"It is over now. You can forget all about it and go back to living your peaceful life."

Are you joking?

"I didn't come to New York to leave empty-handed."

"Your breakfast is getting cold." Angelo tucked another pillow behind her back so she could sit up. Crisscrossing the knife and fork, he cut exact-sized pieces of the strawberry crepes and fed them to her.

"Angelo, if you are trying to distract me, you need to change your tactic. It's not working."
Julienne said in between chews.

"You don't want this kind of life. What Viktor said is true. I am not a nice guy."

If you were a nice guy, I would be dead right now. You told me once there are no such things as coincidences. Angelo, God planned for us to be together. I know it won't be easy, but I have faith in us."

Angelo sat on the edge of her bed; his jaw tensed. "Viktor was not just my informant. He was a friend. His kid brother, Alexi, got into trouble with some powerful people. Viktor always provided excellent intel for me. He always had my back. The least I could have done was to rescue his brother."

251

"I am sure you did the best you could."

Angelo stroked his thumb across her knuckles as he heard the helicopter blades of the past whirling in his head. "Alexi had been sold to a guerilla group who ran a drug trafficking ring. I found him in the middle of the Chocó jungle in Colombia. He was suffering from untreated Malaria and an infected gunshot wound. He was in bad shape, Juls. I tried to get him out. We were under heavy fire and he just gave up. He stopped running," Angelo sighed heavily, the knowledge of what he had done twisting and turning inside him. "I barely made it to the helicopter myself before it took off. Viktor had every right to want to kill me. He trusted me and I failed him." The agent's head hung low; his body slumped forward hiding his inner misery from her probing stare.

"You are not Superman. Not every mission can be a success. Only God is perfect. I mess up every day. When you disappeared, I blamed myself. I thought it was my fault you were dead. If I had listened to you and met you that morning, you wouldn't have been in the building when the planes hit. But God is a God of second chances, and we have been given one." Julienne rubbed his back," Angelo we have to stop living in the past. –look at me."

Unshed tears sat at the edge of his eyes. "It was my fault Viktor attacked you. I would have never forgiven myself if he would have…"

"But he didn't. I'm a big girl. I knew it was dangerous to come looking for you. But I can't live without you. I won't lose you again. I know what I want."

Angelo outlined the curvature of her cheek with his finger. "And what is it that you want Miss Gutierrez?"

"To be your wife and I have the ring to prove it," she said showing him the diamond on her finger.

He couldn't fight it anymore. He was drawn to her like a desert wanderer looking for water.

"I love you, Juls. Even during the amnesia, there was not a night I didn't dream of you. My mind didn't remember us, but my heart did." His lips brushed against hers. In a fluid motion, he crossed the room.

"Hey wait! We are not done here. I still don't know your real name!"

He turned briefly, "I suppose you are one step closer to earning that right."

"Excuse me? I have been blindfolded, cuffed, kidnapped, dragged through the woods, not to mention almost killed by a giant. What else do you want?"

The blank, silent stare was getting on her nerves. She threw a pillow in his direction, but it landed by the foot of the bed. He pointed to a black box sitting on a vintage writing desk about ten feet away.

"All you want to know is in that box. Get up and walk to it."

Julienne swung her legs over the side of the bed and sat up. He brought her a pair of crutches, then stepped away. She propped them under her armpits. She gripped the crutches by their handle and bent the knee of her injured foot. Moving the crutches forward, she gave a little hop on her good foot. She repeated the process until she reached the writing desk. Flashing the agent, a complacent smile, she put her foot down momentarily to rest. She yelped, the pain throwing off her balance.

"Sit down before you land on your face," he said aiding her to the chair. "Never put your weight on a broken bone."

"Gee thanks. I'll remember that the next time I break a bone and you make me walk on it."

"Juls, our conversation was cut short at the safe house. Before you open the box, I think we need to go over the facts."

"Go on..."

"We've established that we love each other. You are wearing my ring, but I don't like to leave any loose ends– I finish what I start."

He picked up the box and knelt on one knee. "Once again for the record, Miss Julienne Gutierrez, will you marry me?"

"For the record, a hundred times YES!" She put her arms around his neck. Her enchanting smile was rewarded with a kiss. It was not an ordinary kiss. It was a kiss that left her breathless and sang through her veins. It was a kiss like no other, one that branded her to him. It was a kiss full of promise from a man deeply in love with her.

"Everything you find inside is what I have been cleared to share with you," he said when their lips had parted. He handed her the box. Julienne opened the lid and took her time looking through the several sheets. She stopped when she reached his birth certificate.

"Roan Yosef, "she read out loud, "you're Middle Eastern?"

"My father was Mossad and my mother, an American Operational Profiler. They met during a collaborative mission between the US and Israel. My parents died serving their country. "

Julienne continued looking through the several fake passports. The one with the female name on it caught her interest. "This one's for me?"

"Yes. The final print will have your picture on it. We will have to disappear after our honeymoon."

"I am okay with going to the end of the earth with you, Roan."

"One more thing, there is someone here who wants to meet you."

46

He was not very tall, but his presence occupied the room making it seem more constricting. His footfall was rhythmic, toe and heel falling precisely on the same count. He wore a fedora that hid most of his graying hair. The man lingered by the window.

"May I have a few minutes of her time?" he asked feeling the material of the linen curtains.

"I will be right outside," Angelo assured her kissing her nose.

The man dusted his hands and tossed his hat on the table.

"*Hola*, Juliana."

Julienne dropped the crutches and fell into the hardback chair.

"*Papá?*"

"*Sí*, Juliana. So many years I have watched you from behind a screen...I never realized you have your grandmother's eyes, but you are strong and brave just like your father."

"My name is Julienne, and I am nothing like you."

"It is understandable you are angry. Anger is a Gutierrez trait, and you, my girl, are a Gutierrez through and through."

"You can't imagine what I feel right now, you left me!" she screamed until she became hoarse.

He flicked a fly that sat on an untouched bowl of fruit. "It had to be done. "

Julienne's cheek turned ruby red, and her eyes glistened with restrained tears. She bit her bottom lip, to calm the fury poisoning her soul. All those wasted years, wondering why her father had left...wondering what she could have done to make him stay.

"So that is all you have to say? Did you know how awful my life was after you left? Mom lost it! She took it out on me!"

He was not angered by his daughter's accusations. Her reaction was warranted. But they did sting. It didn't matter how many years he had been away from her. To him, she was still his little girl.

"Juliana, I know exactly how your mother treated you. I also know how strong you were through it all. I wish I could go back in time and change those horrible moments you endured, but I cannot. What I did accomplish more than you could ever know... and you were not alone. You had Ana and Angelo."

"Angelo? That is another slap in the face! You sent him to keep tabs on me. My whole life was a lie! Everyone in it was planned... and Ana... don't even mention her name! She was killed because of you! How can you justify that?"

The head of the Agency shifted uncomfortably as his daughter's accusing eyes bore into him. "Juliana, I am not going to defend myself. What I did was for the ultimate good of all involved. In the end, you and Angelo won; you both found true love. That is rare in our line of work. Ana's death— America is on the brink of disaster. It takes sacrifice to stop those threatening our freedom. While I have breath in my body, I will do whatever it takes to protect this country. "

Julienne clapped her hands. "Bravo. Hiding behind the flag; that's admirable. But you're right; the only good that came from your deceit was Angelo. I plan to marry the real Roan Yosef, and neither you nor anyone of your stupid goons is going to stop me!"

He took his hat and placed it back on his head. He threw a kiss to her.

"Never lose that feisty Gutierrez spirit. It will do you well in your new life."

Julienne threw a candlestick in his direction. Her father skillfully caught it in his hand before it could hit his hat.

"Practice your throw and catch, next time I may just throw it back at you."

***

Julienne shifted her eyes from her father to her future husband. The older man placed his hand on his future son-in-law's shoulder.

"Juliana Gutierrez, you may hate me right now, but I want you to listen very carefully. Angelo has sacrificed life and limb to be with you. At first, I wanted him dead for thinking he had any right to my daughter. You are no longer just a mission *hija*... I mean, the man has had the gall to break every rule. Technically he has been acting against protocol." Javier

258

dropped his hand from Angelo's shoulder and walked closer to her.

"*Mija...*," He continued tossing the candlestick up and down catching it with his bare hands,"...you have to understand the predicament *Agente D'Marco* has put me in. If he had been anyone else..." He flung the candlestick at his best agent.

Angelo lifted his hand just as the candlestick was about to hit his head and caught it in mid-air.

"What's wrong with you? You could have hurt him!" she hollered in annoyance.

"This man is one of a kind, he has one of the best reflexes in the business. But that does not impress you much. What you want to know if he has a heart... he does, a great, big, disgusting heart that makes him do heroic things like stand in front of a flying bullet to save an old man. Imagine what lengths he would go for the woman he is in love with. Angelo will protect you with his own life. You will do well to marry him."

"Roan Yosef..." Julienne corrected her father, "but you already knew that."

Angelo moved, closing the space separating him from his future spouse.

"That's correct, Mrs. Yosef. There are no more secrets to keep us apart," Angelo answered.

Javier shut the door giving the couple privacy.

Julienne dropped the crutches and melted into his arms. Their eyes met; their lips touched as the silent promise of forever burned in their hearts.

47

Isla del Corazón was an uncharted island in the Atlantic Ocean. The closest landmass was the Tenerife Peninsula situated on the African Coast. Pristine pink sands stretched across the entire perimeter of the island hedging in the mountainous terrain and fertile rain forest. From the pool located on the second floor of the mansion, she had a front-row view of the Teide Volcano and the snow-covered peaks of the Pyrenees Mountains She stretched out on the floating pool lounger trying to relax. It was all surreal.

She had arrived on the island on a private boat. Before she could blink, she was transferred to a limousine that drove her to where she would be staying.

Casa del Milagro was a clay-tiled three-story mansion, with manicured gardens that sat on the peak of a mountain. The smell of saltwater and gardenias permeated the air. It had an open courtyard, with a rectangular pond that ran the length of the courtyard. Bright orange Koi swam peacefully between the floating lily pads. The fresh water pond led into a large fountain. In the center was a tree made of iron, with hollow open branches where water flowed down into the rectangular tiled basin. On the base of the fountain, there was a caption that read: *The Tree of Life.*

The courtyard's semicircular arches were a replica of the ones in the Alhambra palace in Granada. Except for one major difference. The Moor architects had the columns covered in fretwork with inscriptions to their god, Allah. The arches in this mansion were designed with Christian Biblical Scripture covering them. The designer of the courtyard had gone through great length to depict his devotion to God.

The guest rooms were also quite elaborate. Each room was fully furnished with different historic period pieces. The Revolutionary War was decorated with patriotic colors. The Renaissance room captured the romance of the times with large canopy beds and rose-colored walls. But the room set apart for Julienne was not found on the second floor.

The Tomorrow room was spaced out over the whole third floor. It had a touch-sensitive voice-activated system that controlled everything from the bathroom faucets to the blinds. The room had a suite size walking closet and jacuzzi. The tour guide handed her a key card and remarked that the advanced technology found in that room was worth millions. After having some difficulty turning on the voice-activated television, she requested to be moved to a less modern room. But instead, she was encouraged to go enjoy the amenities on the grounds while the voice recognition program was adjusted to fit her needs.

Julienne ran her foot through the pool water and sighed. Her fiancé was probably finishing up paperwork at the agency and would join her soon enough, at least that is what she

261

wanted to believe. Yet she was certain her father couldn't' let his golden boy leave without squeezing the last bit of his marksman expertise. She splashed the water. If her father thought he would make it all better by throwing money at her, he had another thing coming.

"I am glad to see you have made yourself at home," Javier said, walking out to the deck. He wore an white cotton *Guayabera* shirt reminiscent of her childhood days, and a straw hat with a thin blue band around the base. "Isn't it a glorious day?" He said putting on his sunglasses.

"Did you dye your hair?" She asked pushing the floating plastic swan away from the stairs.

Javier moved the deck chair closer to the edge of the pool. With his fingers, he smoothed his hair and smirked, "I darkened it. You can't expect me to walk you down the aisle looking like your *abuelo*."

"What makes you think *you* will be walking me down the aisle?" She had lost the last argument with her father, but this time she was ready for him. "The person that walks me must be someone who had my back when I thought Ang…I mean, Roan was dead. That would have been Ana. I'm walking by myself."

"*Mija,* I think it's time you learn the truth about my disappearance."

"Don't bother, Angelo…Ugh, Roan, he briefed me on it."

"Why don't you join me for a nice lunch? I will have Romero bring it out to us."

Julienne sat up on the inflated lounger, "I'll pass, I want to work on my tan."

Her father took out a cigar from a wooden case and took a whiff. "Okay Juliana, you work on your tan and I will tell you the story of our lives."

262

"You know those will kill you. Not too smart for the man who holds our National Security in his hands."

Would you mourn me like you mourned Angelo? He asked, replacing the Cuban back inside the box. "I take your silence as a no. Juliana you have a right to be angry, you even have the right to hate me. But even the guilty get to have their day in court. That's all I ask, please."

Child forgive....

She heard that familiar voice in the depth of her soul. "Fine, go ahead, tell me what could be so urgent that you had to leave our family, and while you are at it, tell me why you had to send out my fiancé on another mission right before our wedding?"

"Do you know I have been studying the Bible? It was Roan's idea. You could say at first, I thought it was boring. Then I noticed the similarities between the Old Testament kings and warriors to today's agents. I read about their battles and how they handled conflict. Very instructional. Take David for instance. He became King. He fought many battles...he had a gift. Roan has a gift too."

Julienne stared at her father. Although he had the lines of time etched on his forehead, his eyes mirrored power and ageless strength.

"I didn't give Roan that gift. He came to us with it. The gift was only sharpened by our training, but it was all his. He has always said that his service to our country is a calling from God. Do you believe God gave him that gift?"

Julienne floated around the pool thinking. *How could you ask that?* Her father was trying to corner her. He knew that if she said yes, she was being a hypocrite because as a Christian she needed to support God's plan for her spouse-to-be. If she said no, well then, she would be lying to herself and God.

263

"Roan learned through the secure channels of an opportunity to apprehend those who plotted the destruction in 9/11. He asked me if he could lead the team."

"You could have said no," Julienne protested, kicking away the inflatable ball that had bumped the side of her floater.

"Let me finish before that Gutierrez blood goes to your head. I couldn't deny his wish. Roan will adapt to civilian life with you, but he has the heart of a warrior. He could get a job in Law Enforcement, which may keep him from losing his mind. Chasing bad guys is in his blood. That won't change because he marries you." Javier bent down and picked up the inflatable ball that had landed by the chairs. He gave it a good whack, sending it flying to the hot tub on the other side of the pool. "Roan was not made to sit behind a desk."

"I know. I just wished he had discussed it with me first before leaving."

"How naïve you are. Evil does not wait until you have the approval to go after it," Javier answered taking a picture of her with his phone. "*Niña*, you remind me so much of your mother."

"Did my mother know about the Agency? Angelo...darn it! I mean Roan told me she was a civilian."

"Don't beat yourself up, it takes a while to get the hang of it, eventually you become your alias, so names won't matter. Now about your *Mamita*..."he said taking a slow deep breath, "she was a civilian and that was my biggest mistake. I brought an innocent girl into my very complex world. I was young and stupid, when I saw her, I allowed my sentimental heart to take over." He strolled closer to the pool. "My father, *tu abuelo*, rest in peace, was in the military when Batista was in power.

264

He sent us ahead with your *abuela* and stayed to fight against Castro's guerillas. He was imprisoned for a few years but eventually, he joined us in the U.S. When I finished high school, I enlisted in the Army. He told everyone his son was going to be a great military leader and protect the freedom of the country that had opened its arms to us. *Mi viejo* died shortly after I enlisted. But that taste of freedom he gave us, is what every human deserves to have, don't you agree?"

Julienne nodded her head, "Yes but—"

"Don't interrupt. Defending and protecting is a Gutierrez legacy. I was moving fast through the ranks of the army, then I met your *Mamá*. You know it was funny, I was at a birthday party for one of my buddies, when she walked in with his cousin. She was barely eighteen, but what a spitfire! It was a fast romance. She was like oxygen and I was lifeless without her." Javier exhaled a long sigh of regret, "I was a hopeless romantic like you. Our dating lasted three short months before I proposed. Her *Papá* had been a Navy Seal, so he was on board. We had a flash wedding and I was deployed overseas. I didn't see her for a year."

"That's a long time."

"But she handled the separation like a pro. Your mother started a welcome committee to help the new Army wives get acclimated to living on base. She went to school on the Army's dime, to become an Art teacher," he looked at his phone ringing on the table, "she loved teaching kids."

"Don't you need to get that?"

He turned the volume off and smiled, "It's not important. Everything changed when I created the Agency. Back then, UPIA was a very small covert unit that was used only in extreme circumstances when the President needed us."

Julienne slid off the floater and swam to the entrance.

265

She went up the stairs and picked up her towel.

"*Mami* didn't tell me she was a military wife. She told me that she met you in college when her car broke down. You were working part-time as a mechanic." She said drying her skin. She sat at the edge of the pool. It was hard enough having to talk about their past, let alone look at him.

Javier Gutierrez sat beside his daughter. He took off his loafers and placed his bare feet in the water. "I bought her an art studio which she destroyed in a jealous rage. I bought a nice house off the base and spent as much time as I could with her when I was in town, but she thought I was sleeping around."

Julienne didn't know what to believe. He was a professional liar, but his eyes told her he was not just looking for sympathy.

He splashed the water with one of his feet, "Come to think of it, the only mistress I ever had was the Agency. Your mother threatened to leave me. She needed an outlet, so I bought her an art gallery. I promised I would be at her every show." He stopped splashing and looked down at the ring on his finger. "Juliana I never cheated on your *Mamá*. She accused me of jet-setting across the world with different lovers. You probably won't believe me, but the last thing on my mind was collecting women. Not that I couldn't have had them, I had plenty of offers, my end game was always the safety of our nation."

"Did you go to her showings?" Julienne asked, more out of courtesy than curiosity.

"I went to the first one. UPIA was growing and it demanded more of my time. I sent flowers and gifts." There was a long brittle pause before he continued. "Out of spite, she put the gallery on the market. How she thought I would

266

not find out...she was never very smart." He leaned back on his elbows and squinted, staring at the fireball suspended in the sky.

"She got lazy, painted only out of anger. It was junk. I took the gallery from her and sold it."

"That wasn't a smart move." Julienne concluded placing her feet in the cool water next to his.

"We tried counseling. I agreed to return to Miami and to work more from home. I left the flying to my sister who oversaw most of the foreign operations." He brought his head down, turned it, and looked at his daughter. "Your *Mamá* and I did have a few good years."

Julienne bit the bottom of her lip. She had painted her father as a horrible monster in her mind but as the conversation continued the dark hues lost their hold.

"Which one of your sister's took over the Agency?" she asked her amber eyes meeting his.

"*Isabel*," he answered, removing his straw hat to cool off his hair with the pool water. "This heat is unbearable, you sure you don't want to sit in the shade and have some lunch?"

"So, it was you, who sent *Tia Isabel*." She stood up, ready to jump in the pool. "I want to hear the rest." The splash she made soaked Javier. He removed his wet shirt and signaled for a towel.

"Thank you for the bath."

Julienne flipped over on her belly and swam the length of the pool and back.

"This is taking too long," she said out of breath, "how about you fast forward to when I was born?"

"*Mi hija,* my beautiful stubborn and disrespectful daughter...

when you came into the world you brought so much

267

happiness, but a lot of worries too. I was responsible for the three of you. You were born during a busy time in the world of undercover work. The chatter we heard about plots against America were multiplying. Then you were kidnapped," he stopped, the words sticking in his throat, "you were just a baby…. It broke me."

His eyes clung to her. His probing set alarms ringing in her head. *He is a trained liar. He feigns emotions for a living. Don't trust him.* Julienne's thin fingers tensed into a ball underwater.

"I was kidnapped. I thought only Ana had been taken?"

"You were six months old. You were only missing for a day." Raw grief cast a shadow over her father's eyes. "Before the kidnapping attempts, I was an ignorant Idealist. I thought that being the Head of the Agency made my family untouchable. I manipulated Nations and made them bow before the United States. Who would dare bring the fight to my house?" He said letting a regretful laugh escape his lips. "When I woke up from my ego trip, I told your mother it was time for me to go underground —I think that is enough for today."

"So, my mother knew you weren't corrupt." Julienne ascertained swimming back to where he was standing.

"I can see you are not going to let me rest until you hear every detail."

"Nope…I want to know all the secrets you have kept from me all these years," she said before submerging. The young woman swam back and forth trying to release some anxious energy. She held on to the side of the pool and allowed the buoyancy of the water to lift her legs until she was horizontal.

Javier didn't like the feel of wet clothes. It reminded him of being a POW in the jungles of Vietnam. He snapped his

268

finger and one of the attendants brought him a plush robe. He removed the wet clothing under the robe and handed it to the attendant.

Julienne was content floating face up. She would have floated in the pool all afternoon if it was not for her father's voice breaking her concentration.

"Your mother knew the drug deal was a cover, but she thinks I was killed in prison. She was told someone else took over the Agency .... We don't belong together...I don't know why I still keep her under surveillance."

Julienne got out of the pool and sat facing her father. "You still love her," she blurted relying on her intuition. "Is that your wedding ring?"

"It's the ring she gave me to replace the one I lost in Morocco. I...tried to forget her, but.... you should have seen her when she was young...so full of life..." His shame-filled eyes shifted as if the reel playing in his mind had ended. His jaw tensed visibly. The inky blackness of his eyes returned as he spoke again. "Juliana, I had your mother arrested a month ago. She was shooting Heroine."

"You didn't! Nobody gets clean in jail. She will find a supplier in there and die from an overdose."

"*Mija*, stop jumping to conclusions. Ana Maria has no priors. She won't do time. I know the judge. He will send her to a state-sponsored rehab," he said rolling up the sleeves of the robe on his wet arms. "I know you have not seen your mother since you went to live with my sister. It might be therapeutic, once she is clean to touch base with her, for your own peace of mind."

Julienne stood up, "I am good. I wrote her a letter forgiving her. I did the Christian thing. We spoke a few times on the telephone, but she made it quite clear she didn't want

269

a relationship with me."

He took the pitcher the servant had left filled with cold water and lemon rinds. He poured them both a glass.

"Will see after she gets out of rehab, it could be the drugs talking," he said handing her one of the glasses. They quietly watched the parade of dogs being taken to the front lawn for playtime. A large Doberman was leading the pack of smaller show dogs.

"Cute dogs yours?"

Javier smiled but said nothing.

"When I was kidnapped, where did you find me? Julienne asked before refreshing her mouth with the lemony water.

"Miramar. The woman who had you must have loved babies. You came back home smelling like talcum powder and violets."

"I guess I should thank you." She said standing up to look over the balcony.

"Those were the worst twenty-four hours of my life. Not even interrogation is as terrifying as not knowing where you were."

Julienne leaned forward against the railing, digesting his words. Her eyes traveled down to the ocean. She tilted her head to the side and took a slanted look at him. Where was the shrew man who had the world in his hands? At that moment all she saw was the man she had once called her *Papá*, broken and humbled by the sins of his past.

Forgive him, my child.

Must I Lord? He has hurt me so badly.

Forgive him.

"Do you love me?" she asked, with the voice of a young girl wrapped in a woman's body.

Javier put his hands on his daughter's shoulders and looked into her tear-stained eyes. "Juliana Gutierrez, I loved you from the moment I found out your mom was pregnant with you. I know our relationship by any standards is dysfunctional, and I would not win any Father of the Year awards. But if the only way I could keep you safe was to disappear from your life again, I would leave right now and never return."

He didn't wait for her to react. He walked back into the house leaving her to her thoughts.

48

It was close to six when she heard his deep voice calling her name. She ran to him leaving the flowers she was picking on the grass. He had only been gone for two weeks but it seemed longer. He gave her a tight hug and a peck on her lips.

He looks tired. Probably has a few bruises.

"It's good to be home," he murmured, burying his nose in the crook of her neck. "I have missed you."

"You could have told me you were going on a mission," she said toying with the hair on the back of his neck.

He touched her cheek; the skin was warm under his fingertips. "I didn't want to worry you. That was the last one. I am hanging up my spy suit for good. See I am not even armed, "he said, turning around with his hands outstretched to his side.

Julienne looked down at his muddy boots. "What about the one you keep in your ankle holster?"

The spy grinned. He looked at her pixie-like face and

pulled up both of his pant legs. He unzipped the zipper on his boots showing her hair and skin. "Satisfied?"

"It will do for now."

"Have you eaten yet? I know this little hole in the wall on the other side of the island. They catch fish and cook it right in front of you."

"I like seafood." She replied.

"You might want to change; we are going on horseback. If the winds pick up, you will end up wearing your skirt as a hat."

***

Julienne found in the room-size walking closet a pair of jean shorts and a pink t-shirt. She tied a lightweight rain jacket around her waist and went to meet Roan at the stables. He was putting the mounting on a white speckled horse when she arrived.

"Juls meet Haven. He is one of the gentler horses we have. Mine is that nightmare kicking over there. His name is Judas."

"Judas?" she asked, brushing the horse's golden mane. "That's weird, even for you."

He went over to the black stallion and slowly brushed him. When he was calm, he mounted him. "Woah, easy boy," he said pulling on the reins as he neighed and bucked.

"Judas doesn't like to be ridden. I got him from a horse trainer who had no business training horses," he explained untying the horse from the hitching post. "He never taught Judas to obey his master, but we understand each other."

While Roan was trying to stay on the horse, Julienne mounted Haven. You should use a different horse, or we could share mine," she offered, watching Judas bouncing her fiancé like a Rodeo bull.

Roan pulled on the reigns keeping the horse's head high enough to allow him to kick but making it harder for him to buck. He held on with his strong legs while the horse moved around impatiently trying to dismount him. The horse paced back and forth as Roan spoke to him in a language Julienne could not decipher. Once he had him under control, Roan clicked his tongue and bent down to whisper in his ear. The horse neighed once and walked over to where Haven waited with her rider.

"What was all that gibberish? Don't tell me you speak horse."

"Judas only understands Hebrew. I am teaching him simple commands in English, but he is a work in progress." He said loosening the reigns so the horse could bring his head down and graze.

Julienne patted Haven, "Just how many languages do you speak?"

Roan pulled the reigns to stop Judas from grazing and get him moving. "I lost count. I can teach you any language you will need to blend in anywhere we go. We better hustle. We want to make it to the restaurant before dark."

They galloped in sync through the island's rain forest leading to the mountainous terrain. They rode their horses up to the highest peak and stopped briefly to take in the picturesque scenery. The sun sat low on the horizon, patches of red and gold stratus clouds bathed the landscape in saffron. Birds flew by, settling in their nest on the trees below. The lights on the Island of Tenerife were beginning to come on, as families returned home from a long day of work.

They climb down the other side of the mountain and

trotted toward the beach. They raced their horses, their strong hoofs pounding the wet sand.

Suddenly, Haven turned and started to climb back up.

"Hey, where are you going?" Julienne yelled, steering the horseback toward the coast. Judas galloped past her. "Haven knows the shortcut!" Roan shouted as his horse stirred up the sand in its haste. Julienne held on as Haven ran after Judas and his rider. She caught up with them by a waterfall. Julienne led her Palomino toward the water so she could drink too.

"This is the most beautiful place I have ever seen," she said watching Roan lead his reluctant Thoroughbred closer to the fall.

"Come on scaredy-cat, it's just water, "he told the reluctant horse as he inched him closer to the waterfall.

Julienne didn't' have to coax her horse. Haven happy to oblige moved close enough to have his fur wet by the drizzle of the thundering water.

"It is amazing, isn't it? It's all ours. I had the house you are staying at built a few years ago and bought the island."

"How do you buy an island that is not even on the map?"

Roan kept a tight rein on the skittish horse. "Easy Judas…. Juls not everything is on a map. The government has certain places that are off-limits to civilians. Take Area 51, for instance…then others are…"

"Non-existent? I got it. You bought *Isla de Corazón* from the government."

Roan stretched his upper body, "I sort of bought it from your father."

"What do you mean sort of?"

"After I saved his life, he wanted to thank me, most bosses buy you a nice tie, not your father. He had me prep for an extraction mission. I was told this was a one-man job. I got on a military plane and parachuted to the island. I was expecting some kind of resistance from the enemy, but instead, I was greeted by a carved sign with directions where to find a mango tree. I was confused and pretty ticked off. Being angry at your father is as useless as being angry at you."

Julienne swatted him on the arm, "That is not nice! I am a lovely person."

Roan dropped his head down and spoke to the horse, "Judas, she is one hot lady. Hot to look at, and hot to handle."

"Okay smart guy, what happened with my father?"

"Like I do when dealing with *all* the Gutierrez, I chewed my tongue and listened to what he had to say. Which was totally unorthodox...You want to guess what your dear old dad had to say?"

"Julienne shooed away a butterfly that had parked itself on the horse's ear. "I don't have the foggiest."

"He told me to empty my gear and pockets. I normally don't carry a lot of cash on missions, but I happen to have ten dollars on me."

"He took it, ripped it up, and told me I had bought his island for ten bucks."

"That is wow, I ... yeah, I don't have words."

"Me either..." Roan said guiding his horseback to the path so they could keep going.

As they rode toward the other side of the island, he told her how the island had come with an open line of credit and a team of top architects and designers. Roan chose to build a modest four-room house, but Javier had it torn down. Her father had a video created from the most prestigious places Roan had been on missions. In it, he included blueprints of palaces, manors, and villas Roan had stayed in and told him to get inspired and build with his heart and not a price tag.

"And that is how *Casa del Milagro* was built," he said as they arrived at a bungalow with tables and chairs overlooking the ocean.

They handed the horses to a servant. Two men carrying a net full of fish led them to the side of the bungalow where they found three young females assisting the cook in an outside kitchen. They greeted the couple with a kiss on both cheeks.

"Woman, what are you cooking? Gumbo water?" Roan teased the older woman stirring a large pot. She flicked him with a rag, "If you weren't so good looking, I'd kill you, now get out of my kitchen!"

"You and what army? "he teased back, picking up a shrimp and wagging it in her direction before popping it in his mouth. "It tastes like chicken."

"Girl, get this fool out of my kitchen. He got no sense coming up in here talking about my food before I even cook it."

"Come on Julienne, I know where I am not wanted," he said taking another shrimp for the road.

They removed their boots so they could walk easier on the sand. The young couple found a table next to the bamboo torches. They pulled their chairs closer together. Spread out like diamonds on black satin, a host of shimmering lights illuminated the sky. Roan pointed at the constellations. Julienne's eyes widen with awe. "I have never seen so many stars!"

"The desert sky is a lot like this," Roan explained. "I kept telling myself that God was unrolling the stars to remind me I was not alone. I had to believe someone who knew who I was, was looking up at the same sky."

"Thank you for telling me. I owe you an apology. I always thought I was the one who had it bad when you disappeared. I was so angry at you for leaving me. I never stopped to think what it must have been like for you."

His gaze traveled over her face and settled on her eyes. "It was Hell."

"Roan, I will always remind you who you are." A twinkle of moonlight caught her amber eyes. He rested his head on her shoulder. In her golden gaze, he was safe from the horrors of war.

***

Roan lifted his head slightly from her shoulder to hear the voices arguing in the kitchen. "I am sorry...that was rude of me to conk out like that," he said, "I promise to be more rested up the next time we come to the beach." He yawned, raising his hands over his head to stretch out his cramped muscles.

"Promises Roan are not your specialty. But snoring sure is. If there are lions on this island you have them beat with your snores!" Like a playful child, she ran toward the shore. The agent took his time getting up. She was at the edge of the water when he dashed after her. Julienne didn't put up much of a fight when he caught up with her.

"So, I snore huh?" he said, effortlessly picking her up. and carrying her into the waist-deep waves. "Do you know how we get rid of auditory hallucinations in the Agency? A good old fashion head dunking!"

Julienne shrieked as he flipped her upside down.

"Angelo...Roan, I swear if you...!" she screamed holding her nose, as the salty water leaped inches from her face.

"I thought you were tough..." he said, bringing her back up so he could cradle her in his arms.

"Jerk!" she complained punching his shoulder.

"Now, let's check, do you still hear snoring?" he said placing her arms around his neck.

"You are a bully."

"Maybe you need some more head dunking Mrs. Yosef?" he asked, noticing the cook directing the men toward the perfect spot for the cookout. "You're getting a break cause of my starving stomach." He told her his eyes following the men carrying long branches to start the fire. Once lit, they put the shrimp and fish on the metal grate so they could grill them.

Julienne whispered in Roan's ear, "Do they know who you really are?"

He nodded his head, watching the men turn the fish over the open flame.

"The snarling cook too?"

"Yes, she is one of us. This side of the island is a sanctuary for retired agents. It is reserved for those who have given their best years to the Agency. Ivelisse was injured while on duty. She was an outstanding Field Agent." Roan explained, trailing kisses from her forehead to her lips. "Her love of combat made her incompatible with sedentary positions. The one thing she loved almost as much as fieldwork, was cooking. She had always wanted to open up a restaurant." He played with her curls, letting them escape through his fingers. "When I built *Casa del Milagro*, I decided to leave this side of the island for her. Currently, we have five agents living on this beach."

"Just five?"

"Plus, all the supporting personnel to make island living comfortable," he explained enjoying the soft flutter of her eyelids against his cheek. "Juls, why do you think I named the house *Casa del Milagro*?"

"Because it's the only place where you can be yourself."

"That is very perceptive of you," he said carrying her back to where the water was knee-deep. "*Casa del Milagro* is not just a sanctuary for me. With your father's consent, I started a program to help innocent civilians who get caught in the middle of our missions," he said releasing her so she could enjoy the frothy waves that rose to kiss her knees. The water was inviting; perfect for an evening swim, but she had not brought a change of clothes. It would be uncomfortable riding back on her soaked jean shorts. They walked out of the ocean hand and hand. Julienne listened intently as Roan continued to explain how he chose those who came to the island.

"I wanted to make sure civilians who can't go under a witness protection program or other avenues, aren't just put back out in the street—you smell that? Let's go eat," he said shuffling his feet, "Crabs, they hide under the sand at night."

They ate till they had their fill, finishing off with Evelisse's tropical fruit cheesecake. Women in colorful sarongs danced barefooted on the sand as the musicians played Island music on their bongos. For the show's finale, the male fire dancers threw the burning tiki torches up in the air and caught them with their teeth. The couple gave them a standing ovation. Roan tipped the entertainment staff generously for their outstanding performance. When the meal was done, the young couple chatted for a while with the feisty cook.

The thunderclouds rolled in. It was agreed it was not safe to ride back during the storm. Haven wouldn't mind, but Judas would be spooked by the lightning and thunder. The cook volunteered one of the fishermen to drive them back to

Casa del Milagro, but Roan decided they would wait out the worst of the storm and ride home on Haven.

On their trip back they discussed the wedding, even some of the honeymoon plans but that's as far as he would take it. She knew their honeymoon would be the same trip they had planned before their wedding was postponed by the terrorist attack. But Julienne silently wondered where on the globe they would start their married life.

Roan was an expert rider, making their trip on Haven comfortable and enjoyable. Julienne felt his breath on her cheek. His strong forearm brushed up against hers while he held on to the reins. The light of the moon peeked out of the clouds stopping the drizzle from falling on them. She closed her eyes and tried to enjoy the ride. That part of her that needed to know what was coming next was pestering her. Being the wife of an agent meant she would have to learn to live with uncertainty. She leaned back against the taut smoothness of his chest and quieted her soul.

Lord, I am not very good at trusting. It's always been my downfall, but I know you have my future already planned out. I am handing this to you. Thank you for Roan who I know loves me.

"You doing okay?".

"I was talking to God."

"About us?"

"Yes."

Roan stopped the horse. "I may be good at a lot of things, but I can't read your mind. I can only guess what you are thinking.... I'm asking a lot, aren't I? ... I wish I was just that accountant you met. If I was Angelo, it would be simpler."

Julienne turned her torso sideways so she could see his face. "Yeah, but that accountant couldn't have kept me safe.

281

Roan, we don't get to choose who we are. I am the daughter of the founder of UPIA. Do you think if I would have had a choice I would have chosen to be born into a family of spies? No, but I am learning to accept it."

"He told you the acronym? Did he tell you what it stands for?"

"Upstanding Players In America?"

Roan let go of the reins to cup her face. "You are so cute...UPIA stands for Universal Protection Intelligence Agency. Those who require our services, know us as *The Agency.* I can't promise you that our future will be easy. I am leaving my agent days behind, but I want you to go into this marriage with your eyes wide open."

"Give me some credit, I have read plenty of spy novels."

"Fiction. Julienne, they are fiction! The truth is I can't guarantee that some evil person from my past won't come looking for me."

"So, we'll be careful. I already passed Escaping Bad Guy 101," she answered smelling the flower Roan had given her. "I almost shot Viktor. I need extra lessons on self-defense, but other than that I am golden."

"Golden huh?" He said shooing a mosquito off Julienne's arm. "In all honesty Juls, I will keep our lives as normal as possible, for as long as possible."

"You still have time to reconsider. I won't hold it against you if you do."

"Roan Yosef, I am not going anywhere. Whatever comes we will face it together. Jeremiah 29:11."

"I am very familiar with that one," he said, taking the flower she was holding and tucking it behind her ear. "For I know the plans I have for you, declares the Lord, plans to prosper you. not to harm you, plans for hope..."

"And a future," she added, taking the reins just as they were arriving back at *Casa del Milagro.*

49

UPIA insisted agent 539 had two wedding ceremonies. One in NY and one on the Island. It was the most efficient way to keep Roan's profile of Angelo intact while keeping Javier's existence from being leaked out. The New York wedding would be filled with friends and family. The island wedding would be a UPIA sponsored event.

"I give up! How am I expected to plan two weddings on the same weekend in two different locations?" Julienne complained to Roan leafing through the wedding planner's idea book.

Roan threw her a kiss and continued his workout. He lifted the lighter dumbbells and did a repetition of curls. "You could just concentrate on the wedding back home and let the Agency take care of the wedding on the island."

She brought her chin down, resting it on her crossed arms. "You mean to let my father take care of it. You think I should let him walk me down the aisle, don't you?"

Perspiration ran down Roan's back. He laid down on the bench press and lifted the bar bringing it down slowly to his chest. He breathed out lifting it back up. He continued benching multiple sets before re-racking the bar.

"Juls, he is your father, but I will butt out."

Forgive, child

"Why don't we just elope?" She mumbled ignoring the heavenly nudge.

"I'm going to take a shower. Pray about it, the answer will come."

Lord I know you said in your Word we must forgive, well I have forgiven him, but to walk me? He was never there! He didn't see me grow up; he doesn't even know me.

Julienne looked through the agenda on the IPAD Roan had gifted her to help with the wedding preparations. The little, pocket-sized device had advanced technological capabilities not yet on the market for regular civilians. For security reasons, the meeting with the wedding planner would be virtual.

Julienne left the gym and walked across the pool house to the other side of the building. She took the stairs to the first floor. A pair of maids were walking toward the elevators conversing in Spanish. Each went down a different hallway. Julienne sneaked behind the one carrying 'Don Gutierrez's' dry cleaning. The maid went down the hall and took the stairs down to the ground floor. The maid used her keycard to open the door. She whistled a Spanish Lullaby while she hung up the cleaned suits in the closet and picked up the dirty laundry basket before going to the next room.

Julienne came out of hiding. Her father was not in any of the staterooms the maid had visited. To the left of a Medieval knight statue, she found a wooden door with a lion carved on it. She knocked, since there was no answer, she tried the knob. The door opened. The curious woman walked around the room calling out her father's name.

The room was dark except for the light coming from behind the curtains. On top of the desk sat a used ashtray, his computer, and a manilla folder. Inside the folder, she found a picture of her mother's mug shot. Ana Maria's impeccable coiffed hair was a blonde mess of uncombed knots. She had a disconnected stare of someone high on drugs. Julienne looked through the drawers, nothing jumped out at her. What was she looking for anyway? For someone who didn't like snooping, she sure had been doing her fair share. She stared at the dark screen of the computer. It was password protected. She thought about possible combinations of keywords and entered them. *Come on, it can't be that hard...think.* Julienne went over some of the conversations she had with her father. One name stuck out like a neon sign:

NEW ART & MORE

She typed the name of her mother's gallery and hit enter. The monitor lit up. *That was too easy.* Why would someone as intelligent as her father was, pick a preschool password anybody could hack? Julienne gasped as the screen bloomed with old pictures of her. There were pictures from when she was born, lost her first tooth, pictures of birthday celebrations, and the first days of school. As the pictures changed, she found herself staring at photos that should not be there at all. High-definition pictures of her first day on the job in New York, pictures with her and Angelo in Central Park, and ultimately pictures of her time in Miami filled the screen.

Even her romance with Carlos was documented. A

pulsing knot in her stomach urged her to click on the desktop folder that read: PERSONAL. The file opened an Excel spreadsheet. Each date she clicked on brought up a video. There were old home movies of her birth and as a toddler, playing with her father's hat collection. The tense lines in her face relaxed reliving the cake fight with her sister and the Disney World vacation with the cousins. Such fond memories, she thought clicking through the early years of her life.

When she progressed through the videos, the quality changed. The videos that showed up were videos of higher quality where strong magnification lenses were often used. A specific video brought the tension back, it was a video of her running to her grandmother's house after her mother had kicked her out. The video was different. It was grainier. It looked like they had used a darker film, or something was obstructing the light. It looked as if had been taken from behind dark windows. Julienne moved the mouse around the edges of the video and saw a reflection. The video was taken by the car that had been following her that day!

Despite her fear, she continued examining her visual history. She watched the videos of the time she had spilled coffee on a customer at the diner she worked. She saw herself feeding the homeless at the Soup Kitchen and she relived the excitement of Angelo's engagement proposal. There were videos, pictures, and recordings covering the time from when Javier had left up to the present. Javier had told her he had been keeping tabs on her, but she had no idea of the extend. She went to a different file and found letters. Letters that were written by her father but never mailed to her.

"Juliana I was never far away," Javier said, his feet making no sound.

"I'm sorry.... I probably shouldn't be in here..." she

stuttered, "I was looking for you and…"

Javier reached over and closed the lid to the computer. "Why were you looking for me?"

She flopped the three-ring binder on the table. "I can't plan two weddings at the same time. It's impossible. Can't we just say we left on vacation and you know…."

"*Mija,* it is hard to leave your present life without being able to say goodbye to those you love. I want you to have closure this time."

Forgive those who trespass against you. My daughter. I forgave you.

Julienne felt the warmth of the words caressing her.

"I read…. the letters, the ones you didn't send. They were beautiful, I never knew how much you missed me."

"I had Ana. I spend time with her at headquarters. But you…I couldn't even hold you when you were hurting…" he said, his voice cracking, "Your sister stopped me once from contacting you. It was after Roan went missing in the Towers. I couldn't stand seeing you grieving like that."

Julienne stared at the closed folder on the desk. "I wish you would have."

"Where logic failed me, Ana was always there to remind me what could happen if I contacted you in any way." He said sitting in his chair.

"I am sure I would have been safe, you had Angelo, Carlos, and who knows how many people planted in my life."

"It would have been war. Contacting you would have set off a chain reaction in the dark web. Every rogue agent and every hitman from around the globe would have come after you to get to me. Your ditzy sister was so much smarter than you ever knew. The real Ana was brilliant."

Julienne went around the desk and knelt in front of her

288

father so they could be eye to eye. "I wish I could have known that Ana. I think I know who Javier, head of UPIA is," she said patting the hand he had curled against his stomach to hide his missing finger. She laid her palm against his heart. "I want to know more about *this* Javier...my *Papá...*You can start by helping me plan the island wedding. We can figure it out from there."

Javier hugged his daughter. There were tears in his eyes, this time he did not wipe them. "*Hija.* I would be honored."

50

The limbs of the trees shivered as the snow blanketed the ground. Inside the church, the lights on the candles made the stained-glass windows glow. The red satin bows adorning the pews gave the sanctuary a touch of class. Julienne's aunts and cousins took pictures of each other as they eagerly awaited the bridal party to arrive.

The pastor's wife popped her head into the Bridal room, letting Julienne know it was time. The Maid of Honor helped Julienne gather her train before proceeding to the foyer. Ushers were waiting to open the sanctuary doors as soon as they heard the organ playing.

"I go first," Veronique said, taking her place in front of Julienne. *Si'l vous plait* do not run. Slow and elegant so Paparazzi can take good pictures of *moi...* and *vous*."

The maid of honor walked in wearing a red gown she had designed for the occasion. In her hands, she carried a bouquet of white roses. The little homeless girl from the soup kitchen walked in next throwing petals in her red Taffeta gown. The grateful mother stood in the back, dressed in her nursing scrubs smiling. The child's selfless act a year ago, of making a cross out of popsicle sticks had not gone unnoticed. Julienne not only chose the little one to be her flower girl, but Roan found the mother a job and a place to live.

The Wedding March played. Julienne's chest constricted. *This is not real. The man up there is Angelo D'Marco, not Roan. It is all for show...why am I shaking?*

She took a deep, calming breath and focused her eyes on the man waiting for her by the altar. Roan, aka Angelo, looked better than in any of her dreams in his black tailored tuxedo. His face sported a smile. She focused on his emerald eyes taking small rehearsed steps disregarding all the television cameras aimed in her direction. The reporter spoke into the microphone announcing to the viewers that Angelo and Julienne's wedding was a sign of hope and healing for New York. The bride continued toward the altar alone. In the back pews of the sanctuary stood her friends from the Soup Kitchen. They waved at her and took pictures.

The altar was dressed in a white tablecloth. Two large standing vases with red roses adorned the altar. Julienne took her place next to her husband-to-be. His fingers reached out clasping hers.

From behind the veil, swirls of liquid gold shimmered beneath a canopy of long dark lashes. Reddish-brown ringlets cascaded under a diamond-encrusted tiara. The dress she wore was the original dress she had ordered before the 9/11 tragedy had taken place. The altered dress fit perfectly. It fitted her every curve flowing outward from her tiny waist to soft ripples of tulle.

Veronique bent down to straighten the bride's monogrammed train. After 9/11 Veronique had watched her protégée lock herself in her grief. It was then that the designer made the decision not to return the wedding dress to the Paris atelier. Instead, she kept the wedding gown preserved in its original box. The only way she had planned on parting with it was if a curator would want it as a historical piece for a 9/11 exposition in a museum. The wedding gown would be sold for nothing less than a million. Then she would have set that money aside to help Julienne rebuild her life.

Veronique was not a religious woman. Growing up there was no talk of God in her home. Her parents were too practical for such silly notions. To her, God was nothing but a nebulous being who had left the world to destroy itself. Jesus was only a figment of some overly zealous men who wanted to bring hope to a world full of hatred and strife. But when Julienne has reunited with her lost love the hypothesis that a creator could care for his creation was found to be viable. Julienne marrying Angelo was the result of a miracle, the stoic French woman surmised. Perhaps she would give this god a try, she thought. Julienne was always talking about a relationship with Jesus, and though she didn't understand any of it, Veronique closed her eyes as Pastor Cates said a prayer for the couple.

Bonjour Dieu... she began in the quiet of her heart.

The wedding moved swiftly like clockwork. The exchange of the customary wedding vows came first. Then the couple participated in the Holy Communion. The last ritual covered was the lighting of the Unity Candle. Then they kissed sealing their commitment as the network cameras flashed.

Pastor Cates proudly introduced them as Mr. and Mrs. D'Angelo. To the New Yorkers watching from their television sets, this was a time of celebration. In Manhattan, a real fairy

292

tale ending had taken place bringing hope that love and faith conquered darkness.

Mr. and Mrs. D'Angelo had a short reception in the Soup Kitchen Warehouse where close friends and family toasted to the couple. Then it was time for them to depart.

***

Back in the bridal room, Veronique removed Julienne's tiara.

"Petite before you go, I have good news for you." She said unpinning the Cathedral train from her gown. She folded the tulle and placed it neatly back in the box where it came. She unzipped the gown and helped Julienne get ready for her ride to the airport.

"Imperial wants you to launch your own designs." Veronique said handing her the travel bag, "

"After the honeymoon, you meet with them."

"Wow, that's … Thank you."

"What is it petite? You don't look happy."

"Veronique, I don't know how I would have made it all these years without you, you are my best friend," she said hugging her with all her might.

Veronique stepped out of her embrace and dabbed her eyes, "*Si'l vous plait* do not wrinkle me. You are not leaving forever. I will see you in two weeks. You bring a nice gift for me, eh?"

Julienne held her tears, "*Oui*, of course. …um, yes it will be very chic."

They joined Angelo outside. The driver opened the door of the stretch limousine. Cheers erupted as they waved their goodbyes.

Snow flurries covered the windows. Cocooned in his arms, the bride let loose the flood of tears she had been holding.

51

The heat of the day warmed the foreheads of the workers. Muscles strained as they finished installing the last wood panel on the Pergola. The women of the island tied a freshly picked spray of coral peach plumerias and turquoise orchids to the guest's chairs. The conductor gave last-minute instructions to the string quartet while they tuned the instruments. Julienne looked down from the balcony window. Apart from the snipers on the rooftops and the security detail, her father had promised her a typical island wedding. Grace Jones stood next to her watching the parade of silver appetizer platters making their way to the reception area.

"I think it's time we get you dressed," said the agent checking the time on her phone.

Her wedding dress design had been birthed under the careful instructions of an agency seamstress who created apparel for all kinds of missions. Julienne stepped into the dress lifting it and holding it in place as Grace buttoned the waist. Julienne walked over to the three-paneled mirror and turned. The backless dress had an embellished bodice of sparkling sequins that twinkled when she moved. This dress unlike the one she wore for her New York wedding, had a whimsical bohemian look about it. Grace added the finishing touches and affixed a crown of gardenias on her head.

"I know I am already married, but the other marriage was only to keep Roan's profile alive. This is real, right?" she asked, her anxiety rising.

Grace applied more blush on her cheeks. "I get it. As spies, we get married and even have families. Sometimes Flesh Covers can be confused with the real thing. Don't worry Julienne, Roan knows the difference."

"We haven't...I couldn't... I would be sleeping with an impostor. Roan was so good about it. Another man would have forced it."

Grace laughed, "He is one of a kind, that's for sure. Are you sure you are human? I couldn't have that much re-strain."

"I am blessed, aren't I?" she asked putting on her sandals.

"Girl, you are *very* blessed! Let's go and get you married before that poor man ends up in the insane asylum!"

***

The violins played. Javier took his daughter's hand and tucked it under his arm.

"Ready?"

"I was born for this, right?"

"Remember this, no matter what name you go by, you will always be a Gutierrez. Gutierrez's are born leaders."

296

Sitting In the isles she saw the faces of some of the world's most skilled agents. There were benches in the front, reserved for the brass and top government officials including General Collins.

On the left side of the altar, Dream Chaser tried to stand still but the knot on his silk tie was choking him. He coughed slightly pulling at it.

Roan chuckled. *Poor kid, he looks as comfortable as a prisoner in front of a firing squad.* Roan Josef had always been a lone wolf and he preferred it that way. Even when he was living as his alias, he did not have any close male friends. For appearances, he would go out with the boys at the accounting firm to see the Yankees and boxing tournaments. Roan was perturbed when his beloved insisted, he choose Dream Chaser, as his Best Man for the island wedding. He had accepted that she had invited Dream Chaser as a guest to the New York wedding. Dream Chaser had been part of the mission and had been added as a friend of the bride and groom to the accountant's background story. Therefore, it was logical he would have to attend. But he questioned why they had to have the computer geek at their island wedding as well. The week before the wedding, Roan Josef had tried to use his powers of persuasion, but his bride-to-be had a compelling argument. Julienne insisted it was Dream Chaser's surveillance videos that had awakened the missing memories in Roan's subconscious, memories. Neither Angelo D'Marco nor Roan Josef could argue with that.

Javier lifted the veil and kissed his daughter. "Are you sure this is what you want?"

Her answer would change her life forever. It was a question that she had wrestled with in prayer for many long nights and found the answer was always the same.

Julienne kissed her father's cheek, *"si papá."*

Roan looked over at the woman whose veil had been lifted. His bride had dressed in white just like two days ago in the little church in New York. But in New York, the bride's hair and makeup were expertly done by a famous make-up artist. His bride could have doubled for a fashion model. Julienne had walked down the church's aisle smiling and waving on cue to the cameras. Though she had appeared nervous at first, she gave a convincing performance. But to Roan's trained ear, the customary wedding vows she said were low on emotion.

In contrast, the woman escorted by the most powerful man on the planet had a carefree look about her. Loose curls framed her face which was dusted with minimal makeup. Her honey-filled eyes danced; she mouthed a soft, "Hi."

Roan noticed how she barely reached his shoulder. "No heels this time?"

"This is reality. What you see is what you get, Roan."

"I like what I am getting Mrs. Yosef," he answered.

The Pastor with the prosthetic arm waited for the couple to stop whispering before addressing the guests. Pastor Rodrigo was an old friend of her father's. He was known around the Agency as *Cobra.* He had been a decorated SEAL until a grenade took out his right arm. He had finished his years of service as a Chaplin to the Agency. After retirement, he was awarded passage to the island where he established a church.

He thumbed the Bible and turned toward the guests, "Welcome friends. We are here to celebrate the union of Julienne Juls and Roan Michael Josef."

"I am sorry but..." the bride interrupted, "my birth name is Juliana Maria Gutierrez, and I would prefer to be married under that name."

The retired Chaplain looked confused, but Javier nodded his head giving him the okay to continue.

"Very well, we welcome you all to be witnesses as Miss Juliana Maria Gutierrez and Mr...," He turned toward the groom, "Roan any other names we should be aware of?"

Roan chuckled, "Aliases many, but not for this wedding."

Laughter and conversation were coming from the Brass until Javier pulled rank and called them all to silence. "You have the floor, Agent Josef," he said sitting back down.

Roan winked at her and took her hands, "Juls, God allowed me to cheat death because he had a plan for us. He knows when I am not with you, my world is incomplete. You bring me peace and I can trust you with my heart. Our paths did not cross by accident. You saw the real me and drew him out. You are my soul mate. Even when I pushed you away, you came back. You never gave up on me. I promise from this day forward, my love for you will create an atmosphere of peace. I promise to protect you from everything and anyone who even breathes the wrong way in your direction. I want to spend my life making all your dreams come true and I vow to love you till eternity."

Julienne felt her heart drop to her toes when Angelo took her hand and removed the engagement ring from her ring finger.

"Juls, this ring has taken you through a lot of heartaches, but that pain ends here."

Dream Chaser handed him another engagement ring which he inserted on her finger then added the diamond band.

"This ring symbolizes our new beginning."

The bride let out a breath and uttered, "Phew, I thought

you were backing out."

There was more laughter, then the pastor queued the bride.

Juliana took Roan's hands and looked into his emerald eyes. She blinked twice clearing the tears spilling on her cheeks.

"My heart told me to hold on when everyone was telling me to let you go. I tried so hard to move forward but I always ended up looking back. You had taken part of my heart. Even breathing was painful without you. God answered my prayers and returned you to me. I want to spend the rest of my life loving you wherever life takes us. "

Juliana slipped the wedding band Grace handed her on Roan's finger.

"Under the power vested in me by the US Government and God all mighty, I pronounce you man and wife. You may kiss your bride, Agent Josef."

Their lips locked sealing the promise they had made in front of God and man.

52

Paris, France January 2003

Juliana pointed to the bookstore display window. "Look at all those spy novels. I am going to be living them."

"Fictional truth, my love," Roan said, as they walked toward the next storefront window. She lifted her hand and admired the encrusted diamond band adorning her ring finger.

"I still can't believe all this is real."

"You mean the million-dollar wardrobe, the penthouse suite, and the private jet?"

"No, silly. I still can't believe you're alive, and I'm married to an s-p-y," she whispered in his ear. He laughed like she had told him the funniest joke.

He hugged her. "Correction. A *former* s-p-y."

Julienne crossed her arms and tilted her head. "You expect me to believe that you are going to be content sitting idle while fanatical maniacs destroy innocent countries?" She glanced at the sidewalk musician playing his saxophone.

"There is a slew of capable professionals. "

"Please! You won't be you if you are not chasing the bad guys across the globe; this time I will be right there with you."

The Eiffel Tower glimmered like spun gold against the afternoon sun. They found a bench in the *Parc du Champ de Mars* and sat down. Roan had purchased two *Saucisse De Francfort* from a street vendor. He handed her the Parisian hot dog and a bottle of seltzer water. Roan scanned the premises, his eyes taking in every inch of the magnificent scenery."

When he was certain he was not being watched, he removed a small cell phone from his jacket and handed it to her. The phone rang. He told her to answer.

"Hello?".

"Hola, Juliana."

She recognized the deep, raspy voice anywhere. It was a voice that brought so many memories and emotions to the surface of her heart.

"Hola, Papá."

"How are you enjoying Paris?"

"It's wonderful."

"Juliana, I know I gave you an explanation why I was not there when you were growing up. But I never apologized. I am sorry *Juliana* for all the pain my decisions caused you. It was not my intention that you would ever have to deal with the fallout."

"I know, it's all in the past now."

"Sometimes we are thrust into roles—I wish I could be a permanent part of your life."

"Will I see you again?"

302

"Perhaps—I am very proud of the woman you have become. I love you, *mi pequeña Juliana.* "

"I love you too, *Papá.*"

They had come full circle. Her heart was free to love both men in her life without any baggage holding her down. Roan draped his arm on the back of the bench as his wife took a few bites of her lunch. Her melancholic eyes reminded him Mr. and Mrs. D'Angelo only had a few days left. At the end of the week, there would be news in the papers of a pair of American newlyweds who had been killed in an unfortunate boating accident.

"Are you ready to go?" he asked, patting her leg affectionately.

"Where are we going?" she said dunking the crumpled napkin in the trash.

"That's top-secret; I could tell you but then I'd have to shoot you," Roan teased lightening the mood.

Julienne wiped away a stray tear and smiled, "Will you aim for my heart?"

He gently cupped her face, drinking in her every feature.

"Always."

ABOUT THE AUTHOR

Ileana M Leon grew up in NJ but resides in Florida with her husband and son. She has spent most of her life helping parents with special needs in the areas of advocacy and education. She enjoys encouraging parents on their homeschooling journey by sharing her experience as a veteran homeschool teacher. Earlier in life, she worked as a Paralegal in the field of Medical Malpractice and Personal Injury.

She has been involved in various church ministries including administrative assistant of private school, teaching, and leading women's small groups. She is one of the co-authors of Walking on Water, a Collection of Christian Stories and Poems, published by Westbow Press.

Her biggest passion is helping women find their worth in Christ. You can contact her at
leonwrites4truth@gmail.com

Made in the USA
Columbia, SC
22 February 2022

56340481R00186